Ready to Forgive

by
LeighAnne Clifton

Ready to Forgive by LeighAnne Clifton
Copyright © 2021. All rights reserved.

Published by Pen It! Publications, LLC in the U.S.A.
812-371-4128 www.penitpublications.com

ISBN: 978-1-63984-104-2
Edited by Dina Husseini
Cover Design by Donna Cook

But you are a God ready to forgive, gracious and merciful, slow to anger and abounding in steadfast love, and did not forsake them.

Nehemiah 9:17 (ESV)

Acknowledgments

A special thanks goes out to the beautiful ladies who read this book in its infancy and provided invaluable feedback. To my sisters in Christ, Jane and Teresa: your support, feedback, and encouragement were fuel for me! Thank you!

This book marked the end of an era in our family... I retired from engineering while writing it! Our family's new way of life would have never been possible without the unwavering support of my wonderful husband Bill. I love you, honey, and hope to continue living out our "sunshine and shadows, hopes fulfilled and dreams shattered" for many, many more years.

My kids are my personal cheerleaders! They keep tabs on the progress of each book, share them with friends and colleagues, and encourage this crazy way of life I've settled into. I love y'all.

And, of course, this book would have never seen daylight had it not been for the amazing staff - which feels like family - at Pen It! Publications. Debi Stanton took a chance on me. Donna Cook remained patient as I strove for the perfect cover... and she delivered! The amazing Dina Husseini, an accomplished author in her own right, made all the tweaks and edits needed to make what I'd written absolutely shine! My thanks to each of you.

Dedication

I could never write a word in my own strength. God has chosen to do through me things I never dreamed possible.

This book is dedicated to all who feel God calling them. I would tell you, "Become the vessel in the Potter's hands. Take on the difficult or uncomfortable thing He's asking you to do."

To God be the glory for the great things He has done!

Table of Contents

1
She Said Yes

Alex juggled the whiny toddler on her hip with one hand and three bulging bags of refrigerated groceries with the other, rushing into her house to beat the impending downpour. A typical spring day in Burton, South Carolina: beautiful sunny weather one minute only to be followed by a sudden cloudburst the next. Pausing only long enough to drop the bags in her tiny kitchen, Alex made a beeline for Lydia's bedroom. Her daughter had missed morning nap time, and now Alex paid the price for trying to cram all of her errands into one day. She'd put them off for so long, she'd lost all track of time. Before she knew it, the day had slipped away, and so had their patience with each other.

Shifting the little girl in her arms to allow Lydia to rest her head on her mommy's shoulder, Alex swayed gently, lulling her tired, cranky daughter to sleep in no time. She kissed the toddler's soft cheek and eased her into the crib, noting as she stroked the child's soft brown curls how huge she looked. Alex still couldn't bring herself to make the leap to a 'big girl bed.' To do so would be admitting her baby was growing up, a fact Alex resisted.

Pressing her fists against her protesting lower back muscles, Alex wandered toward the kitchen, intent on putting the cold items away before they spoiled and retrieving the remaining bags from her old but trusty SUV. She turned the corner to enter the large, open room that served as her kitchen and living area to see Chad bumping the door shut with his hip, straining under the weight of Alex's purchases. Everything she'd plopped on the counter was already safely stashed away. Chad grinned when he saw her.

"Hey," he said. "I hope you don't mind. I saw your open car door, and a whole bunch of bags were still in there. Looked like you needed a hand."

Alex shook her head, smiling. God had truly blessed her and Lydia when He brought this thoughtful, caring man into their lives. She acknowledged her blessing with a quick prayer of *thanks*, as Miss Matilda had taught her.

"Thank you, Chad. We tried to catch up on some errands I should've done weeks ago. Lydia missed her nap, so this afternoon has been challenging, to say the least." Alex sighed and swept a hand through her short dark brown hair.

Joining him in the teensy kitchen, she reached for a box of cereal to stash in the pantry, but Chad intercepted her and planted a quick kiss on her forehead.

"You look beat," he said, holding her close a second longer. "Go sit down, and I'll put water on for tea. Then you can tell me about your crazy day."

"Really?" she asked.

What a delightful suggestion.

Exhaustion washed over Alex, but the guilt of allowing Chad to complete her responsibility overtook the fatigue. He continued to work, but she posed an alternate plan. One she was sure he'd go for.

"How about you finish with the groceries and I'll whip up a quick stir fry? I bought some fresh veggies and a package of chicken at the grocery store. I can have an early supper ready for us in about twenty minutes."

His big grin was the answer she'd anticipated. Even though she lived in the guest house behind the sprawling home Chad and his sister Charmain shared, Alex and Chad rarely had an opportunity to spend uninterrupted one-on-one time together. After Chad inherited his dad's mechanic shop a few years ago, his responsibilities there consumed him most days.

Alex didn't live a life of leisure, either. Her business creating home décor items from other folks' unwanted junk meant she could almost always be found either thrift shopping, dumpster diving, building, or selling. Her last semester of business school at the local college was almost over, and it hadn't been easy. She'd attended classes year-round since shortly after welcoming Lydia into the world almost four years ago.

For her, the isolated year they'd spent during the global pandemic had been anything but slow. With so much time at home, she'd juggled completing her virtual assignments, providing pieces to her on-line clients, and caring for her daughter. Now that all that was behind them, she hoped life would settle down and allow her to concentrate on things other than homework and studying.

Alex chopped vegetables and listened to the steady patter of rain on the metal roof. Letting her mind wander, she thought about where she might be if she'd made a different choice a few years ago when her car ran into a tree and stranded her in Burton. A smile turned up the corners of her mouth as she recognized the sovereign hand of God guiding her.

"I thought chopping onions was supposed to make you cry, not smile," Chad joked as he placed the final box in the pantry. "Whatcha thinkin' about?"

"Just reminiscing a little bit. Realizing how blessed I am the Lord led me here to Burton." She stopped chopping, put the knife down, and was wiping her hands on a towel when he crossed the kitchen in two long strides to stand in front of her.

"That's funny," he said. "I think I'm the one who's blessed because of your atrocious driving." He grinned as she directed a playful swat with the dishtowel in his direction.

"Miss Matilda saw everything and told you exactly what happened. Besides…"

She'd been prepared to remind him of God's abundant blessings, but he stopped her. She didn't even care that he interrupted her. He cradled Alex's face in his hands and looked into her eyes.

He kissed her – gently, lingeringly, in no hurry. Altogether unlike the quick goodbye pecks that they usually exchanged. No. This kiss rocked Alex to her core. She had to catch her breath as he pulled away, leaning his forehead against hers. His familiar citrusy-spicy scent tickled her nose, and she inhaled deeply, wanting to remember every detail of this moment.

"Sorry," he whispered. "I've been wanting to do that since I saw you walk into the kitchen. You are an amazing woman, Alex Powell. Has anyone told you that lately?"

Alex giggled past the lump in her throat. What had she, a previously-spoiled rich kid, done to deserve the love of this kind, decent, God-loving man?

Nothing, that's what.

Not trusting her voice, she bit her bottom lip as she shook her head. Not so much in answer to his question, but rather as a statement of her disbelief at the depth of their feelings for one another.

Flustered by Chad's grand romantic gesture, Alex broke away and returned to the stove, trying without much success to regain her composure. Though her life had been rocked by the discovery of an unplanned pregnancy, Alex couldn't think of a single detail she'd change now.

She felt settled. Blessed. Happy.

As the fragrance of sizzling veggies filled the room, Alex stirred and asked Chad to put some rolls in the oven. When he didn't answer, she turned around to see what caused him to ignore her. Alex's questions died on her lips.

A single rose in a crystal bud vase sat between two glimmering taper candles, adorning her kitchen table much more elegantly than the finger paint and markers usually found there. Standing beside the table, Chad shuffled his feet, fidgeting as if he didn't know what to do with his hands. Alex turned off the stove, confused by his out-of-character behavior. She hoped she hadn't hurt his feelings by pulling away from their kiss.

"Chad, what's all this? I'm just throwing together a quick supper, not some fancy four-course feast."

Puzzled as to why he'd gone to such lengths to make this impromptu meal so special, her confusion must have shown on her face. Chad grunted, blushed, and rubbed his neck the way he did when he got nervous.

"Gosh, Alex, I have no idea what I'm doing here," he said.

Alex wished she could reassure Chad. When they were first getting to know each other, he'd get tongue-tied and shy, but after four years, they shared a companionship to rival any old married couple. They agreed on foundational issues: managing money, working hard on the relationship, fostering friendship and respect, and, perhaps most importantly, abstinence until marriage. It hadn't always been easy, especially considering the close proximity of their living quarters, but as a conviction strongly held by both of them, they waited and dreamed of the day God would bless their union.

Alex turned toward the stove to wipe her hands one last time and stir their supper, speaking over her shoulder as she did. "I know you pretty well, Chad White, and you're a nervous wreck. What's the matter?"

When she turned back around to hear his answer, her breath caught in her throat. Chad was on one knee, a small black velvet box in his shaking hand extended toward her. Gasping, Alex felt her knees become jelly and her hands fly to her mouth.

"Chad, what in the…?" Alex couldn't even finish her sentence as she raked her gaze from his gorgeous green eyes to the little box and back again.

"Alex, you do know me well. So you have to know how much I love you. At least, I hope you do. And I love Lydia, too. I want us to be a family. Officially. Alex, I had beautiful words planned to say to you, but I'm messing this up so bad. I just want to know, will you marry me?" By the time he choked out his proposal, they both cried happy tears and clung to each other. "So, is that a 'yes'?" he asked. The pained expression in his eyes told her he needed to hear her say it.

"Yes, Chad. Of course, I'll marry you."

Alex extended her hand in front of her to fully appreciate how the ring made the light dance. A delicate filigree setting held a large princess cut diamond, which sparkled with every move of her hand. All the tiny stones encircling the band glinted in the late afternoon sunlight streaming in the window after the brief but powerful thunderstorm.

"It's beautiful," she breathed, admiring the vintage vibe of the piece.

"I'm really glad you like it. It was Mom's."

Again, Alex felt it difficult to breathe as she stared at Chad, trying to gauge his emotions. At the age of twelve, Chad had found his mother after she took her own life. Her death rocked their family, sending Chad's dad into a workaholic frenzy until he was diagnosed with cancer a few years before Alex arrived in Burton.

Chad's formative years, from what Alex had been able to piece together from the two siblings, were defined by the tension dividing him and his dad and by Chad's perceived need to be the stand-in parent for his sister Charmain, two years his junior. Miss Matilda had been a life-line for the kids, taking them to church, having them out to her home for Sunday afternoon dinners, always providing the listening ear and the guiding voice they needed.

"Oh, Chad. I don't know what to say." Alex wasn't sure if seeing the ring on her hand for the rest of their lives would be a constant reminder of his tragic childhood. She voiced her concern, trying to put it as delicately as she could. But he put her fears to rest.

"I had a strong and courageous young woman teach me you can't live your life looking backward," he said, making Alex smile. "There's nothing back there I can change. But I can be the man God has called me to be right now, and every day after today. I'm ready to make this tiny little piece of jewelry bring happy, positive memories. Shoot, I want our home, our marriage, everything about you and me to model the way a Godly life is supposed to look. Not just for us, but for our kids, too."

Alex let his use of the plural 'kids' pass without comment. She did want more children, one day. And she did want Chad to experience the joy of holding his newborn child. He was so good with Lydia, so patient and kind. But given Alex's situation, she worried sometimes. She'd never dreamed her own step-father J.T. would do to her what he'd done. Alex knew in her mind it was wrong to compare Chad to J.T. and in some twisted way believe Chad capable of repeating J.T.'s horrific deed. Her traumatic past, however, still held her in its illogical and unrelenting grasp.

"Mama," Lydia's voice crackled over the baby monitor.

"Well, I guess our dinner alone can wait until another time. Let's celebrate with our girl," Chad said, grabbing another plate from the cabinet and blowing out the candles. "Hey," he said before Alex tossed her apron on the hook and headed down the hall.

"Yeah?"

"I love you." He pulled her close and kissed her again, not as long or as leisurely as before, but she knew she'd been kissed.

"I love you, too. And I can't wait to be your wife."

Chad's face lit up like a neon sign. She tapped the tip of his nose before turning to get her daughter.

Alex settled Lydia into her booster seat, then the three of them joined hands to say the blessing. Chad gave thanks for the food; 'his girls,' as he referred to Alex and Lydia; and the rain. When they all said 'Amen' and were ready to eat, Lydia held onto her mother's hand.

"Mommy, I want a pretty ring, too," Lydia told her mother, her eyes never leaving the sparkly adornment.

Alex rolled her eyes. This child didn't miss a thing!

"Well, sweetie, maybe one day you'll get a pretty ring."

Alex tried to dodge the topic for now. Her inquisitive three-year old kept Alex on her toes, always having to stay one step ahead of the questions pouring from the toddler's mind and mouth.

"When Lydia get one? Who gave Mommy one? It new?" Lydia peppered her mom faster than the physically and emotionally exhausted Alex could think.

"Why don't we eat our dinner. Then maybe we could head over to Miss Matilda's place and show her the pretty ring. How's that sound?" Chad directed his question to the child, but Alex knew he was asking her.

"Yay. Miss 'Tilda's! Can we go, Mommy? Can we?" Lydia clapped and bounced in her seat, excited at the prospect of seeing the chickens.

Of course, Matilda would be thrilled with their news. She was, without a doubt, the person Alex most wanted to share it with. Miss Matilda had been Alex's rock during her first difficult days in Burton, welcoming her into Together for Good. Matilda continued to show the girls at the crisis pregnancy home how a tiny human life grew within them, in the hopes they opted to carry their children to term. If they needed a place to live during their pregnancy, Miss Matilda took them in. Each resident received health care, adoption services, career education, and home-making skills, thanks to the generous support of donors.

"That sounds fun," Alex said, excited to tell her older friend and mentor the big news. "Now, eat your veggies like a big girl," she encouraged her picky eater.

A fun incentive, like seeing the chickens, never failed to encourage the girl to eat healthy fare. Alex didn't know what fueled her daughter's endless energy or constant growth spurts, but the pediatrician assured her Lydia was well within normal height and weight ranges.

Still, Alex worried. She worried about everything when it came to Lydia. Not tonight, though. Tonight was for celebrating.

Alex stared into space and smiled, basking in the bliss of her engagement to this man who'd almost restored her belief in honor and trustworthiness. Almost. Her stomach did a sickening flip when an unbidden memory flashed in her mind. Alex had no reason to believe anyone, especially Chad, would ever perpetrate a cruel, painful act such as J.T. had. Before she could halt the downward spiral of thoughts, this single irrational idea established a foothold in Alex's brain, despite all attempts to file it away and deal with it later.

"Earth to Alex," Chad said, waving a hand in front of her face, oblivious to the dangerous path her mind roamed.

Alex's daydreaming propelled her out of the joy of the moment, sending her into some far-off place plagued by fear, pain, and uncertainty. Chad stared at her, genuine concern making the corners of his eyes crinkle. Blinking, Alex attempted a smile, but it felt fake and weak. What a horrible and inappropriate time to fall victim to the fears and insecurities rooted in her past.

Would there ever be a "good" time? A better question was, *could she ever just leave all that baggage behind her?*

Alex had spent the last few years striving for super-human status, but she'd never allowed herself to fully explore the lingering vulnerability, doubt, and anxiety still lurking in her heart. She turned her head and stared out the window, not wanting Chad to pick up on the hurricane of destructive thoughts brewing in her mind.

"You okay?" Chad asked, oblivious to the turmoil swirling in her frazzled brain.

"Yeah, I'm fine. Let's stack these dishes in the sink and go. I can load the dishwasher later."

Alex's decision elicited squeals of delight from the toddler, who squirmed in an attempt to escape her booster seat prison.

"Hold on there, cowgirl. Let me get that buckle for you," Chad said, chuckling as he reached for the clasp at the girl's waist. He'd done it dozens of times. On the heels of Alex's illogical musings, however, she watched him reach for Lydia, and something in her snapped.

"Let me do it," she said, shoving Chad's hands away from her daughter before he had an opportunity to help her.

Chad's eyebrows shot up. He backed away and raised both hands in surrender. Alex averted her eyes, not daring to respond to the hurt or questions evident on his face. As she busied herself releasing

Lydia from the confines of the seat, Chad stacked plates and carried them to the sink, wordless. Alex stole a glance at him and noticed the muscle in his jaw twitched with the clenching of his teeth. Lydia ran to her room to retrieve Lammy, her constant companion on all outings, play dates, and bedtime. As she left, Alex turned to find Chad staring at the sunset.

"Chad?" Alex touched his arm.

"I'm not him, you know," he said, his back still to her. He knew her so well. How did she believe she'd be able to hide her fears from him, justified or not? He spoke again without moving. "It's not right for you to compare me to some monster of a man when all I've ever done for you and Lyddie is try to make you happy. Make you feel secure and loved. Doesn't that count for anything?"

As he voiced the question, he finally faced her, and Alex saw misty pools forming in his eyes. Hurting the man who'd given his all for her and her daughter slugged her in the gut.

But how did she put the gnawing, nagging doubt behind her?

How did she release the memory of her aloof mother, who'd always had time for anyone but Alex?

Even harder, how did she erase the memory of J.T.'s attack?

He'd been the person she turned to for homework help, bake sale provisions, and girl-drama advice. J.T. had even sent Alex off to her prom. Alex never knew what transpired on that fateful night between her departure and her return home from prom. All she knew was she'd discovered her step-father uncharacteristically and thoroughly drunk. As she'd attempted to help him to his room to sleep it off, he had turned on her.

This disastrous and defining event in her life confirmed an important point for Alex: one can never be sure what's hiding beneath the surface in someone else's life. She'd used this truth as a reason for keeping others at arm's length, not forming close connections. She had friends, but not many she considered close and trusted and unconditional.

Except, of course, for Chad.

He was the exception to her rule, and now she found herself questioning the wisdom of making the exception. With a great sigh, she guided him to the table they'd recently vacated and looked him in the eye.

"Chad, I love you so much. I do want to be your wife. Really, I do. And I want Lydia to be your daughter. But I'm scared." Alex's last words were hardly more than a whisper, as if saying them aloud may somehow give credence to them. Make them more real.

"I'm scared too, Alex," Chad admitted. Alex wrinkled her brow in confusion, and he continued. "I'm scared I won't be good enough for you. I'm scared I'll let you down. And, most of all, I'm scared you'll compare me to someone I don't even know. Someone who hurt you to the core. That's not fair, Alex."

His whole discourse was a plea to allow him to love her. Could she?

"Chad, I don't deserve you," Alex said, tears now streaming down her cheeks. "How do I get a grip on all of these fears I've got? My heart knows what a kind, generous, God-loving man you are, but for some reason, it isn't getting through to my head. Why am I overthinking this so much?"

"I hate to interrupt this conversation, because I know how important it is," Chad took her hand. "I thought Lydia was just going to get Lammy. She's been gone a long time."

Guilt washed over Alex as she realized the man she was practically accusing of being untrustworthy was doling out parenting advice. And rightly so. They both hurried back to the girl's room, smiling as they peeked around the doorway. Lydia lay snuggled up with her Lammy on the plush area rug, sound asleep.

"Well, I guess we'll tell Miss Matilda tomorrow," Chad whispered as he moved to pick Lydia up and put her in her crib. Then, recalling their recent conversation, he stopped and backed away.

Alex's heart broke seeing sadness cloud his handsome face. She didn't trust her own voice, so she motioned for him to continue, then wrapped her arms across her body, assuming her default self-protective position. Chad bent and lifted the girl with little effort, kissing her forehead before placing her gently in the crib.

With his hand resting at the small of Alex's back, Chad led her back to the kitchen. They loaded the dishwasher in silence, each lost in thought.

"I'm gonna go now," Chad said when the last crumb had been wiped away.

"Do you have to?" Alex asked.

She felt they needed to talk some more about the strain she'd caused between them. She took responsibility for this unexpected and sad turn of mood. They should be celebrating tonight.

"Yeah. We've both got some thinking and some praying to do." Chad placed a quick kiss on her forehead, and Alex thought how different it was from the kiss they shared earlier.

"I love you, Alex. It's gonna take a lot to change my mind about that. Let's face this together so we can move on with our life, okay?" With his hands resting on her shoulders, it was impossible not to pay attention to him.

"I love you, too. And, thank you. Thank you for believing I'm worth the trouble."

Chad smiled for the first time Alex could recall since her unexpected outburst. "A very wise lady once told me you were worth it. I believed her then, and I believe it now. Just don't give up on me, Alex."

2
Church Ladies

As the couple predicted, Matilda was over-the-moon excited at Alex and Chad's news when they arrived at her home on Saturday morning. She whooped for joy, raising both arthritis-gnarled hands in the air and dancing around the spacious kitchen in the main house, where the aroma of brewing coffee drew both young people. Their puffy eyes and wan smiles implied a sleepless night for both of them. Matilda wondered what could cause them both such anxiousness at a happy time like this.

Lydia, on the other hand, had risen more than a little miffed at not having visited the chickens last night. As soon as hugs and kisses and a hearty prayer of thanks had been offered up, Chad gulped down a hot cup of black coffee and scooted the little girl, armed with a big basket, out the back door to gather the morning eggs.

The two ladies poured themselves large steaming cups and sat across from each other at the kitchen table. Matilda wished they were in her guest cottage behind the main house, ensuring privacy from the ears of current residents. Alex stared into space as Matilda waited. When no information came, she took matters into her own hands.

"Something is bothering you, sweetie."

Matilda didn't beat around the bush. If something needed saying, she said it.

"Yes, ma'am. I've messed up pretty bad, I'm afraid."

Alex related the previous evening's events. Matilda reached across the table and patted her hand.

"You're still hurting, dear," she said to the girl.

Matilda had seen this happen before in 'her girls,' as she considered them. It was difficult to move beyond the hurt and betrayal of the past. But in order to live in the present, they had to trust God enough to believe that He would deal with whatever and whomever caused the hurt. Matilda knew first-hand that dragging guilt around for a lifetime didn't do anyone any good and tended to weigh heavy on a heart and spirit. Similarly, unforgiveness also proved to be a weighty burden. Matilda didn't want this precious girl to lug that weight around any longer.

"I guess I am," Alex nodded, agreeing with Matilda's observation. "I really do love Chad. So much. But I'm scared. What if something happens? Something changes?" Alex averted her eyes as she voiced her concerns to her trusted mentor. "Maybe I'm just paranoid and petty. Am I terrible person, Miss Matilda? I don't know why Chad would even want me."

Matilda recognized the girl's emotions were in a free-fall. She knew she herself was neither qualified nor prepared to deal with the pain and challenges Alex experienced. To ensure the best start possible for their marriage, Alex needed to deal with her lingering emotional scars. Matilda had watched Chad navigate his own healing process following his mother's death. It had been difficult and emotionally exhausting, but he'd emerged a stronger person with a deeper faith. She wanted nothing less for Alex.

Matilda rose from her seat and shuffled to the coffeepot, asking her question over her shoulder. "Why did you quit going to counseling with Reverend Drummond?"

"I felt like I was done. Besides, I got really busy with a baby, school, the business…" Alex allowed her voice to trail off.

"How do you feel now?" Matilda knew the answer, but she needed to hit home with her question.

"I guess I could use a tune-up," Alex said as Chad and Lydia walked back in the kitchen, carrying a basket brimming with eggs. Chad heard only Alex's last comment.

"You don't need a tune-up, honey. I just checked your car from front to back last week. It's running smooth as silk."

His out-of-context reply was the comic relief Alex and Matilda needed, sending them into giggles at first, soon followed by guffaws. Chad and Lydia looked at each other and smiled at the raucous laughter of the two women, who eventually settled down enough to hug the egg-gathering pair close to them.

The next morning after church, Alex asked Chad if he would mind picking up Lydia from the nursery while she spoke with Reverend Drummond. Her request triggered a million questions in Chad's mind, but he replied in the affirmative and set off for the brightly painted children's area. The church adhered to strict security procedures, so, Alex had long ago put him on the list of approved adults to pick up Lydia.

The little girl squealed with delight at the sight of him, running to him with arms held high. Chad was sure her laughter and joy would never grow old for him. He scooped her up as she approached, making sure she didn't trip at the last second as she'd been known to do. Lydia wrapped her arms around Chad's neck in a tight hug, squeezing her eyes shut.

"Chaddie!" she shouted. All her friends had a daddy, but she had her Chaddie.

"Lyddie," he responded, picking her up in a hug and spinning around, making the girl giggle.

"I telled my teachers 'bout mommy's pretty ring!" Lydia announced, as proud as she could be, but Chad thought he might choke as he set her down to look for her Bible and sweater.

"You did?" Chad squatted down, eye-to-eye with the toddler.

"Yes, she did," Mrs. Drummond said from behind him. "Anything you'd like to tell us?" she asked. Lydia's Sunday school teacher leaned against the doorway, arms crossed and one foot propped casually over the other.

"Um..." Chad stalled, wondering why Alex had sent him today, of all days. He and Alex hadn't even discussed how or when they were going to tell folks around town. Chad knew once the church got wind of their engagement, the whole community would know.

He rubbed his neck, trying to formulate a response when his beautiful fiancée appeared at the classroom door. Chad breathed a huge sigh of relief, rose from his squatting position, and held Lydia's sweater for her to don. He always loved seeing Alex, but right now she was nothing less than his God-sent rescue from a formidable situation.

"Hello, Mrs. Drummond," Alex greeted the pastor's wife. "Hi, guys," she said to Chad and Lydia.

Her daughter ran to Alex, sweater forgotten, spouting words about a pretty ring and telling Miss 'Tilda. Mrs. Drummond looked on with interest.

"And, Mommy, I told my teachers you and Chaddie are gonna get a gage." The look of triumph on Lydia's face was equaled only by the confusion on Chad's.

"I think what you mean, sweetheart, is that we got engaged." Lydia nodded her head several times as Mrs. Drummond clapped her hands to hear the news finally confirmed.

"Oh, congratulations, you two! I'm so happy for you. Let me know if there's anything I can do to help plan the wedding," Mrs. Drummond said, overcome with excitement at the prospect.

"Well, we haven't set a date yet," Chad said, reaching for Alex's hand. She smiled at him as she laced her fingers with his.

"But you'll be the first person we call if we need anything," Alex assured her, ushering Lydia out the door as Chad picked up her belongings.

As they buckled Lydia into her car seat, Alex finally met Chad's eyes, mischief clear in her stare.

"Well, I guess you're stuck with me now," Alex said. "By my calculations, most of the church will know about our engagement by tonight's service."

The laughter in her voice was barely disguised. As she chuckled, Chad relaxed for the first time since she'd asked him to pick up Lydia.

The three of them headed to Miss Matilda's for Sunday dinner as they'd done for years, laughing and happy. Chad wondered how many of the little things he took for granted would change after they were married.

As she raised her head from Chad's prayer of thanks for Sunday dinner, Matilda heard the phone in the kitchen ring. The newest resident rose to answer it, but when she saw everyone else ignore it, she shot a questioning look at Miss Matilda.

"Have a seat, Hannah, dear. We never allow anything short of a baby's arrival to interrupt Sunday dinner at Together for Good."

Miss Matilda patted Hannah's hand, and the girl returned to her seat to finish her meal. Matilda caught the glance that passed between Chad and Alex, no doubt remembering how Terry's ex-wife had caused chaos at the dinner table a few years ago. Chad had heard the account second-hand, but he knew full well how Gail manipulated facts to fit her reality.

No sooner had Hannah scooped up her next forkful of mashed potatoes than the phone rang again. Matilda, not missing a beat in her conversation with Chad, barely shook her head at the expectant look in Hannah's expression. Pretending to ignore the persistent individual vying for Matilda's attention on a Sunday afternoon, everyone concentrated on their own plates. The sounds of utensils tapping the china resonated throughout the room. When the caller began to leave their message on the machine, all the dinner attendees stopped eating and strained to hear what was so important.

"Matilda, dear, it's Evelyn, from church. I was calling to see if the news was true. I heard that the girl who used to live with you and that adorable young mechanic are getting married? It's so wonderful, isn't it? We'll have to plan a bridal shower for her. And, do you know if she has a wedding coordinator. My niece does that, you know? Call me, sweetie, so we can get caught up. Bye now!"

Click.

"Wow, that news traveled fast," Chad said. "But I'm just gonna tell you, I could get used to being the adorable young mechanic." He chomped down on a fried chicken leg, oblivious to the implications of having a Southern church lady involved in one's wedding plans.

The women at the table released their breath collectively before dissolving in a storm of laughter. Matilda sneaked a glance at Alex, whose mirth didn't quite make it to her eyes. She'd seen the same haunted look on her face before. Matilda whispered a silent prayer for this girl who'd been through so much and now stood on the edge of a lifetime of happiness.

Was she willing, or able, to reach out and accept it?

3
Letting Go

Dabbing her eyes, Alex heaved herself out of the deep comfy chair in Reverend Drummond's counseling office. Today had been a challenging session, draining her both mentally and physically. The pastor had questioned her in depth about her childhood, her relationship to both parental figures, and how she felt right now about each of them. Exhaustion gripped her as she prepared to leave, but Reverend Drummond asked her to wait.

"Alex, please excuse my next statement, because my wife would have my hide if she knew I said this to someone. You look exhausted, dear." Concern darkened the white-haired pastor's expression and tinged his voice. Alex knew he'd seen many clients in his long career, and he'd helped them through some dark and difficult times. The fact that he would fret over the toll her situation and counseling sessions took on her told Alex her utter fatigue was obvious.

"I know, Reverend. I do believe my time with you is helping me deal with forgiving my mother and J.T., but it's also dredging up memories I've pushed away for a long time." She refused to cry another tear over the two people who had, in her mind, sent her life spiraling off into a direction she still struggled to navigate.

Her goal was to trust Chad without reservation and move forward in their relationship as the godly wife she knew he deserved. She reminded Reverend Drummond of her aim.

"You know, Alex, I've found the Lord sometimes takes us on a winding route to get us where He wants us. Sometimes the scenery is beautiful, but at other times we have to travel through some desolate wastelands to get where God ordains." He hugged her and opened the door, leaving Alex with even more questions as his closing statement rang in her ears. She trudged through the waiting area toward the exit, not looking where she was going as she searched the depths of her huge purse for her keys.

When Reverend Drummond said, "I'll be right with you, Terry," Alex jerked her head toward the sofa beside the window.

"Hi, Terry. I thought I was Reverend Drummond's last appointment today," Alex said, crossing the room to hug her daughter's half-brother. She never lost her awe at how the Lord had orchestrated her exodus from Woodvale, North Carolina to ultimately land in Burton, South Carolina.

California had been her original destination, but God…

"Yeah, he agreed to squeeze me in this afternoon."

Terry looked worn out. Defeated. An understandable result of the bitter divorce he'd recently endured. Everyone in Burton had known for years what a ladder-climbing, self-serving narcissist Gail Lovell was. That's why she'd secured the services of one of the highest-paid divorce attorneys from her beloved hometown of Atlanta to represent her.

Alex had heard through the local rumor mill Gail vowed to "take down Terry and everything that he holds dear." Although Alex didn't put much stock in gossip-mongers or rumors, that one detail sounded so much like something Gail would say, it gave Alex cause to believe a degree of truth rested in it.

With everything Terry had gone through, Alex appreciated him agreeing to re-negotiate their partnership agreement, giving her more control of her own business decisions. At first, Terry had suggested releasing her from their partnership. Consumed by the divorce proceedings, he hadn't wanted his poor judgment or lack of focus to damage her reputation with clients.

Alex had convinced him, after several clashes of wills and impassioned exchanges, she needed his expertise and the legitimacy his name brought to her product line. At the time, she was still a minor, and getting people to take her seriously was almost as important as the quality of her work. She'd convinced him to mentor her until she graduated from college. Then she'd be on her own.

"Hey, you'll let Chad and me know if there's anything you need, right?" Alex asked her friend and business partner. She'd seen little of him in the past few months, and Lydia had started asking where he was.

"Yeah, I will. I'm finally listing the house this week. When I paid Gail for her half, I underestimated the amount of time it would take to get it ready to sell. I know," he said, raising a hand to halt her complaint at not being asked to help. "You could've been a big help. But, Alex, you've got your side of the business to keep up, as well as finishing school in a few weeks and a toddler. You don't need to take on my problems."

"That's what family does," she said, quoting Miss Matilda's often-used reason for performing extraordinary acts of love for those close to her. It brought a smile to Terry's face, a rare occurrence of late.

"Thanks," he said, hugging the girl whose arrival in Burton had turned so many lives upside down, including his own.

They said their goodbyes, Alex retrieved her keys, and Terry resumed his spot on the sofa as Alex headed out the door with a wave. Her diamond glinted in the late afternoon sunlight that poured in the waiting room windows.

"Alex, wait," he said as he rose again to halt her exit. "I've heard congratulations are in order for you and Chad." The smile he attempted didn't reach his eyes, but Alex knew what a difficult season he was in right now.

"Thanks, Terry. We'll have you out for dinner soon. You know I pray for you every day," she said, squeezing his arm before departing with a wave.

Terry knew he was lifted daily in prayer by the girl who'd learned about the power of God in a real way. What he didn't know was where his head and heart had been lately. Clearly, it wasn't on the people who mattered most to him. He chided himself for his inattention to both his business partner and his sister. He'd neglected his dear Aunt Tilley, too. Between the divorce and the discovery of his adoption, he'd experienced such upheaval and hurt he sometimes had trouble performing simple daily tasks.

Reverend Drummond opened his office door, drawing Terry's attention to the impending session. He didn't know it, but his plea to the kind pastor would be similar to Alex's. He needed help learning how to forgive, but the forgiveness Terry sought to extend was to a stranger and to people who had long ago made their homes in heaven. He'd made his peace with how things had ended with Gail; she didn't occupy his mind anymore. But his parents were another story, both biological and adoptive.

Terry entered the book-lined office, shook hands with the preacher, and took a seat in the deep leather chair. Reverend Drummond rolled the large chair from behind his mammoth mahogany desk before he sank into it a few feet in front of Terry. He handed Terry a bottled water and motioned for him to begin.

"First, I want to thank you for squeezing me in today, Reverend Drummond." Terry steepled his hands and looked his pastor and friend in the eye. The reverend held up both hands.

"Terry," he said. "We've been friends a long time. You can call me Charlie." He'd said this several times, but childhood teaching ran strong in Terry's blood. He'd been taught to address the clergy respectfully and by their title. He chuckled and shook his head at Charlie's request.

"OK, Charlie," Terry said, placing emphasis on the man's given name. "I'll try."

The little exchange served to relax Terry somewhat, allowing him to take a deep breath, lean back in the chair and take a long gulp of water. The pastor asked what brought him there with such urgency.

"I just can't shake this feeling, sir. It's keeping me awake at night. I don't stay in touch with the people I love anymore because I'm scared they'll betray me, too."

"Is that how you feel? Betrayed?" Reverend Drummond asked. Terry nodded. "What about Miss Matilda? Do you feel she betrayed you as well?"

"I'm not really sure how I feel about what Aunt Tilley did." Terry leaned forward, running one hand through his salt and pepper hair that had quite a bit more 'salt' than it did a couple of years ago. "She says at first she followed the example that Mom and Dad had set by not telling me about my adoption. But later, maybe when I started high school or college, I don't understand why she didn't do it then." Terry heaved a sigh, trying to release some of his pent-up frustration.

The rest of the hour flew by, with Charlie encouraging Terry to consider Matilda's point of view. Right after Lydia had been born, Aunt Tilley had told Terry that Carol Ann, his biological mother, died during Terry's birth and the father had never made any effort to get in touch with the family. He understood Aunt Tilley's urge to protect him from unnecessary pain by keeping the secret. But, after Alex found Carol Ann's diary, Matilda realized the time had come to reveal the truth...with a bizarre twist. Jimmy, Carol Ann's boyfriend and Terry's biological father, was also J.T., Alex's stepfather, making Terry and Lydia half-siblings.

"Terry," Reverend Drummond said, closing the leather-bound book he used to record session notes. "The apostle Paul reminds us in Colossians 3:13 to 'bear with each other and forgive whatever grievances you may have against one another.' He finishes that verse with this instruction: 'Forgive as the Lord forgave you.' Do you think that's something you can think about? Maybe you could search your heart about the grievances you're still holding onto." As he asked the question, the preacher reached for a slip of paper and handed it to Terry. "I wrote a list of references to verses on forgiveness," he said. "I'd like you to read them. But also read the text of the chapters in which they appear to give yourself some context of the words. Will you do that?"

Terry nodded as he took the slip of paper and tucked it into his wallet. He asked his friend what he should do in the meantime. Reverend Drummond smiled and took Terry's hands in his.

"Remember, Terry. God's not surprised by any of this, and He won't be surprised by your next steps. Trust Him, read His word, pray with expectation. He's walking you through this for reasons we can't begin to understand. But, one day, we'll see it clearly. Can you trust Him in this time?"

Terry didn't see that he had any choice. He could either trust the Lord to bring him out of this darkness and uncertainty or keep trying to deal with it on his own. He'd tried the latter for a long time and botched it at every turn. Understanding that he no longer had to bear the burden alone but could turn it over to the Lord gave Terry a freedom he hadn't felt in months. Aunt Tilley would be disappointed to learn it had taken him so long to relinquish it to God.

Terry was ready to move forward, knowing more hurt and disappointment could await him, but also knowing he didn't face it alone. He smiled his first genuine smile in quite a long time, rose from the depths of the huge chair, and embraced Charlie. The pastor returned the hug, patting his hurting friend on the back. The freedom of surrender and relief flowed over Terry, allowing him to fully relax as Reverend Drummond prayed.

Terry left the office noticing the tightness in his chest no longer threatened to suffocate him. The sunshine felt warm and welcoming, not blinding and harsh as it had when he'd arrived. He considered what was different, and one word came to his mind. Hope. When he had called Reverend Drummond earlier in the day, Terry had lost hope of moving on from his despair. But the pastor's gentle urging and not-so-subtle reminder prompted Terry to relinquish control of the situation.

As if I ever had any control, he smirked at the thought.

Pushing the ignition button of his car, Terry decided to visit his aunt tomorrow. They had quite a bit to discuss. The long-absent smile crept onto his features. It felt good to smile again.

4
Two People, One Decision

Alex pushed Lydia in the tree swing Chad had installed a few weeks ago, while Miss Matilda relaxed in her rocker on the huge wraparound porch and sipped from the glass of sweet tea Alex had brought her. Alex reveled in the glorious spring day. She had so much in her life to be thankful for: her healthy daughter, a man who loved her more than she could've ever imagined possible, a thriving business, a close-knit church family. Still, she felt unsettled. Discontent. As if something had yet to be completed which, once done, would give her the closure and finality she longed for.

Alex scooped her laughing toddler off the swing with the promise of a cookie and her coloring book. She situated the girl on a blanket on the porch then curled up in a rocker next to Miss Matilda. After her meeting with Reverend Drummond yesterday, Alex needed to bounce a few ideas off her trusted mentor. Sometimes the plans that seemed so clear-cut and rational in her mind sounded ridiculous and half-baked when given voice.

"Go ahead and tell me what's bothering you, dear," Miss Matilda said. Alex shook her head with a sigh, amazed again at how the lady could read Alex like a flashing neon sign. Alex prepared her heart to speak the words she dreaded.

"Well...you know, I met with Reverend Drummond yesterday and I've been thinking... What I mean is..." This was much harder than she'd imagined it would be.

"Just say it dear. Like ripping off a bandage. Quick and clean."

Alex nodded and took a deep breath, drawing what little courage she could from the crisp late spring air. "I'm going back to Woodvale." She exhaled in a whoosh, relieved at finally saying it.

Miss Matilda's face went white and the hand holding her tea began to tremble, making the ice clink against the glass. Alex rushed over to set the lady's quivering, sweating glass on a nearby table before she dropped it, shattering it into a million diamond-like shards. Alex knelt before her dear mentor and friend, taking both of her hands in her own and looking her in the eye.

"I'm not going to stay, Miss Matilda. I'm going back to see J.T., to make sure I have the forgiveness in my heart I need in order to move on with my life."

"Sweetie, you can forgive the man from here, you know." Miss Matilda tempered her hard-earned wisdom with a healthy dose of caution.

But Alex shook her head.

"I ran from my problem once. I need to face J.T., tell him the outcome of what he did to me, maybe tell him that he has a daughter... and tell him I forgive him because of the love of Jesus in me. I owe that to him. I owe it to me. Most of all, I owe it to Chad."

"Will you tell him about Terry?"

Alex hadn't considered that wrinkle in her plan. As she mulled the possibility over in her mind, the ladies heard gravel crunch in the driveway, indicating an approaching car. Alex rose from her kneeling position, looking over the porch railing to see the object of Matilda's question exiting his red sports car.

"Hm. I wonder if his ears were burning," Alex said as she helped a smiling Miss Matilda from her seat. As soon as Terry saw them, he threw his hand up in greeting and called out to them. From her quiet spot on her blanket, Lydia's ears perked up at the sound of her brother's voice. She dropped what she was doing and sprinted off the porch, launching herself off the brick steps into his waiting arms. Together they twirled and laughed until Alex was sure she'd see Lydia's lunch returned onto Terry's expensive designer suit.

By the time the happy pair made their way up to the porch, Miss Matilda had slipped inside and fixed her beloved nephew a glass of tea. Alex knew it had been a long time since Terry had been out to visit Miss Matilda, so she thought it would be best if she and Lydia excused themselves and allowed Terry and Matilda some time alone.

"I think I'll take Lydia home for her nap," Alex said, gathering up the blanket and crayons. Terry and Matilda both objected, but it was Terry's announcement that caught Alex's attention.

"Don't leave. I've got some important news I want to share with both of you," he said.

Alex couldn't leave when he started a conversation like that.

Within seconds of Terry's announcement, Lydia's head rested on his shoulder and her eyes drooped as she neared the sleep she dreaded. Terry eased into the rocker, moved back and forth a few times, and the girl was soon in a deep slumber. He took her inside to the cushy mat in the front room that Matilda kept there for situations exactly like this.

When he returned to the porch, he found his Aunt Tilley and Alex rocking in silence, staring at the garden in the distance. How would his decision affect these two women who meant so much to him? He acknowledged it could bring a different type of hurt to each, but he prayed that they would be able to find it in their hearts to understand why he needed to do what he was about to tell them. Bracing himself, he leaned up against the porch rail facing them, prepared to accept the full force of their hurt, anger, disappointment, and any other emotion churned up by his decision.

"I'm going to Woodvale." He stated it as simply and matter-of-factly as he could. No need to beat around the bush. However, Terry was altogether unprepared for the response he received from both women.

As soon as the words were out of Terry's mouth, Aunt Tilley and Alex looked at each other, then looked back at Terry. Then they looked at each other again. Then...they laughed! Terry had an argument prepared for every response except that one. He searched his brain for how a trip to make peace with a past he knew nothing about, kept him awake at night, and had sent his life into a tailspin could be amusing in any way.

"I hate to rain on your little private joke, but could you please tell me what's so incredibly funny?" Terry crossed his arms and set his face in a displeased scowl.

Matilda, recognizing the annoyance in Terry's voice and body language, sobered and patted Alex's arm, who dabbed at the corner of her eyes.

"I'm sorry, dear. There's nothing funny about your announcement," Aunt Tilley said, reaching out a hand to her nephew. He knew she'd missed him in the past couple of years, and he sensed her reluctance to do or say anything that might drive him away.

"Terry, we're really sorry. It wasn't your news that got us tickled," Alex said. "It's just that it's so coincidental that you would come here and say this today when I just told Miss Matilda exactly the same thing barely half an hour ago. God really does work in mysterious ways."

Terry smiled, reminded of his lack of control over his own life. He asked Alex about her desire to return to the origin of her painful memories. When Alex explained her need to make peace with her past, Terry understood her desire to offer forgiveness, even though it had not been sought. Terry had made that breakthrough with Gail last year, freeing himself to deal with other, deeper issues. The recipients of the forgiveness he now longed to give were either strangers or deceased. He wrestled with the intricacies of letting go of hurts inflicted by people who no longer walked this earth or who didn't even know he existed. The only living person he hadn't made peace with was the one who'd sacrificed her entire life to raise him, ensure he had everything he ever needed, and supported him, even when she didn't agree with his decisions.

"Aunt Tilley," Terry said kneeling in front of his dear aunt, ready to put this step behind him and move on with the more difficult parts.

"I'm so sorry I've been so distant toward you since finding out about my adoption. I didn't understand how or why you wouldn't tell me such an important piece of information about myself, but I know you've got your reasons. And, if my suspicions are correct, you prayed about it for many years." This last part evoked the smile he hoped for.

"Oh, sweetie. I wanted to tell you so many times. But right after your parents died, you were simply too distraught, and I didn't think you could handle it." She gripped Terry's hands in her own soft, arthritis-bent ones, fixing him with her gaze. "As you finished middle school, you were having some issues fitting in, so I rationalized not telling you then. You were so driven through high school to get good grades and excel at baseball. By the time you were away at college, the seasons had floated in and out like the tide, and I thought I'd missed my chance. I didn't think there was anything to be gained by telling you."

Terry remembered each of these time periods his aunt referenced. He had made every effort to excel, attempting to fill the hole in his heart where his parents used to be. The result, however, had been an aloof young man, difficult to approach and almost impossible to get close to. Only his Aunt Tilley had really known him, and even she had been uncertain about introducing life-altering information into his carefully constructed world.

"Can you forgive me for waiting so long to tell you the truth?" Aunt Tilley asked, her eyes pleading for them to be able to return to the closeness they once shared. Terry reached out and embraced his aunt, assuring her of his love for her.

"Of course, I do. If you hadn't shared the past with us, look at all I'd have missed out on. But can you forgive me for being such an ungrateful dummy?" Terry knew he should have had this conversation with his aunt months ago, but he hadn't felt anywhere close to being emotionally prepared to do so.

"You're no dummy. You're my sweet boy who's had to walk through a tough time. I'm so glad you're back," Aunt Tilley had risen from her rocker and wrapped her arms around Terry's midsection, her

31

face pressed to his chest. Tears of joy threatened to stream down her face.

"Terry, this may sound crazy," Alex hated to interrupt, but she'd just had a flash of inspiration. "Why don't we go to Woodvale together?" she asked. This was a huge step for both of them, and they could both use the support.

"Really?" Terry asked. "You'd do that for me?"

"After everything that you've done for me since I've come to Burton, I think it's the least I could do." Alex attempted to downplay the offer. "We may need to wait until after the wedding, though. I'm probably going to be pretty busy with planning, working, and taking care of Lydia."

"Yeah, of course. By the way, have you and Chad set a date?" Terry asked.

"We're thinking maybe November."

"Oh, my!" Aunt Tilley cried, clapping her hands together. "That doesn't give us much time at all."

"Miss Matilda, we're just having a small ceremony. Family and a few friends. We don't even know where it's going to be yet." Alex's voice took on a warning tone as she addressed Terry's aunt.

"Maybe we can go up right after Thanksgiving?" Terry asked.

"That might work out. I'll mention it to Chad."

As Terry took a long sip of tea, he thanked God for drawing him to his aunt's house after such a long absence. Maybe things were starting to turn around.

5
Secrets and Dresses

A few days later, Chad played with Lydia in his living room while Alex fixed dinner in the spacious gourmet kitchen in Chad and Charmain's childhood home. Before Charmain joined them for dinner, Alex wanted to mention her plans to visit Woodvale after the wedding. With Charmain being notorious for interrupting important moments, Alex understood the importance of choosing both her words and her timing with the utmost care.

Ever since Chad had discovered the details about Alex's past, he'd never hidden his dislike for J.T. Alex worried her decision to seek closure and attempt to move on with their lives together by facing J.T. would be met with some resistance from Chad. She understood. He worried about hers and Lydia's safety all the time, seeking to protect them from any future harm. But Alex had broached the idea with Reverend Drummond at her latest session, and he agreed it could be the key to achieving the peace she sought.

Sliding the chicken into the oven, Alex wiped her hands on her apron and prepared to lay out her plan for Chad. Before she could turn around, however, she heard the screen door slam, followed by Charmain's lilting voice calling to them down the entry hall.

"Hello. Where is everyone?" She hurried into the kitchen. "Surprise! I was able to leave work a bit early, so I can help fix dinner or watch the baby or whatever you need me to do. Yum! Something smells delicious." Charmain filled a room from the second she entered. Besides being beautiful to look at, with flowing blond hair and jade green eyes, her personality drew people to her like a magnet. Despite

33

her knack for showing up at the least opportune moment, nobody could stay miffed with Charmain for long.

Alex smiled at the girl who'd become her friend and would soon be her sister. She had an important question to ask her, and she needed to do it soon before the "Charmain train," as she and Chad referred to the fast-paced, mostly single-sided information dump, barreled over them.

"What's a better color on you? Blush or mint green?" Alex asked.

"Blush, for sure. You know, mint green doesn't complement my eye coloring at all. Why?" Charmain was picking at the broccoli pieces arranged on a baking sheet. She had one half-way to her mouth when Alex answered her.

"Oh, I'm just trying to decide on bridesmaid dress colors." Broccoli forgotten, Charmain scooped Alex up and twirled her around the kitchen.

As Alex hugged Charmain, she recalled the day Lydia was born and how Charmain had stayed by her side, encouraging, coaxing, and, ultimately, marveling as Alex brought her daughter into the world. They'd been through quite a bit, and Alex wanted Charmain to be beside her and Chad on their wedding day.

"So, you'll be one of my bridesmaids?" Alex asked when her feet were once again planted on the floor. The commotion had brought Chad and Lydia into the kitchen to see what was going on.

"I'm going to be a bridesmaid!" Charmain squealed, dancing around the kitchen with an invisible partner. Chad put one arm around Alex and pulled her close to himself, enjoying his sister's happiness.

"Man. You'd think she was the one getting married," he whispered to Alex, who elbowed him in the ribs.

Charmain stopped her revelry almost as abruptly as she began it. "Wait. Who are your other attendants?" she inquired.

"Just Brittany, my best friend from high school," Alex said. Charmain looked defeated.

"Just two attendants? Really?"

"Char, we already told you, it's going to be a small wedding. Remember?" Chad had had this conversation with his sister at least half a dozen times, but she had other plans. She frowned as her dreams of an extravagant wedding for her brother and friend began to fade before her eyes.

"On a happier note," Alex attempted to cheer her friend up as she took Lydia from Chad, "I've got a dress shopping excursion planned weekend after next. Are you free? Brittany is flying down from New York."

"Are you kidding? I wouldn't miss it! I'll ask for the day off first thing tomorrow. Now, you two go take a walk or something, and Miss Lyddie can sit in her highchair while I finish dinner. Don't wander too far. I'll call you when we're ready." Charmain reached for the child as she spoke, indicating that "no" wasn't an acceptable answer.

"So, I guess we're going for a walk," Chad said, holding out his hand. Alex took it.

"I guess we are."

Alex's stomach knotted at the thought of ruining this perfect moment with talk of returning to her childhood home and the scene of her brutal attack. She could wait a day or so and then mention it when the timing was better. For now, she wanted to enjoy some alone time with her fiancé.

Hand in hand, they strolled through the pastures that long ago were home to a herd of cows. Now, overgrown weeds and broken fences were all that remained of the once-thriving cattle farm. When Alex first moved into the guest cottage, Chad told her his plans to one day restore at least part of the property to operating farmland. He loved what Miss Matilda had, and he longed for a large garden, a decent chicken coop, and some goats. When Alex expressed an interest in alpacas and a small vineyard, Chad had laughed it off at first. But after doing some research into the financial viability of those two ventures, he discovered that they weren't such a bad idea. The one thing from the old farm days that Chad kept in decent shape was the old barn. He knew that letting it get too run down would require more costly renovations than he was willing to make.

As they walked in the waning afternoon sunshine, Chad and Alex discussed wedding plans, ideas for chicken coops, their favorite vegetables they'd like to plant next spring when all of the craziness of this year had settled down, and a dozen other things. Theirs was a relaxed, companionable discourse, based in love and respect and fueled by the promise of a lifetime together.

More than once, the thought to tell Chad about her conscience-cleansing trip to North Carolina niggled at the back of her mind. She knew he'd be against the idea. He might even want to go with her, to protect her. But she needed to do this, regardless of Chad's opinion of the mission. Maybe having Terry with her would make Chad feel better about the trip since she wouldn't be alone and defenseless. Alex didn't think of herself in those terms, but she knew that Chad saw her as much more fragile than she really was.

Their cell phones chirped, interrupting Alex's thoughts. Both Chad and Alex had finally bitten the bullet and gotten updated phones. Alex hated to admit it, but she didn't see how she had existed without it. Looking at the screen of her phone, Alex saw Charmain had texted her and Chad to come to dinner.

"I guess we just got summoned by the 21st century dinner bell," she said. Chad laughed as they turned around and picked up their pace back to the main house.

Still holding hands, Chad halted right before they reached the back door, pulling Alex up short. Startled, she turned to face him to see what was wrong. He drew her close, taking her in his arms. She wrapped her arms around his waist, closing her eyes and inhaling the heady citrus spiciness of his cologne as she rested her cheek on his chest. She felt so safe in his arms.

"Soon, Alex. So soon we'll be a real family. Are you sure you're ready?" He still held her close, so he couldn't see her face blanch.

She needed to tell him about her impending trek to Woodvale and explain why she needed to go. But not tonight. She wasn't going to ruin this rare and perfect moment alone with the man she loved.

Even as he kissed her before they went in for dinner, a funny feeling in her gut told her she'd squandered an opportunity to be honest. She hoped she wouldn't have to pay too dearly for it.

On the day of the dress shopping excursion, Alex wondered how she could be any more excited on her actual wedding day. Alex, Charmain, and Miss Matilda were making the short trip into town to the one and only bridal shop, and Alex's high school best friend would meet them there. This was the first time Brittany had been to Burton, so Alex was more than a little giddy for their reunion. Brittany would spend a couple of days in Burton before returning to her internship at a design firm in New York City. One of the girls at Together For Good had agreed to watch Lydia for the morning, giving the grownups some rare and much-needed 'girl time.'

An old home had been renovated into the upscale boutique dress shop. Opening the door, Alex heard a tiny bell chime, signaling their arrival. The ladies were greeted by the calming scent of lavender and patchouli, and a middle-aged saleslady in a black A-line dress hurried toward them. She wore her hair pulled back in an elegant chignon. Her expensive black pumps tapped on the gleaming hardwood floor as she approached, her hand extended in greeting.

"Good morning, ladies. I'm Gretchen, and I'll be assisting you today. Who is my bride?" She scanned the three of them, even eyeing Miss Matilda, before Alex raised her hand. "Lovely," Gretchen said, a slight French accent barely detectable. "Let's head into the bridal gown salon, shall we?" Gretchen placed her hand on the small of Alex's back and guided her to an adjoining room.

As they turned the corner, a delighted squeal greeted and startled them.

"I thought you'd never get here!" Brittany said, running to her bride-to-be friend and scooping her up in an embrace.

"Britt! What are you doing here? I thought you wouldn't be here for another hour." Alex had no idea how Brittany had pulled off such a surprise.

"I found an earlier flight, so I took it. And here I am. Let's buy you a dress!"

"Okay. But first, let me introduce you to Miss Matilda and Charmain."

Introductions behind them, the ladies began shopping in earnest. Alex tried on several styles, but none of them blew her away. Every time she stepped up onto the little pedestal and looked at herself in the mirror, disappointment washed over her. She had a vision in her head of the woman she wanted Chad to see walking down the aisle. Plus, when she looked at the price tags on all of the dresses, she almost went into sticker shock. Some of them were four times what she had budgeted for a dress. And that didn't even include alterations, shoes, something for her hair…

The list went on and on.

Spinning around in a lovely, poufy ball gown, Alex heard the 'oohs' and 'aahs' of her friends, but even though it was the fifth dress she'd tried on, it still wasn't quite right. She plopped down beside Brittany on the squishy sofa, leaning her head back in exhaustion and frustration.

"Maybe I'll just go to a department store and buy a simple white dress," Alex said, discouragement tingeing her outlook. She was ready to move on to selecting Brittany's and Charmain's dresses.

Gretchen walked into the room, arms loaded with a mountain of frothy white creations, and Alex almost groaned. This was not her vision, but she had no idea how to communicate her wishes to the helpful saleslady. Ever her right hand, Brittany rose and approached Gretchen, following her into the dressing room. When they returned, Brittany motioned for the group to follow her.

"What did you do?" Alex whispered to her friend. She'd seen Brittany's boldness in action, so Alex cringed to think what Britt may have said to the sweet, misguided saleslady.

"I just explained that, while all of the gowns that you've tried on were stunning, they didn't exactly match your aesthetic of vintage chic, and I asked if she had something that might be more appropriate."

Alex didn't even know what it meant to have 'an aesthetic of vintage chic,' much less have the sense to ask for that style. She trudged along behind Brittany, still in the enormous ball gown, to a room toward the back of the home-turned-boutique. A sign above the door read, 'Gently Used.'

"It's their consignment section," Brittany declared, ushering them into another huge room packed with racks of not only bridal gowns, but colorful formals as well. Alex found the rack with her size and began sliding the dresses, one by one, selecting a few to try on. Her excitement for the process now gone, she didn't even notice that her bridesmaids had also found a few creations for themselves that fit the bride's requested color palette. Alex gathered her own selections and once again headed to the dressing room.

She didn't even bother to come out to show her friends the first two choices, but when she put the third one on, they could hear her gasp from their positions on the sofa. The ladies looked at one another, eyebrows raised.

"Hurry up," Charmain said. "The suspense is killing us." It was the first time today they'd gotten one bit of a reaction from their friend. When Alex stepped onto the platform in front of the mirror, they understood why.

Alex had found a simple champagne-colored silk sheath, barely more than a wisp of material that reached the floor. Exquisite matching lace adorned the front across the upper bodice and trailed down to the hem. The same delicate lace formed tiny cap sleeves and meandered down the back to a small train. Tiny seed pearls scattered across the lace gave it just the right amount of shimmer.

The dress fit Alex as if made for her, skimming over her slender curves and reaching the floor in a smooth line. As Alex stared at her reflection, it began to swim with the tears pooling in her eyes. Turning to her friends, she saw they were armed with tissues, dabbing their eyes and noses.

"I guess this is it," Alex said, laughing with relief as she watched their emotional reaction to the dress.

"How much is it, dear," the ever-practical Miss Matilda asked. Alex's stomach flipped as she tried to reach the price tag behind her back. Brittany jumped up, picked up the tag, and blinked. This caused Charmain to join Brittany, and when she saw the price, Charmain said, "Wow!"

"Is anyone going to tell me how much this dress, which has now become my dream dress, is going to cost me? Please tell me I'm not going to have to take out a loan just to afford it." Alex's stress level over the dress buying process had reached its peak, and she was in no mood for games.

"Alex, you're not going to believe this. It's only $200." Brittany, who was a regular shopper in the fancy stores in New York City, delivered the news in awe.

"What?" Alex asked, not able to believe it herself. "Those dresses I tried on earlier were thousands of dollars. There must be a mistake."

Gretchen walked in as they all stood gathered around the lovely bride gaping at the price tag. They asked her about the price, certain it was an error.

"Oh, there's no error. That dress has been on the rack for quite some time because nobody has the shape to pull it off." Gretchen walked slowly around the podium, eyeing the lovely dress on Alex. "But I do believe the right bride has finally come along," she declared, smiling and clapping her hands.

"I'll take it!" Alex announced, thrilled with her choice and equally thrilled to have the decision behind her. Now, if she could get the painful process of selecting her bridesmaids' dresses completed, she would feel so much better. Sighing, she stepped down and went into her dressing room to change, not noticing her friends slipping into another changing room where they had stashed the dresses they'd found.

Back in her street clothes, Alex joined Miss Matilda on the sofa, looking around for Brittany and Charmain. She heard their giggling but didn't see them anywhere. Then the fitting room door opened and they stepped out, visions in pale beige with pink undertones. The dresses weren't exactly alike, but each one complemented the girl who wore it. The effect was beautiful, and Alex could imagine them standing beside her and Chad.

Alex sprang from the sofa, rushing across the room to embrace these two girls who meant the world to her. How blessed she was to have friends who understood her. What could have been a stressful, disastrous shopping trip had turned into a delight, more successful than she'd even planned.

"Let's go get some lunch," Alex suggested. "My treat. I just saved a ton of money!" The ladies erupted into giggles, which is how Gretchen found them when she returned.

Shaking her head, she retreated silently, allowing the laughter to subside.

"Customers leave either in tears or over-joyed," she muttered, though nobody was listening to her. "Thank heavens we accomplished joy today." She carried the gowns to the register to ring up the day's first purchases.

6
Getting Off the Carousel

After a long morning of dress shopping, the ladies grabbed a hasty lunch at a nearby sandwich shop. Charmain returned to work, but the other three ladies decided to take advantage of the beautiful day. They strolled past the downtown shops, Miss Matilda doing an amazing job of keeping a steady pace.

When Alex spotted a beautiful pearl and crystal hair comb in the antiques shop, they ducked in to check it out. Since moving to Burton, Alex had allowed her pixie cut to grow out to a chin-length bob. Her hair had just enough waves to give the style a tousled look, which suited Alex. Trying to get a toddler and herself ready every morning barely gave her enough time to run a bit of gel through her hair and allow it to air dry.

Looking at the comb, Alex thought how perfect it would look with her lovely wedding gown. Brittany, Alex's stylist in high school, pulled the sides of Alex's hair back, twisting as she went, and fastened them at the crown with the antique comb. The salesman appeared out of nowhere with a hand mirror, motioning them to the full-length mirror in the nearby vintage clothing section.

Alex inspected her reflection.

"What do y'all think?" she asked. She loved it, but she didn't want anything too ostentatious. "I'm not planning on wearing a veil, so this would be my only accessory."

"I think it's gorgeous," Miss Matilda said.

"Stunning. It'll be perfect with your dress," Brittany agreed.

That settled it. Alex paid for her treasure, and the trio returned to Alex's car. After dropping Miss Matilda off at Together For Good and retrieving Lydia, the younger girls returned to Alex's house, despite pleas from Miss Matilda to stay for a glass of tea. Alex was exhausted and she was sure Brittany had to be, considering she'd flown from New York this morning.

Brittany commented several times at the lovely countryside. Lydia chattered from the back seat, regaling the women with tales of how she'd spent her time at Miss Matilda's. By the time they reached their destination, however, Lydia's active day had caught up with her, and she slept soundly in her car seat.

"What're you going to do?" Brittany asked, still amazed her friend was a mom. A really good one, from what she could tell.

"I'll take her to her bed. She'll sleep for a little while and we can get you settled." As she spoke, Alex unstrapped her daughter and hefted the sleeping baby into her arms. Brittany retrieved all of their packages from the day's excursion and followed her into the cottage behind Chad's house.

Returning from Lydia's bedroom, Alex found Britt checking out her tiny abode.

"This place is adorable, Alex," she told her friend. "You told me you'd fixed it up, but I never dreamed it was this cute." Much of the décor was Alex's own creations, which Brittany hadn't seen yet.

"Do you want the full tour? It takes about five minutes." Alex headed down the hall, quietly opening the door to Lydia's room with its soft aqua and chocolate brown color scheme. They moved on to Alex's room, done in a clean white with touches of pink accessories. Since Brittany had already explored the living room and kitchen combination space, Alex decided to show her the shop.

Alex opened the door to the former garage, which Chad's dad had turned into a workshop for Chad's grandparents when they lived in the guest cottage many years ago. It was the part of the house that had sealed the deal for Alex. Well, that and the fact that she was just a few steps away from the greatest guy in the world.

"Wow!" Brittany breathed. She looked around at Alex's projects in various stages of completion.

"I know," Alex answered, thinking Britt was impressed by the garage itself. "I barely had to do anything to get the workspace functional. It's insulated, got running water, and I've put a little fridge over there to keep bottled drinks and juice boxes," Alex rambled on about the virtues of her workshop, but Brittany wasn't listening to a word she said. She moved from one project to another, marveling at the creativity and craftsmanship.

"These are beautiful, Alex," Brittany said. "I had no idea you were so talented. Why haven't you told me how successful your business has become?"

Alex, never one to seek the spotlight, waved her friend off.

"I just take the stuff other people don't want and make useful things out of it."

Brittany shook her head, continuing to inspect Alex's work. When Alex saw the gleam in her friend's eye, she knew it could only mean one thing. Britt had an idea.

"What if I took some of the smaller pieces back to New York with me? The company I'm interning for is a home furnishings store that specializes in eclectic accessories." Brittany's eyes shone at the possibilities, but Alex hesitated.

"I don't think that's such a good idea, Britt."

"Why not? Your designs are amazing and unusual. There's nothing like this out there."

"It's one thing to sell my stuff around here. I don't know about New York, though. That's really scary." Alex didn't tell Brittany that the shipment she made occasionally to a little shop on the outskirts of Atlanta generally sold out within a week.

"Well, let me know if you change your mind. I know these would do well." Brittany didn't push her friend too hard, but Alex knew she hadn't heard the last of it.

As the pair headed back inside, Alex heard her little girl calling out.

"Nap time's over," Alex announced, heading down the short hall to get her daughter and leaving Brittany alone to consider how to get Alex to agree to sell her work in New York.

"So, when do I get to meet your mystery man?" Brittany asked as she and Alex took their plates loaded with spaghetti and garlic bread to the little table in Alex's kitchen. Lydia was already in her highchair smearing spaghetti sauce in her hair, so the big girls settled in to enjoy catching up over their meal.

"He said he'd drop by as soon as he got home from work and washed up." Alex had seen how filthy Chad could get working on cars, and she knew he wanted to make a good first impression on her life-long friend. "Until then, tell me what you've been up to." Their phone conversations were brief, so Alex knew very few details of Brittany's life in the Big Apple.

"It's hardly glamorous!" Brittany smirked, then launched into an animated description of her closet-sized apartment, the exorbitant prices of everything, and cut-throat competition at the design firm where she worked. One of the five interns would land a permanent job after graduation.

"I honestly can't decide if I want to stay in New York or come back down South and start my own business," Brittany sighed.

Alex smiled. Her friend would always be a small-town girl at heart, and the sooner she realized that, the better off she'd be.

"I'll pray that you make the decision that brings you peace," Alex told Brittany, scooping a forkful of spaghetti into her mouth.

Alex saw the shock register on Brittany's face. She'd told Britt about her faith in Christ, but she'd never talked to her about it so openly. She smiled and reached for Brittany's hand.

"It's okay, Britt. I'm not going to yell and scream at you about a relationship with Jesus. But, if I'm totally honest, I do pray that you'll come to know Him one day soon." Alex peeked under her lashes at her friend, trying to read her receptivity for a further conversation.

"If you're going to pray for someone, it really should be for your mom and J.T." Brittany declared, shoveling her own large bite into her mouth. As soon as Brittany spoke the words, Alex swallowed wrong, causing her to choke. She gulped from her glass of water to try to ease the constriction in her throat.

"Mommy, it go down the wrong way?" Lydia asked, repeating what she'd often heard her mother say when the little girl had problems with food going down the hatch. Alex smiled at her daughter.

"Yes, sweetie. It went down the wrong way. Now, eat your carrots so your eyes sparkle like a princess." Alex busied herself with her daughter's meal, attempting to compose herself.

"I'm sorry if what I said upset you, Alex," Brittany said. "As sick as J.T. is, I just thought maybe praying for him would help." Brittany's eye pleaded with Alex to forgive her.

There was nothing to forgive, Alex thought, *but much that needed to be explained.*

"What do you mean, 'as sick as J.T. is'?" Alex asked. The only contact she ever had with her mother and J.T. were a couple of notes a year to let them know she was doing well. She never included a return address, and Brittany always mailed them from New York. They had no idea where Alex lived.

"Wow, Alex. I thought you knew. The doctors don't give him much time. Mom was telling me about it when I was home for spring break. He's got some strange illness that they can't seem to treat effectively, and his health keeps declining." Brittany looked uncomfortable at having to deliver news that upset Alex so much.

"Britt, I'm planning to go to Woodvale in December after the wedding to talk to J.T. I need to tell him everything that happened, forgive him in person for what he did."

"To tell you the truth, Alex, from everything Mom told me, I don't think he's gonna make it that long. I'm so sorry to be the one to break this to you." Brittany reached a hand out to cover her friend's, noticing as she did how Alex trembled at the shock of the news.

Seconds later, Alex heard Chad's familiar rap on the door before he let himself in, bearing a huge bouquet of flowers in one hand. Lydia bounced up and down in her seat, begging for him to rescue her from her confinement. Chad approached the trio, all smiles and happiness, until he saw the somber looks on the ladies' faces.

"Hey, babe," he said, dropping a quick kiss on the top of Alex's head. "What's wrong?"

"Mommy's going to the woods!" Lydia announced, pleased with herself.

Alex groaned. Chad fixed his gaze on Alex, unspoken questions obvious in his expression. Brittany guessed from Chad's reaction that Alex had not yet shared her travel plans with her fiancé. She sprang into action, attempting to defuse the tension. Or, at least excuse herself from it.

"Lydia, why don't you and I go get you bathed and in your jammies? I think you're wearing more spaghetti than you ate. You can show me what mommy does. How does that sound?" Brittany could make a root canal sound like fun, Alex remembered with a weak smile. Lydia, having been released from her chair by her Chaddie, grabbed Brittany's finger and pulled her toward the tiny home's bathroom.

"Maybe you two can take this chance to talk," Brittany suggested as she disappeared down the hall.

Something wasn't right. Chad had felt it the minute he walked in the door. Already nervous about meeting Alex's best friend, Chad's senses went into hyper-alert at their tense expressions and hunched posture. He sank into the chair vacated by Brittany and took Alex's hand.

"Do you want to tell me what's going on?" he asked. Alex nodded, but didn't meet his gaze.

"J.T. is sick," she said, eyes still averted. Chad wasn't sure how he was supposed to react to this news. Alex was visibly shaken, but he couldn't understand why. The man who'd changed the course of her life didn't deserve Alex's worry. At last, she raised those beautiful chocolate-colored eyes, misty with unshed tears.

"I've got to go back to Woodvale, Chad."

He blinked; he must not have heard her right. His mind spun out of control at the possibilities of what she might be suggesting.

Back? For a visit? Forever? What was she talking about?

Chad sucked in a huge breath, trying to maintain his composure. "Baby, do you think that's a good idea?"

He needed to try to make her see reason. He needed her to know he went crazy thinking about her safety. He knew he couldn't risk coming off as controlling. Alex defended and maintained her independence, a position she'd been forced to assume as a single mom and entrepreneur.

All before the age of nineteen!

Alex recounted for Chad her recent sessions with Reverend Drummond, and her overwhelming need to extend forgiveness in the hope it would allow her to move on with their life together. Chad listened in disbelief as she told him Terry had also been struggling with ghosts from his past. Without her knowledge, he'd also decided to visit Woodvale, seeking the closure so vital for him to move forward and heal.

"So, Terry and I decided we would go up together after the wedding and make our peace with the demons that plague us," Alex said, her eyes begging Chad to understand.

It was too much for Chad to grasp.

"Alex," he said, "we're going to be husband and wife. A family. Don't you think this is the kind of decision you discuss with your husband-to-be, not your business partner?" Chad had never thought of his and Alex's relationship as being threatened by Terry, but right now, he wasn't so sure.

"It's not like that, Chad." Alex took both of Chad's hands in hers, her eyes pleading with him. "I would have gone anyway. It's something I need to do to heal, to move on from that painful chapter of my life. But when Terry said that he wanted to go, too, well…" She let the thought trail off.

"You were going to go anyway. Without even talking to me about it? How do you think that makes me feel, Alex?" They rarely disagreed about anything, making this a pivotal moment in their relationship.

"I'm sorry, Chad. I didn't think you would be upset. All I was focused on was doing what I needed to do to get my heart and mind right so I can be the best wife possible. I don't want to bring all of my past hurts into the marriage with me."

Chad reached out, stroking her cheek. "Sweetie, don't you understand it's our hurts that shape who we are? I've got 'em, too. Remember?" She nodded, gazing into his green eyes intently. He continued, his words barely above a whisper. "But you know that God doesn't waste anything. He'll use our past pain in a way we can't understand right now." Chad released a long breath before asking his next question. "Do you really believe that going to Woodvale is what you need to do?"

Alex nodded.

"Reverend Drummond explained it like this. When we don't or won't or can't forgive someone who's wronged us, no matter how bad the offense, it's like we're hanging onto the stirrup of a carousel horse. We're always going around and around, up and down, holding onto that hate and bitterness.

"The carousel horse doesn't know, or even care, we're down there, getting dragged through the gravel, bounced on the platform, made dizzy from all the spinning around. But as soon as we release that stirrup, we fall away from the source of the dragging and bouncing and dizziness. The source of the pain. Wounds still need to heal, but we're free to walk away. You see, Chad, it's my choice to release it. I need to do that."

"But why can't you release it from here? Why do you have to go to Woodvale and face him?" Chad appreciated her need to move on, heal, and face life whole. What he didn't understand was why it required an eight-hour road trip back to where her hurt began. As the thought raced through his head, everything crystallized for Chad. She had to go back to where it all began in order to make it all end.

Chad tugged on the hand he still held, inviting her to come to him as he stood before her. He wrapped her in his arms, holding her sobbing body until the shaking subsided. If a trip to Woodvale would purge the fears and anxiety from this woman he loved more than anything, he'd agree to it. She deserved nothing less than his full support in seeking the restoration she needed, for herself and for them.

7
Graduation Day Surprises

The lovely town of Burton enjoyed a delightful, albeit brief, spring time. Colorful flowers, budding trees, and freshly tilled soil perfumed the air. Alex loved the new life and fresh starts spring brought. However, it also brought graduation season.

Against her better judgment, Alex agreed to participate in the graduation ceremony for her college. Miss Matilda made persuasive arguments about being an inspiration and motivation to the girls currently living at Together for Good. Alex knew the path she'd chosen hadn't been the easy one, but the decision to spend late nights studying while caring for her daughter and continuing to make a name for herself in the home décor business now seemed worth all the sacrifice. If one girl learned something from Alex's example, it would be worth the struggles.

Graduation morning dawned sunny, but the weather forecast promised thunderstorms by the afternoon. Glad to be having the ceremony in the town's large indoor concert venue, Alex paused with her hands on the steering wheel before pulling out of the driveway. She took one last quick look around her SUV to make sure she'd left Lydia's car seat with Chad and Charmain.

Check.

Did she remember the tassel to go on that silly looking cap? *Check.* Saying a quick prayer of thanks for the many blessings the Lord had showered on her, Alex guided her car onto the road to make the last trek into town for college.

It hadn't been so long ago that she and Brittany had driven together to their high school graduation ceremony. Those four short years stretched across time, packed with immense change in Alex's life. She considered the person she was now versus who she'd been when she attended her first graduation. Alex could honestly say that, despite the long nights of studying and tending a crying child and working to complete a customer's order, she liked the woman God was growing her to be.

Feeling free and ready to take on the world, Alex checked in with the administrator, Mrs. Gunby, who lined up the graduates alphabetically before giving them their final instructions. Soon, the group stood ready to process into the auditorium. Right before they started walking, Mrs. Gunby consulted her notes one last time, emitting a shrill squeak as she did.

"Oh, my goodness. Where is Alexandra Renee Powell?" she called out, gazing over the top of her readers and scanning the line in front of her. Alex raised a shy hand, trying not to stand out in the crowd.

"I'm Alex Powell." No sooner had the words crossed Alex's lips than Mrs. Gunby swooped in and grasped Alex's wrist with instructions to follow her. They made a beeline for the front of the line.

"Mrs. Gunby," Alex protested, "I think there's some kind of mistake. My last name begins with a 'P'. I shouldn't be up here." Alex's protests fell on deaf ears as the middle-aged lady, a veteran at herding crowds of cap and gown-clad college kids toward the fruits of their labors, inserted Alex in her new place in line.

Looking around, Alex found herself third in line, behind the guy she recognized from on-campus posters as the student body president and another guy she'd seen in one of her math classes. Alex remembered he was brilliant, but reserved and shy. Even more so than Alex. Realizing she wouldn't get much info from her math buddy, Alex attempted to address the student body president, figuring it had been his job to interact with all kinds of people. Maybe he'd know why she'd been whisked to this spot.

Before Alex could question him, however, the familiar strains of *Pomp and Circumstance* echoed through the building, signaling the graduates' entrance.

Off they went. Alex strode past the place where her friends took turns holding her toddler in their laps. She tried not to smile as Lydia, recognizing her mommy near the front of the line, squealed. "Mommy!"

Chad was prepared with a bag of Cheerios and a coloring book. Once Alex was out of Lydia's line of sight, she'd be easily swayed with Chad's bribes.

The graduates filled the rows designated for them to await the distribution of diplomas, then the provost of the college took to the podium to address, encourage, and challenge the graduates. Some looked on intently, others fidgeted in their seats more than Alex's toddler. Most were ready for this day to be over so they could launch themselves into their well-planned futures.

Alex smiled at the thought.

She'd believed her own future to be carefully formulated when she attended her high school graduation and delivered a salutatory address meant to motivate her classmates. At the time, her big uncertainty was when and how to deal with the tiny life growing in her. Alex had considered having an abortion once she reached her destination of California, but God had other plans for her and the sweet little girl currently sleeping on Miss Matilda's shoulder. Alex understood the importance of making plans, but these days, she also recognized Who was truly in control of her life.

Bringing her attention back to the ceremony, Alex realized her math-whiz friend had vacated his seat to go to the stage and receive an award. Alex clapped, happy for him and not surprised he had earned the award for highest GPA in their class.

"Congratulations," Alex whispered to him as he took his seat, patting him on the back.

"Thanks," he said, still beaming. "Your turn now."

What was he talking about? Alex whipped her head around to give her full attention to Dr. Connelly, the business school dean, who was smiling as she approached the podium. All Alex could muster was a terrified grimace. What was going on?

"As many of you know," Dr. Connelly began, "each year we recognize one student who exhibits the traits of hard work, academic excellence, teamwork, and drive in an extraordinary fashion."

Dr. Connelly's spiky gray hair, pointy up-turned nose and narrow chin gave the impression of a magical little pixie. Alex had taken several of her classes, and she'd been anything but magical. In fact, she more closely embodied the ferocity and tenacity of a ferret, demanding nothing short of excellence from her students. Alex had thrived under Dr. Connelly's sharp business acumen and exceptional teaching skills. Now, however, Alex listened to her professor speak as if from far away, barely able to wrap her head around the things Dr. Connelly was saying. Her voice seemed to be coming from down a long tunnel. Alex forced herself to concentrate.

"This year, we are pleased to honor a young lady who has not only demonstrated these traits in exemplary fashion every day in her academic pursuits, but she already operates a successful business, carving herself a niche and making a name for herself in the home décor industry. We are proud to present Alexandra Renee Powell with the Award for Outstanding Graduate."

The applause began, but Alex remained glued to her seat, gawking at Dr. Connelly. Math whiz guy elbowed her, tilting his head toward the stage. Dr. Connelly motioned with her hand for Alex to come up. Alex stood, certain her watery knees would give way before she arrived in front of her professor. After what seemed an eternity, but was actually only a few seconds, she found herself onstage. Later, she'd have no recollection of how she got there. The beaming professor greeted Alex, who glanced at the line of dignitaries seated on the stage and realized they too were clapping for her.

She shook Dr. Connelly's hand and accepted the envelope containing her plaque. As Alex turned to go, the older lady placed a hand on her shoulder, halting Alex's planned hasty exit.

"As is our tradition," the professor told those assembled, "our outstanding graduate will be the first to receive her diploma, followed by the student body president and the academic award recipient. We will then proceed directly into the alphabetical listing shown in your program."

By the time Dr. Connelly had explained what was happening, the provost had taken his place beside the stack of diplomas, assisted by his trusty secretary.

"Alexandra Renee Powell," she announced, signaling Alex to proceed toward the provost to receive her diploma.

"Yay, Mommy!" she heard her daughter cheer from the crowd, bringing the first smile to Alex's face since she'd arrived on the stage. Alex waved the folder containing her hard-earned diploma at her friends and family.

"On top of Miss Powell's other outstanding accomplishments," Dr. Connelly announced as Alex navigated the shaky steps off the stage, "she is the mother of an adorable little girl, who is apparently very proud of her mommy." This elicited laughter from the crowd.

The remainder of the proceedings passed in a blur for Alex. She wondered if Miss Matilda had known about the award, thus encouraging Alex to be present for the graduation ceremony. Could Miss Matilda really keep a secret that important without spilling the beans? Alex smiled at the thought of her dear friend and mentor being entrusted with such exciting news and not being able to tell anyone.

Then again, Matilda had kept another secret for a lifetime, until the discovery that Terry and Lydia's biological father was the same man. Alex couldn't imagine the burden she'd borne for so long, while at the same time raising her nephew, grieving her sister, and running a home for girls facing unplanned pregnancy. No wonder the lady was a fount of wisdom, patience, and Godly counsel.

Dragging herself out of her reverie, Alex realized her friend Zack Zykowski had made it across the stage, indicating the end of the diploma distribution. At the provost's signal, the graduating class rose, moved their tassels to the other side of their caps, and filed out of the auditorium by the same route they'd entered.

Whereas their entrance had been dignified and almost somber, the crowd and the graduates were now in celebration mode. Applause, congratulatory shouts, whistling, and a general air of merriment accompanied the class to the huge lobby, where they would meet up with friends and family.

Alex hugged her classmates, trying to deflect the accolades she received from the students, their families, and the faculty. At last, she saw Chad's recognizable red hair, which would turn to a pale strawberry blonde during the upcoming summer months. Alex waved at her group, squeezing and pushing past the throng of people to get to them. As she pressed through the mass of humanity, her heart overflowed.

Here to celebrate her hard work and accomplishment were not only the man she loved and her precious daughter. They were accompanied by Miss Matilda, Charmain, and Terry. How her life had changed since her high school graduation. And she wouldn't trade it for anything.

Chad handed Lydia to Terry, giving himself more freedom to press through the crowd to his fiancée. He still loved the sound of that. He'd love it even more when he could call her his wife. At the sight of her waving to him from a sea of people, Chad doubled his efforts to part the crowd, not ashamed of the elbow he gave some clueless man standing in the midst of the melee yelling into his phone.

When he finally reached her, Chad scooped Alex up in a big bear hug and twirled her around, as much as he could without slinging her legs into bystanders. They sneaked a quick kiss before he grabbed her hand and pushed his way back to their family and friends. His height and substantial shoulder width encouraged folks to step out of his way more effectively than Alex's diminutive stature.

"Mommy!" Lydia strained against her brother's grasp. Terry refused to set her down for fear of losing her.

"Hi, sweetie! Come here and let me see your pretty dress." Alex handed her diploma and award to Chad before reaching for her daughter. Alex was well-aware that holding Lydia required two hands.

"Bubba bringed it to me. It's pretty." Lydia proudly ran her hand down the front of her dress, admiring it as she told everybody of its origin.

Chad knew Terry spoiled Alex's daughter more than she liked. She'd once told Chad the little girl was the closest Terry would probably ever get to having a child. Besides, he was Lydia's brother, no matter how bizarre the circumstances that brought them together. Lydia was the one and only person in the world who was allowed to address him as 'Bubba', and he beamed when she used the oh-so-Southern moniker.

Miss Matilda reached out to hug her favorite former resident.

"Miss Matilda," Chad heard the hint of accusation Alex's voice held as she embraced the older lady. "Did you know about the award?"

"Well, we may never know, hm?" Matilda patted Alex's cheek gently, then busied herself with admiring Lydia's dress.

Chad herded their little group to the courtyard outside the lobby, allowing for more room to move and breathe. Once there, Miss Matilda invited them to her house for a huge lunch, and everyone jumped at the chance to enjoy her hospitality. Chad decided he'd earned a few minutes after lunch to catch a little shut-eye on one of those porch rockers.

Back at Together for Good, the ladies who lived there had created a festive atmosphere, setting the table with the good china, arranging beautiful blossoms from the garden in a lovely centerpiece, and even adorning the front porch rails with colorful balloons. It made for a spectacular welcome for the guest of honor, but Chad knew she'd be uncomfortable with all the fuss over her.

Once seated, Miss Matilda asked Terry to say the blessing. He offered a sweet prayer of thanks for friends and family, for wisdom and discernment, and for safety. Chad thought it was an odd petition for a celebration lunch, but he understood praying as the Spirit led. He caught a look that passed between Terry and Miss M., but he couldn't decipher the meaning.

"Well, everyone dig in," Miss Matilda said with a little too much enthusiasm.

Something was off, but Chad couldn't put his finger on it. The past couple of weeks had been insane, with Alex completing all of her assignments, Charmain changing jobs…again, and, the most stressful for him personally, Chad's business receiving word that his business records were being audited. He'd been at the garage so much he'd hardly seen Alex since the night she had told him about her trip to Woodvale after the wedding. Chad decided to talk to her about it right after his cat nap.

He discovered he wouldn't need to wait that long.

"When do y'all leave for North Carolina?" Miss Matilda addressed her nephew, but Chad's senses went on high alert. He felt Alex tense up beside him.

"Monday morning," Terry answered around a bite of fried chicken. Chad looked from Terry to Alex in confusion.

"Like this coming Monday?" He directed his question at Terry, afraid to meet Alex's eyes.

Clearly uncomfortable and recognizing he'd spilled a piece of information that had yet to be discussed by the couple, Terry nodded and looked to Alex for help out of the uncomfortable situation.

"I thought you said you were going after the wedding," Chad said, turning to face Alex.

"I know, and I'm sorry. We've been so busy over the last couple of weeks I haven't had a chance to tell you that we've decided to go now. J.T. may not be well enough, or even alive, after the wedding."

Alex's explanation made sense. But Chad felt foolish and hurt at having been left out of the decision-making progress.

"What about Lydia? Is she going with y'all?"

"No," Alex said. "Miss Matilda has offered to keep her during the day and Charmain will stay in my house at night with her."

Chad's features froze, his face becoming like stone. He wiped his mouth and placed his napkin on the table.

"Miss M., would you please excuse me?" Even in his state of hurt and anger, good manners prevailed.

"But, dear, you've hardly touched..." She stopped mid-sentence when Terry touched her hand and shook his head almost imperceptibly. "Of course, dear. You may be excused."

Chad slid his chair back from the table, being careful to put it back into its place, then took a few long strides to reach the front door. His exit was quiet and controlled, but inside, his emotions were in a turmoil.

He needed time to think, pray, and make some decisions.

Alex stomped down to the chicken coop where she found Chad tossing corn kernels over the fence. Not discussing their departure with Chad may have been a hurtful mistake on her part. She could've made the time to tell him what was going on. But, over the last few weeks whenever they had a few minutes together, something more pressing required their immediate attention. Besides, he wasn't in charge of her life. She didn't need his permission for every little thing she did.

The chickens pecked the ground and strolled around their pen, clucking and squawking with each morsel Chad tossed in. Alex approached Chad, crossed her arms, and cleared her throat. Startled, Chad jumped and scattered the remaining corn across the chicken yard, sending the hens into a frenzy.

"Dad gummit, Alex!" he said. "You 'bout scared me silly." His warning tone told Alex he was in no joking mood. Neither was she.

"I'm sorry I scared you, Chad. That was pretty rude what you did. Leaving in the middle of a meal." Alex moved to stand in front of Chad, but he still wouldn't look at her. "What do you want from me,

Chad?" she asked. Following a pause that seemed like an eternity, he answered.

"Alex, don't you understand? Y'all are leaving in three days, but you couldn't find ten minutes to tell me what's going on? When were you going to let me know? When I went looking for Charmain at home and found her at your house instead? Alex, running away, avoiding people who care about you...that's not how you solve things, you know?"

These last words cut Alex to the core. True, she had run before when she'd been hurt and scared and couldn't imagine any other way out. But the current situation in no way resembled her past. Chad had never done anything to hurt her, with the exception of his last comment. This time, though, she was going to Woodvale to seek the closure she needed to heal her emotional scars, not running away from Burton. Alex closed her eyes and counted to ten, trying to rein in her temper. She needed to reason with Chad. To make him understand where she was coming from.

To do that, she required full control of her faculties.

"I'm not running away, Chad," Alex fought to keep her voice steady. "I'm working on making myself whole again. For you. For us." Afraid she'd lose her fragile grasp of her emotions, she paused again for a deep, steadying breath. "I was going to talk to you this afternoon. You've been so stressed with the audit at the shop and Charmain's new schedule, I wanted to tell you when we had a little bit of time alone. I'm sorry you found out the way you did."

Gulping back tears, she tried to make him understand her position.

"Chad, I've been on my own for a long time now. I'm not used to asking permission to do what I have to do."

Needing to exhibit the strength and independence she claimed to have, Alex drew another long, controlled breath, hoping to stave off tears. She hated crying whenever she had an extreme emotional response, whether sad, happy, angry, or remorseful. It made her appear weak and transparent. The opposite of the image she tried so hard to portray now. She swiped at her face and waited for Chad to continue.

"Babe, don't you understand?" Chad asked, his gaze not wavering from hers. "I'm not here to give you permission. You're a grown woman. You don't need my permission to live your life. I'm here to listen to you. Support you. Offer my opinion... when you ask for it." He lowered his eyes, looking at the dirt he toed with his shoe. "I thought we were a team. How can I be on your team if you don't even let me know what play we're running?"

He dragged his eyes to hers before reaching out and pulling her close. Alex felt her irritation melt away. She wrapped her arms around him and rested her cheek on his chest, feeling protected and loved. How could she stay angry with him? They stood holding each other, talking of her trip, his work, their future. Alex looked at her watch and pulled back, reluctant to leave their little bubble and rejoin civilization but aware of her responsibilities as a mom and her obligations as the guest of honor.

"I'm sorry, Chad. You're not the controlling type. I'll try to do better sharing my plans and asking your opinion. Can you forgive me?" she said, taking his hand and attempting to move toward the large house. But Chad pulled her close one more time for a sweet, tender kiss. Alex closed her eyes and drank in everything about the moment. The bright spring sunshine warming the tops of their heads. The smell of the flowers in full bloom. The strong, safe, gentle arms that held her.

"Don't forget how much I love you while you're gone," he told her.

Keeping her eyes closed, she shook her head.

"How can I forget," she asked, blinking and cupping his cheek in one hand, "when I'm always thinking about how much I love you?"

One more kiss, then they walked hand in hand to rejoin the party. Alex hoped the group inside had saved them some cake. She felt like celebrating now that things were once again right with Chad.

8
The Journey Begins

To Alex, time went at warp speed for the next couple of days. She was caught up in a blur of packing, writing detailed instructions for Lydia's care, shipping the latest collection of home décor items to both Atlanta and her new contact in St. Augustine, and through it all, praying. She prayed she'd have the strength to face her mother and J.T., recognizing two different kinds of strength would be required. She prayed she'd also have the strength to extend forgiveness and, in the process, find the peace in her life to enable her to move on. She also prayed for Terry, that all of his questions would be answered and he too would be able to extend mercy to a total stranger, who just happened to be his father.

Amongst her never-ceasing prayers, Alex felt the overwhelming impulse several times to pray for physical strength, clarity of mind, and the right words. She had no idea what purpose these esteemed yet mysterious traits could possibly serve, but having been led by the Holy Spirit before, Alex learned not to question the gentle, and sometimes insistent, promptings to petition the Creator of all things.

A beautiful sunrise greeted Alex on the day of their departure. *Too bad my mood doesn't match the weather.*

Not one to prolong a disagreeable situation, Alex rose, stripped the sheets off her bed, remade it with fresh linens, and spritzed the pillows with her favorite fabric freshener. She smiled thinking of Charmain falling into bed tonight and enjoying the gentle lavender fragrance. After an evening of chasing Lydia, she may need the relaxing properties of the soothing herb. Alex made a mental note to place the box of chamomile tea in a prominent place on the kitchen counter.

Charmain didn't have a clue about the ride she was in for.

Then Alex set her mind on the business of last-minute preparations. A quick shower lifted her spirits, but it was the enticing scent of coffee coming from the pot she'd programmed last night that lured her to the kitchen with a bounce in her step as she tousled gel in her hair. She'd barely chugged two huge sips from her giant mug before she heard Lydia calling. After one more bolstering gulp, Alex smiled, set the mug on the counter, and strode down the short hall to retrieve her baby.

The next couple of hours somehow disappeared like a morning mist. Alex got her daughter fed and dressed while Lydia chattered non-stop about today being the day she went to Miss 'Tilda's and Aunt Charmain spent the night. The little girl's excitement tugged at Alex's emotions. She was already missing her baby before she loaded even one piece of luggage into the car. When the time came to start toting suitcases to the front door, Lydia ran to her, a serious look on her tiny face.

"Mommy, you can take Lammy with you," Lydia said. Alex's heart melted at the unselfish offer, knowing how much the little blanket with a plush lamb's face stitched onto it meant to Lydia.

"Oh, sweetie, that's so nice of you. But you know what? Mommy's suitcases are packed pretty full. If I put Lammy in there, I don't think I'll have any space to bring you back a surprise."

Alex had said the magic word. Lydia sucked in her breath, her eyes getting big before she retreated to her room, Lammy dragging on the floor in her wake. When she returned, she was empty-handed and ready to oversee her mom's departure preparations, as soon as she finished coloring at the coffee table.

Alex had never left her daughter, and she worried Lydia didn't understand what all the scurrying about truly meant. Her mommy wouldn't be there if she scraped her knee, or needed her sandwiches cut into triangles, or wanted to be pushed in the swing, or... Alex tried to silence her worries, reminding herself she'd only be gone for two or three days.

A knock at her door dragged her out of the anxiety-ridden thoughts. Seeing Chad standing on her doorstep, Alex acknowledged God knew what she needed to calm her down. She greeted him with a smile and a kiss, opening the door wide enough for him to enter. He spied her luggage waiting by the door.

"Wow, babe. I thought you were going for a couple of days, not a month," he joked.

Alex reached out to swat at his arm, but he dodged her adroitly, experience from a lifetime of dodging the same playful, and sometimes not so playful, swipes from his sister giving him the advantage.

"I've only got a suitcase and an overnight bag. The other bag is Lydia's. Charmain will take it when she drops her off at Miss Matilda's in the mornings," Alex explained, bending to start carrying the luggage to the driveway to wait for Terry.

Chad stopped her, took the bags out of her hands, and set them down before turning her around to face him.

"I'm going to miss you so much." The look in his eyes spoke of the caring and protectiveness he showered on her every day. He pulled her to himself, and Alex feared neither of them would be able to let go.

"I'm going to miss you more." Alex tilted her head back so she could see his face. "I don't know how I can ever thank you enough for your support of me in doing what I'm about to do. Please, don't stop praying." She searched his face, committing every freckle and morning beard stubble to memory.

He leaned in for a farewell kiss, but before he could reach his goal, they heard Charmain calling out for them.

"I don't give a darn how bad that girl's timing is. I'm going to kiss my fiancée goodbye." Alex giggled a little at the running joke regarding Charmain's uncannily bad timing. Within a couple of seconds, though, Alex forgot about anything but her dear man.

What was she thinking, leaving the two people most important in the world to her to chase some unknown, unnamed longing to close a previous chapter of her life for good? She could think about that on the road.

For now, all she wanted was to remember everything about this kiss.

Terry arrived precisely at eight o'clock, making Alex smile. Punctuality was imperative to him, and he considered arriving early as rude as arriving late. Terry and Chad loaded the bags into the trunk of Terry's little Mercedes sedan while Alex reminded Charmain of all the details of Lydia's care.

All six typed pages.

"Let's see, I feel like I'm forgetting something. Oh, this is really important. I went to the pediatrician and told them I'd be out of town for a few days, so if you need anything, be sure to give them Lydia's name and remind them I'm gone. You have authority to have her treated if necessary. You have their number, right? And poison control? What about the fire department? What if you leave the stove on or something?"

Alex worked herself into a full-blown tizzy going through all the what-ifs, while Charmain stood nodding like one of those dashboard bobble heads.

"I'll call 9-1-1. For heaven's sake, I'm not a child, Alex. I can take care of a little girl for a couple of nights."

"You're right. I'm sorry." Alex hugged Charmain and went to sit down next to Lydia at the coffee table.

"Mommy's about to go, sweetie. I'll see you in a few days." She lifted the little girl onto her lap, feeling the tears threaten.

"What is a few days, Mommy?" Lydia asked. As Alex had guessed, her daughter had no concept of what Alex's impending leave-taking meant in her life.

"After you and Lammy have slept this many nights," Alex held up three fingers, "Bubba and I will be back. OK?"

Lydia raised three fingers, pointing out that she was that many. Alex held her close and kissed her one last time, drinking in the scent of her, the tears dropping onto her daughter's light brown curls. She again questioned her sanity and the wisdom of the decision to take this impulsive trip. Charmain saved her by swooping up Lydia and announcing it was time to go outside and wave goodbye.

Alex grabbed her purse, her water bottle, and a sweater. Outside, she hugged Lydia and Charmain again, then clung to Chad for all she was worth.

"It's gonna be OK, babe. We'll be here praying you through it. And I'll be here waiting for you when you get back."

His whispers were loud enough for only her to hear as Charmain took Lydia to hug her brother. Alex nodded, not trusting her voice. Chad kissed the top of her head, released her, and opened her car door.

Within minutes, Terry backed out of the driveway, but Alex turned in her seat to watch the house get smaller and smaller until it disappeared from view. With a deep breath, Alex scrounged in her purse for a tissue that hadn't already been used by a three-year-old, only to have Terry present her with a pristine pop-up box. She smiled through her tears.

"Did you buy these just for this trip?" Alex popped two and blew her nose with gusto.

"Yep. We'll both be needing them, I guess. Help yourself." As he said this, he pressed the accelerator, and they sped toward their destination.

The send-off committee stood waving until they could no longer see Terry's cherry red car. Chad hugged his sister and pulled his keys out of his pocket, ready to hit the road himself. They had a ton of folks bringing their cars into his shop today.

Why do people wait until the last minute to get their car serviced before a summer road trip?

He watched the girls, not sure how Lydia would react.

"Are you ready to go see Miss Matilda?" Charmain asked Lydia, still carrying the girl. They needed to retrieve her meticulously packed bag Alex had left right inside the door. Lydia nodded, but both adults noticed her chin quivering and big tears pooling in her eyes.

Chad guessed the toddler was trying her best to put on a brave front. Maybe this wasn't going to be the cakewalk Charmain had thought it would be. Alex had warned them that she and Lydia had never spent any time apart. Charmain had told Chad she thought her friend was exaggerating or, at the very least, being over-protective. Regardless of Alex's motivation, right now Charmain had a real problem on her hands. Chad knew he'd better leave before this situation got out of hand. He turned, intending to escape to his truck, but he stopped in his tracks at what he heard.

"I need my Mommy!" Lydia wailed, her body shaking as she sobbed.

Her pitiful, plaintive call squeezed Chad's heart. Turning back around, the sight of the two girls made him question which one needed rescuing most. Charmain held Lydia, whose arms and legs wrapped around his sister like a starfish, holding on for dear life. Chad wondered if Charmain even needed to support the child. The little girl's head was thrown back and she howled exactly like the coyotes he'd seen on documentaries.

At the sound of Lydia's pitiful cry, Charmain's face looked as if someone had just asked her to walk across a pond full of alligators. Chad saw the fear and uncertainty and, yes, sheer terror emblazoned across her features. He knew Char needed to get Lydia to Miss M.'s before going to her job in town. Under the current circumstances, it was looking unlikely that she would make it to work on time.

With a sigh, Chad returned to the chaos, hoping he could calm both girls down. He suggested Charmain go inside, fix herself a cup of tea in one of Alex's insulated travel mugs, and let him try to soothe Lydia. Charmain bolted at the first suggestion of removing herself from the pandemonium occurring in the driveway. Chad had Lydia join him on the wooden steps that led out his own back door, just a few steps away from the only home Lydia had ever known.

Chad wondered if Alex had mentioned to Lydia that they would be moving into "the big house," as it was laughingly referred to around here, just like at Together for Good. They hadn't been sitting there more than a few seconds when Lydia scrambled into Chad's lap, seeking comfort, security, and consistency where she knew she could find it. Smiling at the feel of her tiny body in his lap, he held her close, rocking back and forth and stroking her soft hair.

Within a few minutes, Lydia's body-racking sobs subsided and she asked, more calmly this time, when her mommy would be back. When Chad told her it would be a few days, Lydia held up three fingers.

"Mommy told me I have to sleep this many," she said. Chad reminded himself never to tell this kid anything he didn't want her to remember or repeat.

"That's right, Lyddie. But until then, you and Char and Miss Matilda and I will get to have fun here. You can color pictures of the things you do and show Mommy when she gets back. Won't that be fun?"

Chad knew he was reaching, but reasoning with a three-year-old wasn't his strength. He did take some comfort knowing he was doing a better job than his cowardly retreating sister. Even if retreating <u>had</u> been his suggestion.

Whatever he said worked. As quickly as the melancholy mood struck her it turned to resolve. She struggled out of Chad's lap, chattering about needing to gather her things and get to Miss 'Tilda's as soon as possible. She descended the steps one at a time and rushed into her own house, reminding Chad of a miniature Alex as she barked directions to Charmain to make sure there were crayons and paper in her bag.

When it came to women role models who could get things done, this little girl had the best.

9
A Penny for Your Thoughts

They'd decided to forgo the insanity and uncertainty of the interstates in favor of driving through small rural towns. By Terry's calculations, it would add about an hour to their trip, but it would be more relaxing and scenic. Since Terry had offered to drive, Alex didn't argue. She hated the interstates, with all of the crazy fly-overs in big cities and traffic at a stand-still if there was a fender bender. And the constant construction delays!

Starting their journey, Alex cried for almost half an hour without stopping. She wasn't sure if Terry listened to her moaning about abandoning her daughter or if he simply kept his focus on the road. Finally, her feelings spent and her energy drained, Alex had slept as if hypnotized for the next half hour and awoke feeling much better, both physically and emotionally. After that, the two business partners chatted like old friends about any subject that came into their heads: weather, politics, church news.

One topic led into the next.

The growling of their stomachs reminded them how long ago breakfast had been. Even though Terry's car boasted all the latest comfort features, by lunchtime both travelers needed rescue from the confined space and the monotony of the center line speeding past them. Alex noted that men didn't take as many restroom breaks as ladies, so she willingly agreed when Terry suggested lunch in the next burg they passed through.

"You know," Terry said, "I know that you like Aunt Tilley's fried chicken, but I don't really know much about what else you like to eat."

Although they met regularly to discuss business, Alex rarely had time to enjoy a meal that didn't involve scanning the menu for chicken nuggets, cutting said nuggets into bite-sized pieces, and sharing some of whatever vegetable was on her own plate. Alex smiled, thinking once again of the little girl who'd sent her life topsy turvy. How could Alex have ever expected the overwhelming, sometimes-chaotic joy her daughter brought?

"Hm," Alex thought about Terry's question. "I like salads, smoothies, veggie wraps. You know, stuff like that." The smile evaporated from Terry's face.

"Alex, that's not people food. That's rabbit food."

Alex and Chad had had this same conversation, so she waited a few seconds to throw her curveball.

"Oh, yeah. And I love a good burger," she said, sneaking a sideways peek at him.

"What? Ha! You had me worried for a minute. I thought I was going to have to search high and low for some froo-froo vegetarian place." His comment elicited a howl of laughter from Alex.

"First of all, you can get vegetarian food at almost any restaurant. It is the twenty-first century, you know? And what's a 'froo-froo' place, anyway?"

"You know, those cute little restaurants tucked into old antebellum houses with wrap-around porches and ferns hung everywhere. They're lady lunch spots, but we can try to find one in this little town if you want."

"Nah," Alex said, still chuckling at Terry's description of the quaint little tea shops and lunch cafes that many ladies frequented. "Let's find a burger place. I'm starving."

"Girl, now you're speaking my language," Terry said, the smile returning as he scanned the roadside for signs of something that looked good. For the last four years, Alex had been able to block from her consciousness the fact that Terry was J.T.'s son. Sometimes, though, especially with the toll the divorce had taken on him physically, she caught a glimpse of the man she grew up with. His smile was the thing that caught her off guard the most, echoing ghosts from her past, but she never said anything to Terry.

They found a little burger place and decided to go inside and sit down to eat instead of trying to deal with messy burgers on the road. Alex gave Terry her money and her order as she excused herself to go to the ladies' room. They had agreed before leaving that the trip was what Miss Matilda would call 'Dutch treat', meaning each would pay for their own meals, hotel, etc. Although Terry could well afford to fund the whole trip, this agreement gave Alex some comfort in knowing this excursion was her own, she just happened to be sharing a car ride with a friend.

When Alex joined him, Terry sat at a small table holding the receipt, waiting for their order to be prepared. Alex noticed a middle-aged lady at a nearby table who kept glancing over at them and whispering to the man with her. He seemed patently uninterested in what she had to say, focused as he was on the enormous burger in his hands.

Alex wondered if people thought she and Terry were together: the stereotypical May to September romance. It wouldn't be the first time they'd gotten inquiries. Several times they had walked into shops or architecture firms to introduce her products, only for the proprietor to dismiss her as the tag-along wife. Although this had infuriated her when it had happened, she'd tried to remain calm and professional so as not to damage either her or Terry's reputations.

However, with the platinum-blonde lady's gestures becoming ever more expressive, Alex began to take offense at the intrusion on their privacy.

How dare that lady, who doesn't know us from a hole in the wall, talk about us as if we aren't even sitting here.

Alex prepared to launch into her theory with Terry but was cut off by the man behind the counter calling their order number. Terry excused himself to retrieve their tray. While Alex watched him, she didn't notice that the object of her agitation had slipped from her chair and was standing on the other side of Alex and Terry's table.

"Hello," Terry said, causing Alex to whip her head around to see who he could be speaking to in this unfamiliar place. "Can we help you?" He had no idea about the concerns dancing unfettered through Alex's head.

"Please, excuse the interruption," the lady said, placing one hand to her chest, stirring up the soft scent of her rose perfume. She extended her other hand...to Alex. "Ma'am," the lady drawled, obviously a Southerner. "Are you by any chance Alex Powell?"

Alex almost choked on the sip of water she'd taken. Terry, polished in all situations from his years on the social scene and in business, slipped Alex a napkin and took over the exchange.

"What can we do for you today?" he asked again, deftly avoiding her question without being brash or rude.

"I'm so sorry. Where are my manners?" the lady gushed as she searched the tiny cross-body bag slung over her shoulder. "I know I've got it here with me somewhere," she mumbled. Finally, she produced her business card, introducing herself as Penny Wyse. "That's my married name, not my birth name. But, I'm not one of these 'progressive girls'," here she made air quotes with her fingers, "who don't take their husband's name, so I got a fabulous man and a hilarious name that folks don't forget. I win all the way around, don't you think?"

By this time, Alex had regained control and stood to speak with the mystery woman. Alex and Terry soon discovered that Penny Wyse was a hands-on kind of person, tapping their forearm to emphasize a point or patting their back to encourage them to talk. Between the invasion of both her privacy and personal space coupled with her extreme hunger, Alex had difficulty concentrating on what the long-winded lady had to say.

"So, who do you think I am, again...and why?"

Alex needed to cut to the chase and figure out who this was and what she wanted. A knot formed in the pit of Alex's stomach. For years she'd feared her parents would send someone to look for her, but she never dreamed it would happen in some little town in the middle of nowhere by a verbose Southern belle.

"Oh, sugar. I still haven't explained that, have I? I told Brian, my husband – now that's Brian with an 'i' and Wyse with a 'y,' isn't that peculiar?- anyway, I told him that I was sure I saw your picture in the store when we got the new merchandise shipment last week. I never forget a face. I may not remember a name, but this time I remembered yours."

Penny finished with a celebratory clap.

"Uh, Penny, I think there's been some mistake. Where is your shop?" Alex knew the names of all the people she shipped her designs to. Penny Wyse was not one of them. Alex knew she'd never forget a name like that.

"Oh, it's right there on the card, see? I own Penny Wyse Interiors right outside of Charlotte. We received some fabulous pieces from our supplier in New York last week. It's for our new collection featuring up-and-coming artisans. They even included pictures and a brief bio of each. You're quite the accomplished young lady." Penny emphasized this point with an elbow to Alex's ribs.

"Brittany," Alex whispered.

How could she do this? Alex had been crystal clear about not showing her work in New York.

"Excuse me?" Penny asked. "I don't think we got any pieces from anyone named Brittany, but I'd just love to see some more of your things. Do you have a website or a catalog?"

"Mrs. Wyse, I'm not..." Alex started, but Terry cut her off.

"Alex didn't bring any of her business materials with her. I'm driving her to visit a sick relative. Can she contact you at the number on your card?" With the practiced smoothness of a socialite, Terry cupped Penny's elbow in his hand and wandered back toward her table as he spoke.

"Well, bless your heart for helping that poor girl. Of course, she can get back to me. Let me write my personal cell number on the back in case she needs to call after hours."

The number neatly inscribed, Penny shook Terry's hand and introduced him to Brian before Terry excused himself. He was chuckling by the time he finally sat down.

"Could we please just bless this food? I'm going to kill Brittany once I get my hands on her," Alex said, livid with her best friend.

Terry offered thanks for their meal, then they both dug in. Despite being a bit cold from the wait, the burgers hit the spot. Conversation waned as they ate, thanks to manners and Alex's preoccupation with murderous thoughts of her dearest friend.

Terry polished off his food faster than Alex then leaned back in his chair and considered the situation.

"I want to make sure I understand why you're upset. What's the downside to Brittany sending this lady a sample of your work? Other than, she also gave her a picture and bio. I wonder how detailed that bio is? Anyway, what's the big deal?"

Having been in the public spotlight for most of his life, Terry couldn't relate to her all-consuming need for privacy.

"Terry, I've worked really hard for the last few years to keep a low profile. I pay for almost everything in cash, my cell phone is in Chad's name, and I pay him for all my monthly utilities. I've done everything I could to keep my name out of systems that would make it easily available for my mother or J.T. to track." Alex grunted a mirthless chuckle. "Of course, that's assuming they would even want to find me. They may have been perfectly content with my mysterious departure."

"What about school? I'm pretty sure your name was in the local paper when you won the outstanding student award."

Terry pointed out the flaws to Alex's plan that she'd already considered. However, while at school, she'd used her middle name in class and on projects. If anyone had ever snooped around the campus looking for Alex Powell, nobody would have known who they were talking about. To students and teachers, she was Renee. Of course, her social security number would be searchable, but so far, she'd gotten no indication of being tracked.

Walking out of the restaurant, she knew her need to hide would soon be over. Once she told Karen and J.T. the truth about the last four years, there was nothing they could do about it. That thought alone lifted a weight off Alex.

Now all she had to do was call Brittany and get this mess cleared up. Checking to make sure she had cell service in this tiny town, she hit the speed dial as Terry pulled out of the parking lot. Britt had a lot of explaining to do.

Alex punched her phone to end the call, still seething. Her annoyance was no longer directed at her best friend, though. Now she wanted to go to New York and strangle Brittany's lying, two-faced, deceitful supervisor. Alex stuffed her phone in her purse with a sigh and threw her body against the seat, wrapping her arms around herself.

"It sounded like that went well," Terry said, attempting to lighten the mood. Alex shot him a look indicating his attempt at sarcasm failed in no uncertain terms. He tried the direct approach.

"Well, what happened?"

"Her boss double-crossed her, that's what happened."

Alex shifted in her seat, adjusting the seat belt so she could face Terry, then she recounted the explanation she and Brittany were able to piece together.

Before Brittany had left Burton, Alex had given her a few of her smaller pieces as gifts. Brittany had taken them to work to decorate her office. When Talia, her supervisor, commented on how lovely and unusual they were, Brittany proudly described her best friend's growing home décor line. Brittany then added she'd tried to convince Alex to allow a few pieces to be displayed in their New York showroom. Talia had brushed Brittany off, commenting that good designers were a dime a dozen.

The next morning when Brittany arrived at work, all of Alex's pieces were missing from her office. Angry and sad, she reported the theft to Talia, whose main concern was obtaining information about Alex, not the descriptions of the items. Talia had been adamant about keeping the police out of the situation, stressing to Brittany the need to maintain the company's stellar image in the public eye.

Heartbroken, Brittany had tried to forget the incident. However, she became suspicious that something wasn't right when she stayed late one evening and overheard Talia telling someone on the phone that she would have the shipment with five artists' work leaving the next day. Brittany had worked on the shipment, and she was sure there had only been four new artists to sign with them.

The next day, Brittany confronted Talia with her hunch, and Talia had come unhinged, throwing things across the office, spewing profanities at Brittany, and ultimately firing her. Alex's friend packed up her belongings and left in tears. She still had a couple of weeks to go until graduation and she worried that this would affect her grade for the class. She apologized profusely to Alex for compromising her secrecy.

"So, I still don't understand where the picture came from that Penny said she saw," Terry wondered.

"Talia must have Facebook stalked Brittany's page from way back and found a picture of the two of us together, then cropped Britt out. What a snake! Now Brittany doesn't even know what she'll do when she graduates in a couple of weeks."

They drove in silence, each lost in their own thoughts. Terry was the first to speak.

"You realize you could hold the answer in your hand," he said.

"Don't be so dramatic. What are you talking about?" Alex was in no mood for games.

"Penny Wyse. Why don't you see if she'd like to interview Brittany? She could be perfect for Penny. She's got a big city vibe, but she also understands the South. What have you got to lose?"

Alex smiled. Sometimes she forgot why Terry's business was so successful. Then he came up with brilliant ideas like this, and she understood what set him apart. He cared about not only making money, but also about people. And maybe not even in that order.

"You know, you have a decent idea every now and then," Alex said, smiling as she dug her phone out of her purse.

"Hello, Penny. This is Alex Powell. I've got a business deal that may interest you."

10
Going Home Is Never Easy

Alex and Terry squinted against the sun slanting through the windshield as they passed the Woodvale City Limits sign. The sense of impending doom growing in her gut since lunch crashed into Alex with the force of a bus. Was she out of her mind for doing this? Stealing a quick glance at Terry, she noticed his white-knuckled grip on the steering wheel. She wasn't the only one feeling the pressure and anxiety.

Only one way to deal with that.

"Terry, how 'bout I pray for what we're about to do?"

"That's a great idea. I think God will excuse me if I don't close my eyes while I'm driving, but my heart will be prayerful."

Alex nodded, then bowed her head. She thanked God for their safe journey, for Penny Wyse, and for family back home who supported their quest. She praised Him for His goodness, His sovereignty, and His complete control over every situation. Including this one. Then she asked Him for peace, strength, wisdom, discernment, and the Holy Spirit's leading in the task ahead of them. As they said Amen, both Alex and Terry agreed they felt a calm unlike any they'd experienced since deciding to make the trek to Woodvale.

Terry asked Alex if she wanted to check into the hotel and freshen up or go straight to the house. Alex decided to rip the proverbial bandage off and be done with the initial unpleasantness. Besides, Karen and J.T. didn't know Alex and Terry were coming, so they may not even be home. The thought of having come all this way for nothing sent Alex into another spiraling panic attack.

"It's fine," Terry said. "If they're not home, we'll leave a note on the door to have them call the hotel and ask for me."

"But they don't know you," Alex said, trying with all her might to maintain her voice at a normal pitch. "Why would they return your call?"

"I'll just say I'm an architect and want to discuss a project with them. Technically, nothing about that is untrue." Terry was splitting hairs, but Alex accepted this plan as an acceptable alternative to finding them at home.

They rode the rest of the way in near silence, only interrupted by Alex giving directions or exclaiming at a newly erected business or home. They approached the huge brick columns flanking the long driveway, and Alex indicated they had arrived.

"Wow. This is where you grew up?" Terry asked, taking in the huge brick mansion set atop the hill in the distance.

Given the perspective gained by a few years of absence, Alex could see her childhood home through the eyes of a stranger. It spoke of opulence, a privileged lifestyle, and people accustomed to having things a certain way.

She and Terry were about to derail things for Karen and J.T., but at last hope began to overtake the dread in her heart. Maybe she and Terry could leave this place having found the answers and the peace they both needed.

Terry guided his car into the brick-paved circular driveway, stopping in front of the two-story Grecian columns that graced the porch. While he commented on the architectural elements of the house, Alex noticed a beat-up old pick-up truck parked at the side of the house. Usually, the gardener and pool staff parked in the back. Only guests parked in the front and on the side. And that was an oddly out-of-place vehicle for someone who was a guest of her mother or J.T.

Standing at the front door, Alex released a huge breath to dispel the nerves that assailed her, then she reached for the doorbell and pressed it once. They heard the chimes reverberate inside, followed by the staccato clicking of heels on wood. Alex recognized the stride as that of her mother and thought she may heave what was left of her burger into the bushes beside the porch. Before she could bolt, however, Terry placed a reassuring hand at the small of her back, and she steeled herself for the inevitable.

Nothing, however, could prepare her for her first encounter with Karen in over four years. The woman who answered the door resembled her mother, but this woman was old, she had unkempt gray hair, there were visible lines around her mouth. It was as if time had somehow sped up for Karen Wickham. Alex wondered if it really was her, until she spoke and removed all doubt.

"What do you want? If you're selling something, I don't want any. If you're one of those holy rollers, just get out now," she said in the same demanding, accusatory tone Alex had heard all her life.

"Mother, it's me. Alex."

Alex managed to choke the words out in a raspy whisper, so great her shock at the change such a short amount of time had wrought on Karen.

Karen's eyes narrowed and she scanned Alex up and down. Her assessment took in Terry, noticing his protective posture. Then she did something that almost knocked Alex to the ground. Karen reached into her pocket, pulled out a pack of cigarettes, extracted one, lit it and took a long drag. She exhaled a steady stream of foul-smelling smoke toward the pair standing on her doorstep before addressing them again.

"Is this why you ran away from home? Is <u>he</u> the reason you threw away your scholarship and everything I ever did for you? Some old guy. You found you some sugar daddy to take care of you so you don't have to work for a living?"

Her insult, not only of Alex but also of her dear and trusted friend, and her implication that Alex was little more than a bum or worse, ignited a fury in Alex unlike any she'd ever known. Never had she wanted to do bodily harm to another person, not even in the wake of J.T.'s assault or Terry's ex-wife's hurtful allegations.

But now, every ounce of self-control, and Terry's hand on her shoulder, were necessary to prevent her from clawing her mother's eyes out of her head. This woman had no idea the trauma Alex had endured, the hard work she'd put in to become the woman who stood here today. Nor did she understand how Alex had agonized over the decision to come here, even to the point of risking losing the love of her life.

This last thought brought Alex to her senses. Chad. Their future together. These cherished reasons were precisely why she'd travelled so far. To forgive Karen for never being the mother Alex needed her to be. That was step one, and it was going to be almost impossible. Closing her eyes, Alex lifted a silent prayer for strength and wisdom…and holy restraint. That last part entered her mind unbidden, making her smile. When she opened her eyes, her mother was looking at her perplexed.

"Have you turned into some kind of weirdo? Are you on drugs?" Karen asked, taking another long pull on her cigarette before dropping it at Alex's feet.

"No, ma'am. I'm neither a weirdo nor a druggie. I'm a college graduate and a business-owner, among other things we can discuss later. I heard that J.T. is ill. May we see him?"

"I don't think that's such a good…" Karen began, but before she could finish her sentence, she was interrupted by a deep, booming voice approaching from behind her.

"Is that my Lexie Bug?" A tall, slim black man stepped out of the shadows from behind Karen. His closely cropped hair was white, but his face held very few signs of the years he'd seen.

"Zeke? Is that you?" Nobody but J.T.'s long-time foreman Zeke called her Lexie Bug. He'd helped J.T. teach her about construction, always offering patient instruction. Now, he pushed past Karen and stepped outside to hug his former protégé.

"Zeke, you look great. This is Terry, my business partner. He's an architect." As Zeke and Terry shook hands, Alex realized she'd given Zeke more information about Terry in two seconds than she had given her mother in five minutes. Karen, hands on her hips, tapped her foot on the floor, obviously impatient for the reunion on her porch to wrap up.

"Anyway, Alex," Karen said, "you'll have to come back some other time to see J.T. He's sleeping." She started to shut the door when Zeke piped up.

"No, ma'am. He's not sleeping. I just left him, and he's wide awake. He'd love to have a little company. Y'all come with me and I'll take you to him." Zeke again pushed past a shocked Karen with Alex and Terry in tow and strode toward the back of the house.

"Suit yourselves," Karen called after them. "I'm going to meet a client." The front door slammed.

Zeke peeked around the corner and verified Karen wasn't following them, then he stopped to address the two guests. He knew Alex hadn't seen J.T. since she left years ago, so he warned her his appearance was going to be a shock. Alex nodded and turned to head toward the stairs, but Zeke stopped her.

"He can't get up and down the stairs, Lexie Bug," he said, sadness in his voice. "We had to have a hospital bed brought in."

Concern wrinkled Zeke's brow and shone in his green eyes.

"So, where is he?" she asked, confused. *Where else was available downstairs?* They had already passed through the living room, the dining room, the kitchen. That left only one room on this floor, making Alex's insides clench.

"He's in his old den. You remember it. He used to have that big leather sofa, but we moved that out and brought the bed in there."

Zeke kept talking as he walked into J.T.'s den. Terry followed close behind, but Alex froze in her tracks. When Terry heard her make a little squeaking noise, he looked around and saw she'd fallen behind. Backtracking, he went to her side, concern etched on his features.

"What's the matter? Have you changed your mind about doing this? I can go by myself if you want."

Alex knew Terry didn't want to leave the matter unfinished after coming all this way. Neither did she. She shook her head, trying to buy enough time to calm her fears and compose herself. Terry deserved an explanation, no matter how it wrecked her to say the words and re-live the event.

"Terry, J.T. assaulted me in that room. I never went back in there. Now I have to go back to the scene and face the one who tore my life apart. Tell him I forgive him. I don't know if I can do it." This was more than she'd bargained for. God couldn't expect this much from her, could He? She searched her heart.

Did you think this trip wouldn't dredge up the horror of that night? she thought. *Then, get on with it!*

"Alex, I understand if you can't do it," Terry said. "But I also know you've come a long way, left behind a lot of people who you love very much, to do this. If you leave it undone, will you be satisfied with the outcome?" His question made so much sense. No accusations, just a reminder she'd traveled a long way to accomplish a specific goal. For Chad. For herself. For them.

"You're right," she said, hugging him. "I'm really glad you came with me."

"Well, I drove, so technically, you came with me."

The light-hearted banter bolstered her courage, and she led the way to the next step in their journey.

11
Revelations and Reservations

Stepping into J.T.'s den, emotions crashed into her like ocean waves in a hurricane. Fear. Anger. Sadness. Alex's knees buckled under the onslaught. Returning to the place of her physical and emotional devastation, the place of which her worst nightmares were comprised, this place made her stomach lurch and her body tremble. Terry again placed a calming hand on her back, and Alex drew strength from knowing she wasn't alone this time.

Looking at the thin, frail man in the hospital bed facing the window, Alex knew she no longer had anything to fear. The decrepit creature in front of her could barely lift a spoon, much less forcibly overtake a strong young person. Alex's mind and heart wrestled with how to react to the heights from which J.T. had fallen, once a mountain in physical stature and a pillar in community standing. Pity, disgust, and righteous indignation fought with each other for the privilege to be expressed. But none of those emotions were her reason for coming here. Alex questioned once more whether she had the strength, the faith, and the heart-felt desire to forgive this sad remnant of a man.

On the other side of the bed, Zeke bent over and whispered in the patient's ear. He straightened, his hazel green eyes catching Alex's chocolate-colored ones. Something in his stare told Alex that Zeke understood why she and Terry had come.

"He's ready to talk to you, Lexie Bug," Zeke said. He patted her shoulder as he walked out the door. "I'll be waiting for you by the pool," he said.

Alex nodded and moved to take the seat beside the bed. Terry positioned himself in a chair in the corner of the room, giving her space. She looked over her shoulder at her friend, unsure how to begin. Terry nodded his reassurance and support. Turning back to the man who lay watching her, no expression on his face, no hint of recognition in his features, Alex voiced the words she'd rehearsed in her head hundreds of times over the last few weeks.

"J.T., you have no idea how badly you hurt me. You changed my life forever, and there have been times I didn't think I'd be able to live a normal life ever again." Alex sniffed, determined to hold back the tears. "But normal looks different for me now. And I'm happy with my new normal."

She held his gaze throughout her discourse, but she dropped her eyes when she finished speaking. Alex had no plans to share any details about Lydia, other than to tell him of her existence. As she paused to contemplate how to bring up the subject of her child, J.T. interrupted.

"Did you have the baby?" he asked.

His voice, weak and scratchy, made her question if she'd heard him correctly. Her head snapped up, wariness in her eyes.

"What did you say?"

Maybe he and Karen had sent a private investigator to find out where she was and what she did. Terrified they knew all about her precious daughter, Alex's eyes sought Terry's for advice. He simply placed one finger to his lips, indicating she should remain quiet for a time and allow J.T. to speak.

"Oh, Alex. How can I ever tell you how sorry I am?"

J. T pushed a button on the little remote by his hand and raised the head of his bed until he sat almost upright, looking Alex in the eye. He didn't seem to notice Terry.

"After you left, I put clues together. When we heard from the school in California that you'd never shown up, your mother was worried, but I couldn't let her look for you. I knew the truth way down deep in my heart, and I couldn't live with myself."

Tears poured down his face. Alex tried to recall ever seeing him cry, and she couldn't.

"Why did you do it, J.T.?" The question had plagued Alex for four years now. Maybe he had no answer, but if he did, she needed to know.

Between sobs, J.T. attempted to piece together a timeline of Alex's prom night. He recounted buying the corsage and placing it on her wrist, watching her leave with her friends in the limo, and reminiscing on missing his own prom. Then he found the wine in the pantry, intending to have one small sip to calm his nerves. As he told the story in painful detail, Alex noticed an inconsistency in what he told them and the facts of that night.

"J.T., when I came home, I found two empty bottles. I'd never known you to have more than one glass of wine on occasion. What happened that night?"

It didn't add up for Alex. *Why had he turned into a binge drinker in a single night?*

"I started thinking of her."

His simple statement could have been about anybody, but the far off look in his eyes told Alex and Terry that J.T. even now remembered someone from his long-ago past.

"Who?" Alex asked, her body tense as she waited.

She knew the answer before the question even left her lips.

"You never knew her. Her name was Carol Ann." Alex almost fell off her chair. Terry turned the color of the bed sheets. They both inhaled so sharply it felt they would empty the room of oxygen.

Terry reached into his jacket pocket and extracted the packet of unread letters his Aunt Tilley had given him almost four years ago when he discovered his biological mother died during his birth. She'd written the letters to J.T., but due to manipulations by her mother, they had never reached him.

J.T. knew nothing about Terry.

"J.T., I'm going to talk to Zeke for a little while," Alex said, needing to put some space between her and J.T. while she processed what he'd told her. "I'd like to introduce you to my friend Terry Lovell. Why don't you two chat?"

As she spoke, Alex rose from her seat beside the bed to allow Terry to sit close to the man whose blood ran through his veins.

Alex slipped out the door, closing it quietly behind her and praying with all her might Terry would find the strength, as she had, to do what he had come to do.

Alex found Zeke right where he said he would be, sitting in the waning early evening sunlight at the outdoor dining table beside the pool with a pitcher of lemonade and three tall glasses. He began to pour two when he saw her approaching, arms wrapped around her body.

She accepted the cool drink, sat in a chair across the table from Zeke, and took a long gulp. Her departure from Burton this morning seemed eons ago, and a bone-deep fatigue from the day's events oozed throughout her body. Alex tilted her head from side to side and then rolled it around in circles in an effort to work out the muscle kinks brought on by a long trip and compounded by stress. Finally, she addressed Zeke.

"Do you know what happened?" Alex had no intention of offering an explanation if he didn't know what she was talking about. That wasn't the case, though. Zeke nodded, took a sip of lemonade, and set his glass down before leaning forward, elbows on his knees.

"Sweetie, you leaving town was all folks talked about for weeks. Your mama tried to convince folks that you'd gone to school early, but some folks remembered when J.T.'s girlfriend left town years ago. She never came back. Way back then, the rumor mill had people believing J.T. killed that girl." Zeke's eyes bore into Alex as he spoke.

"He didn't kill her, Zeke," Alex said.

Zeke nodded. He told Alex about going on a fishing trip with J.T. years ago, before Karen and Alex came along. J.T. had just bought a lakefront cabin in the mountains with plans to remodel it and sell it. After a long day of fishing, both men were exhausted and collapsed into bed. Zeke was awakened by J.T.'s screams in the night. He'd been able to piece together a few details from J.T.'s anguished, dream-fueled monologue. The next morning over breakfast, J.T. told his friend of seeing the car leaving town with Carol Ann crying in the back seat.

"He never saw or heard from her again," Zeke said. "But he never got over her."

"She tried to write to him. To tell him what had happened." Alex told him, smiling a little at his startled expression.

"How do you know?" he asked.

It was Alex's turn to tell a story. She recounted her discovery of Carol Ann's diary and how she'd asked Miss Matilda about the girl. She told Zeke how Carol Ann's parents had sent her away because she was pregnant, but she hadn't survived childbirth. Her baby had been adopted by the couple who ran the home where Carol Ann had gone, but they had died in a car accident ten years later. Miss Matilda's sister was the child's adoptive mother. Matilda had raised the child, but never told him about his adoption.

"The pieces are starting to fall into place," Zeke said, nodding. "But I still don't see how the man you brought with you – it's Terry, right?- how he fits into the story."

"Terry is Carol Ann and J.T.'s son."

Alex's statement could have been a sledgehammer. Visibly shaken, Zeke couldn't speak for several minutes, and Alex left him alone in his thoughts.

"And how did you get to know this Matilda lady?" Zeke asked. He almost had the whole story pieced together. He prayed he wasn't right about this last part.

"Through a set of unbelievable circumstances, I ended up at the home for girls in a crisis pregnancy. The same one Carol Ann's parents sent her to all those years ago. I was trying to decide whether to abort the baby I was carrying." Alex knew that sugar-coating the facts of the situation served no purpose at this point, so she shot straight with Zeke.

"And what did you do?"

93

"Even though she was the result of being raped by J.T., I carried her to term. I named her Lydia." That was enough for now.

"Lydia," Zeke said, mulling the name over. "There was a Lydia in the Bible. A mighty strong woman. I hope your baby's got the character of that Lydia."

Alex sat stunned at Zeke's words. She's never known anyone who read the Bible, believed in God, or went to church. She described her salvation experience to Zeke, whose eyes sparkled as she told about seeking Miss Matilda in the middle of the night to pray the sinner's prayer. She finished her story with a shrug and a small smile, but Zeke felt it called for a celebration. He stood up, waved his hands in the air, and danced around the pool deck. Alex worried the man would fall in the water, but all she could do was stare, dumbfounded. He cackled as he returned to his seat.

"Lexie Bug, God is so good. I've been praying for this family for years and years. I've had my whole church praying for y'all." Zeke shook his head in disbelief, patted his heart, and pointed to the sky. Alex chuckled.

"What do you mean, 'your whole church'?" she asked.

"Baby, don't you know that running J.T.'s construction crew is just my Monday through Friday daytime job? I pastor a little church just outside of town. I have for probably twenty-five years," Zeke said.

Alex had no idea.

They'd have to discuss Zeke's church and Alex's salvation later. Alex took a bracing gulp of tart lemonade to prepare herself to talk to Terry. He approached the pool, head bent, tissues in his hand. Alex rose to meet him, but Zeke placed a hand over hers.

"He may need a few moments to compose himself, Lexie Bug."

Alex nodded at Zeke's wisdom, and together they waited to hear how the news had been received.

Terry dabbed his eyes one final time as he stepped onto the pool deck, attempting to calm his frayed nerves by inhaling the early evening air. He noticed Alex pouring a tall glass of lemonade, and he hoped it was for him. She extended the glass to him and he accepted it with much thanks.

"How'd it go?" she asked, settling back into her chair and motioning for him to occupy the third one at the table.

"Whew," Terry exhaled sharply.

He replayed the past hour in his mind and thought he'd lose control of his emotions...again. He questioned whether this had been the right thing to do, even after giving Alex the speech about coming such a long way to accomplish a goal.

"That was much more difficult than I expected. I guess I don't know what I expected." He took a long drink from his glass and stared into the gathering dusk.

Alex and Zeke exchanged glances with brows raised, communicating without words their curiosity at what could have happened that left Terry so shaken and emotional. They didn't have to wonder for long. Terry drained his glass but held up his hand when Zeke offered to pour another. He launched into a description of what had transpired in the den.

Terry told J.T. about Alex finding the diary and asking Miss Matilda about Carol Ann. As soon as Terry spoke her name, J.T. became so distraught Terry thought he'd need to fetch the other two for help. Within a few minutes, however, J.T. regained control of his raw emotions and asked Terry to continue, promising to remain calm.

"Aunt Tilley saw Alex's Woodvale address on her driver's license the day she arrived in Burton. She recognized the town name from the letters addressed to Carol Ann's boyfriend years ago," Terry had recounted to the old man.

As Terry had since learned and relayed to J.T., Carol Ann had decided to give her baby the gender-neutral name of Terry because Jimmy's middle name was Terrence. When Alex slipped up one day and said J.T.'s name, Aunt Tilley had begun to put the pieces together.

Terry offered J.T. the diary and all of Carol Ann's unopened letters, given to Aunt Tilley when Carol Ann's parents had come to retrieve her body.

"Then he asked me to read the diary to him," Terry said, his voice flat, drained of emotion.

"Did you?" Alex asked.

Terry nodded, running both hands through his graying hair as he recalled the pain the girl had poured out on those pages.

By the time Terry finished recounting Carol Ann's journey of discovering she was pregnant and being carried off by her parents, both men's bodies shook with sobs and regret.

One man looked backward in time and wondered what he could have done differently to change how things turned out. The other wondered what it would've been like to meet the woman who had given him life.

Both mourned the same person.

"That was one of the most difficult things I've ever done. Before I left, I reminded J.T. we'd be reunited with her in heaven someday," Terry stated, his faith the rock he clung to, especially when things were tough. But J.T. had shaken his head.

"God doesn't want me. Look at everything I've messed up, Terry. Why would God want someone as vile and dirty as me?"

"Then he turned his head and motioned for me to leave." Terry's eyes shone with unshed tears.

"I stepped outside the door and cried the tears of a desperate man. I fell on my knees and called out to the Lord to show J.T. the truth."

Despite how difficult it had been to open up the past and read it aloud, learning that J.T. felt unworthy of the salvation offered to everyone undid Terry. How could he make this broken man understand his worth?

12
An Accident

The sun dipped below the flowering trees, and the lemonade pitcher had long ago been drained. Alex and Terry, both exhausted from their physical and emotional journeys, rose from the table by the pool to leave.

"Do you have to go so soon?" Zeke asked as he hugged Alex and shook Terry's hand. Alex smiled at the familiar parting words reserved for dear friends or family.

"Oh, Zeke. It's been a long day, and we're beat. We'll be back tomorrow, though," Alex promised.

The prospect held little appeal for her, recognizing she'd probably have to face her mother again and delve deeper into uncomfortable conversation with J.T. She couldn't shrink from the reason they'd made this difficult trip in the first place, and she steeled herself for the difficulty ahead of her. She owed it not only to herself, but also to everyone she loved.

The physically- and emotionally-spent travelers trudged around the house to where Terry's car sat in the driveway out front. Before they got in the car, Alex asked Zeke if he had a cell phone.

"Lexie Bug," he said with a twinkle in his eye, "I may be old, but I'm not a dinosaur."

"I know, Zeke. You probably got a phone before I did," she told him, smiling as she punched her number in. He reciprocated with her phone. After one last hug, she and Terry made their exit.

Alex released her breath in a huge gush as Terry eased the car out of the driveway and punched the accelerator. She flung her head back against the seat, eyes closed.

"Are you O. K.?" Terry asked, glancing at her every few seconds while trying to keep his eyes on the unfamiliar road.

"Yeah. You?" she asked, not wasting words.

"Did you know that J.T. isn't saved?"

In spite of all he'd been through that day, it seemed the reality of his biological father's spiritual situation weighed the heaviest on Terry's heart. Alex nodded before she answered.

"We never really talked about God in our family. I guess I'm just a terrible person for never wondering why my friends went to church but we didn't. Or even how everything came to be. I didn't give it much thought." Alex tried not to dwell on her past, but sometimes she wondered how she could have been so clueless, misguided, uninformed, and blind.

She reclined her seat in an effort to get more comfortable. Terry had the directions to the hotel a few miles away, and Alex decided to catch a little catnap before they arrived. As soon as her eyelids drooped, however, she heard her phone, the insistent buzz making her purse vibrate.

"Ugh. I wonder what Zeke forgot to tell us," she guessed as she dug in the contents of her mammoth mom-purse. By the time she recovered it from the depths of her bag, it had gone silent. Punching the 'missed call' button, Alex saw that Chad had tried to reach her. Six times.

Fear gripped her heart and knotted her stomach as she considered the possibilities. Chad wouldn't call that many times to simply check on their trip. Lydia! If something had happened to her baby and she wasn't there, Alex didn't know if she'd ever forgive herself.

Hands quaking so badly it took three tries to connect her finger to the redial button, Alex drew a deep breath to steel herself for the worst.

Chad checked the hardwood floor in his living room to make sure he'd not worn a rut pacing for the last two hours. Lydia finally slept with her head on his shoulder, her tiny body becoming heavier with each lap around the room. Her bandaged arm hung like a wet noodle at her side, but she clung to him, even in her sleep, with the other.

As Chad leaned over to lay his precious cargo on the sofa, his phone punctuated the silence with the customized ringtone of Alex's voice indicating she was calling. He chastised himself for forgetting to put the stupid thing on vibrate. When Lydia heard her mommy's voice blaring "Hey, sweetie" over and over from Chad's phone, her eyes popped open, erasing all of Chad's efforts at comfort. Lydia's wailing resumed as Chad sat next to the little girl and stabbed at the phone.

"Hey, babe," he said, trying to act nonchalant even with the caterwauling going on beside him.

"Chad! Oh, my goodness. What's going on? Why is Lydia screaming like that? Do I need to come home? Oh! I knew I shouldn't have done this. You tried to warn me. What have I done?"

Chad felt Alex's desperation escalate with each question. He wondered for a brief second how he'd gotten himself into this position of having a screaming injured toddler beside him and her hysterical mother on the phone.

As fast as the thought entered his brain, he remembered that these girls, whether in crisis or celebration or anything in between, were his blessings from God. He had to step up and provide the comfort they both needed in this moment.

"Alex, everything's fine."

Chad spoke calmly and softly into the phone as he sat on the sofa and allowed Lydia to climb into his lap. The little girl settled against his chest, her hiccups now the only remnants of the intense crying.

"How can you expect me to believe that, Chad? You called six times. I just now heard Lydia screaming in the background. Please, tell me what's going on." The tremor in Alex's voice gave away her level of panic.

"OK, babe. We had a little accident, but..." Chad started.

"You what?" Alex shrieked.

Chad cringed as the sobbing started on the other end of the line. He rolled his eyes heavenward, praying for any help the Lord might be willing to dole out.

"Just calm down, honey. I've got it all under control. Although, I gotta tell you, Charmain and Miss M. were Godsends this afternoon." Chad prepared to break the news to the little girl's mom in a way that wouldn't send her into orbit. "Just take a few deep breaths and I'll fill you in."

He heard Alex inhale and exhale several times before going silent, obviously waiting for him to continue.

"So, well, there's no easy way to say it, so I'm just going to tell you. I promise we were keeping a close eye on her. These things happen with kids. The doctor said he sees it all the time."

"Doctor! What? She had to see the doctor?" Chad heard Alex starting to come unhinged again, so he tried a different approach. Something more direct.

"We were visiting Miss M.'s chickens. See, I went to check on Lyddie during my lunch break. I was standing at the gate to the pen, shooing the pecking little beasts back. But Lydia slipped by me and tried to squeeze through the partially open gate." Chad took a deep breath, hoping he gave enough information, but wanting to spare Alex the details of what transpired. "Before I knew what had happened, she was howling. I looked down and she was holding her arm." He spared Alex the account of how much blood poured out of that little arm. He also omitted the part where his stomach heaved at the sight of Lydia being hurt, especially while he was supposed to be protecting her.

"So, she scraped herself," Alex momentarily returned to the role of rational mom. "Why would she need to see the doctor for that? She's up to date on her tetanus immunization."

"You see, the thing is, we thought... That is, Miss M. and Charmain and I thought that considering how it was... Well, there was so much... Wait, that's not what I wanted to say."

Chad stumbled over the explanation, adamant about remaining vague concerning the blood, the ride to the Emergency Room, and the screams of pain. He wiped a hand over his face, trying to erase the memory of this afternoon. Alex's panicked voice brought him back to the present.

"Chad. I know there's something you're not telling me. Please," her voice cracked. She cleared her throat. "Please, tell me what happened to my daughter."

"We took her to the ER, sweetie. They put seven stitches in. Your doctor wants to see her in a week."

There. He'd ripped the bandage off. He smiled at his own play on words.

His humorous thoughts met with silence on the other end. He began to think she'd hung up on him. "Alex. Are you still there?"

"I'm here."

"You OK?"

"I'm not sure. Can I talk to her?"

Chad glanced down at the little girl now sleeping in his lap. He hated to say his next words to Alex, but he knew Lydia needed to rest after her eventful day.

"Um, honey, I know you really want to talk to her. I'm sure it would put your mind at ease. But the truth is she just fell asleep. She's exhausted after everything that's gone on today." He waited to gauge Alex's reaction to the news.

"I understand." The words came out stilted and jerky.

Chad knew she held back the tears she wanted to cry. His heart broke for her.

"Hey, how 'bout I send you a picture? Would that help? Then, when she wakes up, I know she's going to want to tell you all about today." He hoped it would appease her.

"Yeah. OK. That's a good idea. Call me back when she wakes up."

"I will. And, Alex, I love you."

"Love you, too. Bye."

Staring at the silent phone, Chad realized he hadn't even asked how her meeting with J.T. had gone.

"Is everything all right?" Terry glanced over to see Alex with her arms wrapped around herself. She stared out the passenger window, but he saw how her body shook with the sobs she tried to muffle. She nodded, never taking her eyes off the side of the road as it sped by them.

"What happened?" After hearing only Alex's side of the conversation, Terry knew only that his little sister had been injured. Not wanting to further upset Alex or push for information she wasn't ready to share, Terry kept his eyes on the road and waited.

"Lydia cut her arm on the chicken pen and had to get stitches."

Alex's abbreviated version of the conversation left much to the imagination, but Terry remained silent. Glancing at her again, he saw her big brown eyes swimming, her face tear-streaked.

"Wanna talk about it?" Terry reached for the tissue box as he asked, offering what small comfort he could.

"How could I let this happen?" Alex wiped her eyes, blew her nose, and drew in a deep breath.

"Alex, you weren't even…"

"I know," she said, holding up her hand, palm facing him as if she could stop his words. "I wasn't there. That's the point. I've come on this ridiculous trek to see the two people who destroyed my life, meanwhile I've abandoned everyone I love. And the kicker is, I all but accused Chad of being capable of hurting my baby, and he's the one who took care of her. Because I wasn't there."

She'd worked herself into a frenzy by the time she finished her self-accusatory rant. Spent, Alex again banged her head back against the seat. The dam broke on her waning self-control, the sobs shaking her small frame. Terry let some of the force of her guilt and doubt play itself out before speaking, praying he wouldn't alienate her in the process.

"You should listen to what you're saying."

Terry knew the truth hurt sometimes. He also knew that sometimes the truth was exactly what someone needed to hear. He'd experienced both situations repeatedly over the last few years.

"What are you talking about?" The edge on Alex's voice told Terry she'd put her guard up. He'd have to tread carefully.

"Well, it sounds like your fears and your past pain are telling you lies. If Chad wanted to hurt Lydia, would he take her to the ER? Then ditch work to stay with her while she recuperates? Were Charmain and Aunt Tilley there when it happened?" Alex nodded. "So, why didn't Chad just ask them to take her?" Alex shrugged. "Because he loves her. And he loves you. Can't you see that?"

Alex turned her face back to the window as the town's homes and businesses passed in a blur. "J.T. loved me, too," she said, her voice so quiet Terry almost missed it.

"Alex, let me give you a piece of advice, even though you haven't asked for it." He needed to share the wisdom he'd gained through his own pain and, hopefully, spare her from experiencing and causing more heartache. "Don't project your fears onto Chad. For years, Gail tried to make me into someone I wasn't. Someone I didn't even want to be. But, I stayed because I thought my love for her could make things right. It never did. Let Chad make his own mistakes. Y'all can deal with that together. But don't make up imaginary ones in your head. He has no defense for that."

It pained Terry to say the words, knowing they cut Alex to the core. How would she respond? He knew she stood at a cross-road in her life. He prayed she'd make the right choice.

13
Redirection

A strange bed and a guilty conscience kept Alex awake most of the night. A few minutes after two o'clock, she opened her phone and tapped on the picture Chad had snapped of her precious daughter sleeping soundly, her tiny arm wrapped in bandages and her long lashes spiky with tears recently shed.

Alex climbed out of the huge king-sized hotel bed, shoved her feet into her flip flops, and shuffled to the bathroom. The harsh light stung her tired eyes. When she caught a glimpse of her reflection in the wall-to-wall mirror, the puffiness from endless crying and dark eye circles from lack of sleep made her do a double take. Bracing her arms against the counter, Alex hung her head, overcome with despair.

What in the world was I thinking? Have I messed up everything with Chad? Is my desire to face my past going to cost me my future?

Doubts raced through Alex's mind, spiraling to new heights even as she tried to get a grip on her situation. She trudged back into the bedroom, too tired to get dressed but too emotional to sleep.

Maybe there's something good on TV.

A quick scan of the room didn't reveal the TV remote. She pulled open the nightstand drawer. No remote. Instead, she found the one thing she needed at the moment.

The Bible tucked away in the drawer beckoned for her to pick it up. Alex hugged the book to her chest as if embracing a long-lost friend. She opened the notes on her phone to the list of verses Reverend Drummond had recommended for when she found herself in times of dark despair. She flipped through the pages, hungry to seek counsel from the One who knew her and loved her anyway.

Alex read for over an hour, drinking in the wisdom, comfort, and strength she always found in God's word. The tears she shed now were those of relief and release and peace. She knelt beside the bed, calling out to the God who'd rescued and protected her over and over. The God who'd blessed her with a beautiful daughter and who'd brought Chad into her life. She unashamedly laid her fears and insecurities at His feet, aware she'd been carrying a weight she didn't need to lug around anymore.

Glad to finally be free of the unnecessary burden.

Her emotions spent and her body exhausted, Alex felt a flood of peace the likes of which had eluded her for many months. She'd allowed herself to ignore God's loving comfort, trading His peace for the insane pace and constant demands of life as a mother, student, and business owner. It wasn't a mutually exclusive choice. She understood with new clarity she could fulfill the many roles life demanded of her and still rest in the Lord. In fact, she could be better at all her earthly responsibilities if she simply allowed God to be in control.

Why is this such a difficult lesson for me to learn?

Her chirping phone woke her at seven o'clock. She groped around the bed, disoriented and searching for the source of the noise. When her outstretched hand made contact with the hard surface of the device buried under the covers, she tapped the screen to answer. She was rewarded for her sleepy efforts by Chad's familiar voice.

"Good morning, sunshine. How are you feeling?"

Joy and gratitude flooded Alex's soul. This man. She'd accused him of being capable of horrible atrocities. Of trying to control her. And how did he respond? With love, kindness, and compassion. She'd done nothing to deserve the unconditional love he continued to pour on her.

Considering his question, Alex sat up in the bed and stretched. She felt good. Once she'd finally fallen asleep, it had been a deep, restorative rest like she'd not had since she'd been a child.

"I'm actually feeling pretty good. How about you?" As she talked, she climbed out of bed and made a beeline for the room's coffee maker, which she'd set up last night. She pushed the button to start the brew cycle. "And how's our girl?" She hoped Chad picked up on her use of the plural pronoun.

"She's doing fine," he said. Alex heard the smile in his voice. "Charmain's off work today, so we're not taking her to school. She may have some pain, so we're just going to let her rest on the couch and watch videos. Is that cool with you?"

"Yeah. I mean, whatever you think is best."

How did she even begin to apologize or try to explain her soul-baring encounter with the Lord? She didn't want to do it over the phone. She wanted to hold his hands, look in his eyes, see if he could forgive her for pushing him away and questioning his motives.

"Sweetie, is everything OK?" Chad's tone held none of the lightness of a few moments ago.

"Yes. Everything is perfect. I'll tell you all about it when I get home. But, for now, know that I love you very much. And I'm so thankful Lydia and I have you to take care of us."

"Gosh, babe. That's all I want to do. You're my girls, my gifts from God. I don't know what I'd do without you two."

Alex knew truer words had never been spoken. They talked a few more minutes, with Alex requesting another picture and reminding Chad to tell Lydia how much she loved her.

She hung up ready to face the day ahead of her with more strength and confidence than she'd felt in a long time.

As they had agreed after dinner last night, Terry prepared to meet Alex at the car after breakfast. Fastening his watch on his wrist, he wondered how she'd slept. They'd both had a pretty rough day, considering the hours in the car, the upsetting encounter with Karen, and their one-on-one time with J.T. And Alex had to shoulder the added burden of knowing her child had been hurt, and she was too far away to do anything to help or console her.

Terry grabbed his keys and room card and strode down the long hall toward the parking lot. He paused in the lobby to fix two cups of coffee and secure the lids before continuing. As the cool North Carolina morning breeze greeted him, he was shocked to see Alex already waiting for him beside his car.

She smiled as she held up two coffee cups.

"I guess great minds really do think alike," she said. They both laughed while Terry clicked the button to open the doors. "I could probably use a couple of cups today," Alex said, settling into the passenger seat.

"Rough night?" Terry didn't want to pry, but he was surprised at how refreshed and relaxed Alex looked today. He'd been expecting more tears and sadness. Instead, she sat beside him chattering about Lydia staying home from school, Chad sending pictures of the little girl, and how well she'd rested.

"Alex?" Terry wasn't sure if she was faking it. Or maybe she was hyped up on too much coffee.

"Yeah?" she said, her face the picture of calm and contentment.

"Are you really OK? I mean… last night when we got to the hotel you were a mess. And now… Well, let's just say I'm surprised to see you so happy." The last thing Terry wanted was to insult her, but he couldn't follow the drastic mood change. He didn't want her to have a breakdown at Karen and J.T.'s house.

"About that. I'm really sorry for being such a pain yesterday. I also want to thank you for your advice. I did a lot of soul-searching and praying last night. I'm in a much better place today." As she spoke, she relaxed her head back on the seat, a smile playing at her lips.

Terry concentrated on the road before him. Maybe she was good to go, but he wasn't sure how his emotions would hold up today. He said a quick prayer for the same reassurance and peace Alex had encountered.

Terry held the stack of letters his birth mother had written, his hands trembling so badly he feared he'd drop them and send them raining down on the polished hardwood in J.T.'s convalescent room. Alex pressed her hand to his shoulder, a reassurance he needed.

"You can sit right here," Zeke said, positioning a wing-back chair beside the large floor-to-ceiling window. "The light's best here." His eyes caught Terry's, holding him in a gaze that spoke encouragement and empathy without saying a word.

When Terry and Alex had arrived a few minutes ago, Zeke had met them at the door and ushered them directly into J.T.'s room. Karen was nowhere to be seen, and Alex hadn't inquired about her. Without preamble, the frail man in the bed had greeted them by jabbing the stack of yellowed envelopes secured with a faded pink ribbon toward Terry.

"I need you to read these to me today," he said.

"Sir, don't you think it might be better if you read these by yourself? I mean, they probably contain ..." Terry tried to object, but J.T. cut him off before he could make his case.

"You're a grown man. There's nothing in here that would shock you. Besides, I'd think you'd want to know a little bit about your mother."

Though his tone was brusque, his eyes pleaded with Terry to do this thing for him.

"Yes, sir," Terry said.

Now, after accepting the stack from J.T., Terry set the letters on a nearby side table and settled into the comfortable chair. Alex leaned down to whisper in his ear.

"I'll just wait for you by the pool," she said. But J.T. wouldn't hear of it.

"No, Alex. I want you to hear this, too. I want you to understand where the pain began that drove me to be the monster I turned into. Please." This final appeal was little more than a squeak.

Terry watched the emotions play across Alex's face, and he was beyond grateful when she perched on the edge of a straight-backed wooden chair. She looked as if she might bolt out the door at any moment, but at least she agreed to provide Terry the support of her presence for a time.

Selecting a brittle envelope from the top of the stack, Terry opened it gently and pulled the letter out. His heart beat out of control as he recognized the slanted, looping handwriting of the teenaged girl who'd written in the diary. His mother. Taking a deep breath, he prepared to begin.

He had one request to make first.

"Before I start, I'd like to ask Zeke to pray. Is that OK with you?" Terry watched J.T. heave a deep sigh and give a reluctant nod. Zeke, however, thought this was a fantastic idea, as evidenced by his bright smile against the deep chocolate color of his skin.

"Father, we enter Your presence today acknowledging that we're sinners in need of Your Son. We ask You to be in this place with us, directing our words and softening our hearts. May we see others as You see them. In Jesus' holy name, Amen."

The prayer took less than half a minute. In that brief span, however, Terry felt tension, his constant companion for the week leading up to this trip, drain from his body, replaced by a serenity he both recognized and welcomed. He finally felt he could undertake this task he'd been given.

"Thanks, Zeke," Terry said, finally able to turn his attention to the crinkly paper in his hands. "Are you ready to start, J.T.?"

J.T. closed his eyes, leaned his head back against the pillow, and nodded. Terry began to read, transporting the occupants of the room to a long-ago time, drawing them into the thoughts and fears of a scared girl. A girl deeply in love. And a girl who couldn't understand why her love had forsaken her.

At some point, Zeke slipped out to get Terry a glass of water. Taking a sip, Terry glanced at the man lying in the bed. J.T.'s eyes were still closed, but a tear rolled down his cheek occasionally. Terry raised his eyebrows in question and glanced at Zeke. Zeke spun his finger in the air, indicating Terry should continue.

Two hours after he started, Terry folded the final letter, the one in which Carol Ann told J.T. about her decision to raise their child alone. The letters had taken them on a roller coaster of hurt, betrayal, hope, and love. Knowing the ending made the words that much more painful to hear.

Spent, Terry closed his eyes and slumped back in the chair, voice shot and emotions frazzled. The whole time he'd narrated Carol Ann's thoughts, he couldn't forget he was the person growing within her. She'd loved him without even knowing him, even to the point of being willing to challenge societal norms to keep him.

When J.T. drew a raspy breath, Terry opened his eyes and looked at the old man with concern. J.T. wasn't looking at Terry, though. He stared across the room to the hard, wooden chair in the corner. He raised a feeble hand and motioned for her to pull her chair up beside him.

Terry prayed Alex had the strength to take this important step toward accomplishing one of the most important goals of the trip.

14

Forgiven...At Last

I *can't do it.*

It was the first thought that popped into Alex's mind when J.T. invaded her quiet bubble in the corner. Terry's deep voice had pummeled them with the agony of Carol Ann's unwilling departure from Woodvale, her salvation experience, and her heart-wrenching belief that the one she'd loved had abandoned her.

Of course, everyone listening to the anguish she poured into those letters knew her love hadn't forgotten her. She'd been ripped away from him.

Now, Alex faced the man who'd lost his first love. The same man who'd brutally assaulted her. She didn't understand how her heart could feel pity. This man had wounded her to the core. He'd derailed her plans, sent her life into turmoil, and even caused her to doubt the love of the most wonderful person she'd ever met.

What is impossible with man is possible with God.

The familiar scripture verse rang in her mind so clearly, she felt sure someone must have spoken it. Alex looked around the room, but all three men were silent as they watched her. Feeling like a puppet whose actions someone else controlled, Alex arose from the hard chair, her bones and muscles aching in protest. She walked toward the bed with all the grace of a robot. Terry vacated the comfy chair by the window and patted the seat.

Sinking into the chair, Alex glanced at Zeke, who mouthed the words, "Thank you," to her. She gave him the smallest of nods. J.T. spoke first, although it took him several tries to regulate the cracking of his voice. Finally, he gained control enough to address his step-daughter.

"Alex, there aren't enough words in any language to tell you how sorry I am for what I did to you. I'll go to my grave tortured by my selfish, unforgivable actions. I don't even have the right to ask you to listen to me, but I thank you for doing so." He leaned back against the pillows again, obviously spent from the effort of talking. Zeke nodded at Alex, indicating she could speak while J.T. rested.

"J.T., you're right about one thing. You have no right to ask me to listen to your excuses or your explanations. When you raped me," the words made J.T. wince, "I was scared, confused, hurt. I didn't understand how it could have happened. You were more of a parent to me than my own mother." It was Alex's turn to stop to gather her composure. After a few deep breaths, she continued. "What you're wrong about, however, is thinking you have to take this terrible thing you did to the grave with you."

J.T.'s eyes opened wide and he looked at Alex, confusion evident in his expression.

"What are you talking about?"

"I'm not here to gloat or remind you of the sins of your past, J.T. We've all got past sins. I've come all this way with one goal. I want you to know I forgive you." A huge whoosh of breath escaped Alex.

How long had she wondered if she could say those words to him and actually mean them? Searching her heart, she knew she did mean it. Holding onto the pain and hurt and bitterness from the past hadn't been a successful way of dealing with her emotions. But she was being urged to go a step further. Without pausing to consider the implications, Alex forged ahead.

"J.T., my forgiveness isn't what matters here. I know Zeke's told you this, but you need to ask for God's forgiveness." Alex's words prompted J.T. to shake his head furiously against the pillow.

"No. I've told Zeke and I'll tell you two. God can't forgive what I've done. Why would he?"

Alex leaned forward in her seat and placed her hand over the frail one that rested on the sheets. It was the first time they'd touched since the night of the attack. The feel of her hand on his silenced J.T.'s protests.

"He'd forgive you because He loves you." Alex knew J.T. heard this explanation because he turned his head away from her, his fragile body racked with sobs.

She felt Terry's hand on her back, and when she looked up at him, he motioned for them to step out. She saw Zeke nod at them, and she accompanied Terry outside. They returned to the table by the pool and sunk into the cushioned chairs, both lost in thought and too spent to talk. Alex broke the silence first.

"Maybe I shouldn't have said anything about God loving him. Like I said, we never went to church when I was growing up."

Doubts assailed her, but Terry shook his head.

"Alex, you said what he needed to hear. Sure, Zeke's probably preached a hundred sermons to him. But until J.T. experienced forgiveness in action, how could he understand the freedom it gives both the forgiver and the forgiven?"

Alex considered Terry's words, knowing he spoke them to himself as much as to her. She knew he'd also struggled with forgiving his late parents and his dear Aunt Matilda for what he saw as a lifetime of lies. Alex prayed Terry knew the freedom of forgiving.

Alex watched as Terry, shoulders drooping under the weight of the long trip and painful exchange, trudged back from the pool house carrying bottles of water for them when her phone pinged notifications of two incoming text messages. One was from Zeke. The other, Chad. She tapped the screen to open Chad's message and was rewarded with her daughter's smiling face covered in chocolate. Alex laughed out loud, reveling in how good it felt to relax, even if just for a second.

She looked up to share the picture with Terry, knowing he loved watching his little sister's antics. However, the color draining from

Terry's face shut Alex down. His eyes locked on something behind her, and she turned to see what had spooked him.

Together Alex and Terry watched in stunned silence as Zeke lowered a wheelchair containing J.T.'s fragile form from the back porch to the ground. As if his brain suddenly engaged, Terry trotted over to help.

"What's going on," Alex asked Zeke as he rolled the chair onto the pool deck. He'd told them yesterday of J.T.'s inability, and unwillingness, to get out of the bed for any significant amount of time.

"I texted you, Lexie Bug. I thought you kids always had those phones on you," Zeke said, smiling broadly despite Alex's concern.

"I got a text from Chad," Alex said, hoping that was enough of an explanation for Zeke. She still wasn't ready for J.T. to know any details about Lydia, so she said no more. Zeke nodded, accepting her short response.

"Well, Lexie Bug, we've got some news. Isn't that right, J.T.?" Zeke patted J.T.'s arm gently, encouraging him to speak up. J.T. nodded but kept his eyes glued to his fingers fidgeting in his lap.

"What's your news, sir," Terry asked, kneeling down to be eye to eye with J.T.

"I did it."

"Did what, sir?" Terry's patience never ceased to amaze Alex. She wanted to shake somebody until they spilled whatever top-secret news they guarded.

"Well," Zeke began, his hand still resting on J.T. as he looked at the two guests, "J.T. may be your father, Terry, but now he's also your brother."

As Zeke's words sank in, Alex's eyes grew wide and her jaw dropped in disbelief. Glancing at Terry, she saw the same fish-faced look of shock. Not trusting her legs, which suddenly turned to jelly, she reached out a hand in search of the chair she'd recently vacated. Sinking into it, she shook her head in awe, her stare never leaving Zeke and J.T.

"I finally get it," J.T. said, his voice quivering from emotion and exertion. "Zeke's been telling me for years about God's love and forgiveness. It never clicked until today. I thought of God as some all-powerful judge, always ready to remind me of my mistakes."

He shook his head, overcome and unable to continue for a few moments. Alex and Terry waited, eager to hear how the story played out.

"I started thinking that if you two could forgive me, maybe God could, too. Then Zeke led me through the sinner's prayer. All those things he's told me over and over again... they finally made sense as I prayed with him. I've been forgiven. I'm free."

Alex rejoiced in the knowing this was the answer to many years of Zeke's prayers. She suspected Terry had peace knowing he'd one day see all of his parents together. And Alex cried in response to the relief she felt, knowing she'd laid her own burden down at last.

J.T. broke the silence.

"So, what's next?"

"Normally, we'd suggest following the Lord in believer's baptism," Zeke answered.

"Is that where you dunk someone underwater?"

"Yes, sir," Zeke said, chuckling a little at the simplistic description. He explained how John had baptized Jesus at the beginning of His earthly ministry. "We can try to get you to my church when you're feeling a little bit stronger."

"Was Jesus baptized in a church?" J.T. asked.

"No," Terry replied. "John baptized Him in a river."

"Will a pool work?" J.T.'s eagerness to take the next step baffled Alex.

"J.T., why don't you wait and let Zeke take you to his church?" she asked.

"Because, in my condition, I'm not promised tomorrow. And I'm definitely not getting any stronger. Will y'all help me? Please." His solid logic, followed by a simple, sincere plea for help, energized the others.

Alex ran into the house for towels. She'd seen some old clothes by the back door stuffed in a bag marked 'Donate' and found a few things that they could change into. Rushing out of the kitchen, a half-eaten baguette caught her eye. She grabbed it, rummaged through the fridge until she found a partially-consumed bottle of wine, and stacked a few paper cups on top of it.

By the time she got back to the pool, Zeke was searching his Bible app for the first chapter of John, which described the baptism of Jesus. Terry raised his eyebrows when he saw her return laden with clothes, towels, bread, and wine.

"You need a snack?" he asked, a teasing note in his voice.

"Um, I guess it was a little presumptuous, but I thought Zeke could help us celebrate the Lord's Supper after J.T.'s baptism." The two younger men voiced their approval of this idea as they relieved Alex of her load.

J.T. refused the offer to change into different clothes, insisting he could change afterward. Alex and the two men went into the pool house change rooms and donned the old clothes. Walking back to the shallow end of the pool, Terry fell into step beside Alex.

"Would you have ever predicted this?"

"Not in a million years," she said. Terry grinned at her, pulling her close for a second in a side hug.

Zeke thought his heart may burst from joy. This had to be one of the best days of his life. It ranked up there with his wedding day, the days his three daughters had been born, and the day they'd each accepted the Lord. How he'd prayed for J.T. Wickham. And Lexie Bug, too.

Zeke knew God heard his prayers. For years, the answer to them had been, "Not now." Today, however, Zeke got a huge "Yes!" to the petitions he'd made for many years. He couldn't wipe the joyful grin off his face as he stepped into the warm pool.

He watched Terry scoop J.T. in his arms with almost no effort. The older man's once-hulking form, now ravaged by illness and inactivity, slumped in his son's arms. His face, however, gleamed with anticipation.

Zeke stood beside his employer and friend as Terry held him. Alex stood behind, ready to help lift him out of the water if necessary. Once Zeke was certain everyone was ready, he began reciting the passage from John he'd read to J.T. a few minutes earlier. He explained that believer's baptism wasn't a requirement for salvation, it was an act of obedience borne of the joy of salvation. J.T. hung on his every word.

"And, now, my brother," Zeke intoned in his preacher voice, "I baptize you in the name of the Father, and of the Son, and of the Holy Spirit. Buried to the old way of life," at which point he tilted J.T. back, submerging him briefly. Alex cradled his head as it went underwater, helping Terry draw him back out. Zeke continued, "Raised to walk in glorious newness."

Tears followed, but Zeke knew these were nothing but joy rolling down everyone's faces. "Why don't we get changed and we'll partake in the Lord's Supper," he suggested, but J.T. wouldn't hear of waiting.

"We'll do it now. It's warm out here. Can't y'all wait just a few more minutes before you get into dry clothes?"

Zeke noticed the look that passed between Terry and Alex. It spoke of confusion, disbelief, but, above all, elation.

"We can do that, J.T." Alex answered as she trudged up the pool steps and retrieved the towels, passing them to each man as he emerged from the water.

The group took their places around the table. Then Zeke recounted the story of Jesus in the upper room on the night He was betrayed, recounting the familiar words from the gospels of Luke and Matthew. Except, this time, he knew these words were heard in a fresh way by one new to the faith.

Zeke broke a piece of bread and passed the loaf to Alex and Terry who followed suit. When it reached J.T., although he looked unsure what he should do, he tore off a piece and held it just as the others did. At Zeke's signal, they all placed the bread in their mouths.

Zeke poured a small amount of wine in each paper cup. He then held up his cup, announcing the ushering in of a new covenant thanks to the shed blood of Jesus. Again, J.T. followed their lead, drinking when they did.

"J.T.," Zeke said, placing his hand on J.T.'s arm, "I know you may not understand what we just did. But, I'll give you a Scripture reading plan. You can read about Jesus' earthly ministry and maybe understand a little better what it means to follow Him." J.T. nodded, shivering in his chair.

"For now, though, let's get you into some dry clothes," Zeke said, spinning J.T.'s chair to face the house.

"Wait," J.T. said, waving his hands to indicate he had something to say. "Thank you. All of you. I have a feeling I just made one of the most important decisions of my life."

"Actually," Terry corrected, "it's the most important decision. Welcome to the family." The double meaning of Terry's words wasn't lost on anyone there. J.T. nodded, the tears still shining in his eyes.

Alex and Zeke strolled around the yard, catching one another up on their respective lives. Terry had volunteered to help J.T. get changed and settled back in his bed, giving the old friends a chance to say their goodbyes. Alex relished the opportunity to learn how Zeke had been getting along. She knew this kind man had been J.T.'s right hand for many years.

"What's going to happen to J.T.'s business, Zeke?"

There were men, like Zeke, who'd worked for the Wickham Land Holdings company for most of their lives. Alex wondered what they were doing now. Zeke shook his head before answering.

"Well, Lexie Bug, that's kind of a long story. Do you want the short version?"

120

Alex nodded, keeping her eyes trained on the gravel path. She didn't think she could bear to see the sorrow in his eyes that turned his booming voice gravelly.

"I'm running the company right now. But at the first of next year, we'll quit taking on new projects. J.T. has instructed his lawyer to begin liquidating his assets at that time." Zeke stopped walking, and Alex felt the weight of his gaze on her.

"But, what about when he gets better? What will he do then?" J.T.'s plan seemed short-sighted and ill-conceived. She turned to face him, seeing the sorrow in his eyes. Zeke's voice barely reached her ears when he answered her.

"He's not going to get better, Alex."

She swallowed. Hard. Taking a few seconds to process Zeke's statement, Alex drew in a ragged breath before speaking.

"What about Mother?"

Though Karen had been distant and uninvolved with her only child, Alex still wanted to make sure she wouldn't be left destitute. The brief encounter they'd had with her left Alex wondering about her current economic situation.

"He's seen to it that she'll be taken care of," Zeke reassured her.

Alex nodded in silence, trying to imagine her mother on her own. Zeke interrupted her thoughts when he placed his hand on her elbow, guiding her to follow him on the path.

"Enough of the sad talk. I want to know about you. What's going on in your life now?"

The instinct to protect her and Lydia's privacy at all costs flared inside her gut. Before she could rattle off her stock evasive answer, though, she reconsidered. Barring some drastic change of plans, this would be the last time she ever saw Zeke. She decided to be open and honest with him. Mostly.

"I'm getting married."

She omitted all the best parts of her life. Those that involved having Lydia, falling in love with Chad, running a successful business, and graduating with honors.

"I figured as much, seeing that beautiful ring on your hand." Zeke's smile encouraged Alex to let down her guard a bit more. Her grin grew wide and joy lit her face as she told Zeke about her fiancé in Burton.

"He's wonderful, Zeke. I think you'd really like him."

"I'm sure I would, Lexie Bug. When is the big day?"

"The weekend after Thanksgiving. Do you realize the planning involved with a wedding?"

Zeke chuckled before answering, "Baby, you're talking to the father of three daughters. I've watched enough wedding planning in my day to practically be an expert." Despite his protests, Alex saw the love for his family shining in his eyes as he spoke.

"Well, if I need any wedding planning advice, I know who to call." Alex nudged his shoulder playfully.

Zeke turned serious.

"Alex, I know I'm just an old man you haven't seen in a long time, but may I give you some unsolicited advice?" When Alex nodded, he continued. "Like I said, I'm an old man now. I've seen a whole bunch happen in my lifetime. And, the one thing that's not changed is folks forgetting tomorrow isn't promised to them. Do you understand what I'm saying?"

Alex squinted and inched her head from side to side. The sudden change in subject caught her off-guard, unable to follow Zeke's train of thought.

"Let me try to put it another way. The Bible tells us we don't know what tomorrow brings. Our lives are like a mist. I've watched J.T. wither away in what seems like no time. I'm not saying rush into marriage. No, ma'am. But, if you know it's God's will, then don't miss out on as many tomorrows as you can have with that man of yours."

Alex considered Zeke's words as they wound their way to the back door.

Am I ready for this? What will Chad say if I suggest moving the wedding up? Do we have any chance at pulling it off?

Zeke reached for the doorknob with one hand and motioned for Alex to precede him with the other.

"You pray about what I said, Lexie Bug."

Alex knew she'd spend most of the trip back doing exactly that.

15
A Change of Plans

Chad saw the fancy red car turn into his driveway as the sun dipped below the tree line. The weary travelers would be exhausted in every way possible, but he longed to see her.

Hear details of the trip. Hold her in his arms.

Although Alex had told him the highlights of the trip, he needed to see her eyes when she spoke of it. He wanted to know if the haunted look he'd seen in her for so long had been replaced by something else. Had the pain that had held her in its grip for so long finally let go? He lifted one final prayer for his beautiful fiancée's healing as Terry guided the car in front of Alex's cottage.

Although he already thought of Lydia as his child, Chad was happy Charmain had taken her to play at Miss Matilda's until Alex got settled. He knew the little girl had missed her mommy, but he really needed some time alone with his future wife. He needed answers to some of the questions consuming his thoughts. Had this trip had been the balm she desperately sought? Could she enter into their marriage without the ghosts of her past tainting every decision? If a toddler demanded her attention, he knew he'd never get the information he so desperately needed.

Terry unfolded his long frame from the low-slung car and walked around to open Alex's door. A pang of guilt jabbed Chad in the gut as he tried to remember if he did the same for her. He chided himself for about the hundredth time for not going with her. But it wouldn't have done any good, and he knew it. What if Lydia had neither her mom nor her Chaddie to read her stories and make her lunch? What if he hadn't been there when she got hurt and needed a strong set of arms to hold her? He shook his head, trying to chase the unproductive thoughts away, knowing he had no time for idle speculation and 'what ifs'.

Chad breathed in the fragrant early summer air and plastered on a smile, trotting to the car to help unload Alex's luggage. He slowed to a stop beside the passenger side and watched her. Alex looked up at Chad as she emerged from the plush interior. The way she crinkled her upturned nose and squinted her beautiful brown eyes when she smiled turned Chad's insides to mush. But he needed to know if something else still hid in those eyes. As Chad explored the rich chocolate depths of her stare, he searched for the guarded expression she'd worn to ward off anyone who dared to intrude on her carefully constructed façade.

Could it really be gone at last?

Closing the distance between them, Chad engulfed Alex in a suffocating embrace, loosening his hold on her only when she whispered assurances of her love in his ear. Not daring to release her, Chad took her by both shoulders and held her at arm's length, tilting his head back and forth as he examined every detail. Alex giggled under his scrutiny, self-conscious at the attention.

"Chad, what are you doing?" She squirmed in his grasp. "I feel like a bug under a microscope. We've only been gone a few days. Have I changed that much?"

Chad stole a glimpse at Terry, who had begun heaving Alex's heavy luggage out of the car's tiny trunk. Terry raised one eyebrow in answer to Alex's question. Chad couldn't wipe the smile from his face as he reached for the bags. He felt giddy, and even a little goofy, as he thanked Terry for taking good care of Alex and waved goodbye. He couldn't help this joy bubbling up within him. He didn't even know if its source was his love for Alex, his relief at her safe return, or the possibility they could finally pursue their dreams together without the burden of the past weighing on them. He didn't care where it came from. She was here now, and that was enough.

Chad grabbed a suitcase with one hand and slung the other arm around Alex before leading the way to her front door. He fidgeted while she found her keys in the mammoth purse she hauled around and opened the door. All he wanted to do was take her in his arms and hold her for the rest of his life. He knew she needed her space, though. And time to process the last few days. Maybe even some time to envision how their life together could be.

Though it cut him to the core, Chad prepared to leave her alone and retrieve her daughter, giving her time to decompress and get her bearings.

"Well, um, so… I guess I'll go get Lyddie now," he said, awkward as a teenager on his first date. "I'm so glad you're back, babe. I really can't wait to hear every detail. That is… whenever you're ready to tell me."

He leaned over to drop a quick kiss on her cheek. In the next second, however, he was glad to be propped up against the kitchen counter. Alex took his face in her hands and kissed him. Alex turned the quick peck he'd planned on into a long, leisurely, loving kiss. When she finally released him, he had to blink a few times to make sure he wasn't dreaming.

"I've really missed you, too." She said, looking up at him through her long lashes.

After that kiss, Chad thought, *I have no doubt.*

He felt the silly grin return to his face, but he had no desire to wipe it, or Alex's strawberry-flavored lip gloss, off.

"I asked Terry to go get Lydia. Miss Matilda has supper waiting for him. That way, we've got some time to have dinner and catch up before he brings her home. Does that suit you?"

Although it was a question, Chad felt sure Alex already knew the answer because she reached for her apron even as she asked.

"Have I told you how glad I am that you're home?"

Her radiant smile and the little wink she gave him sent his heart into a tailspin. Again.

Alex's dinner sat cold and untouched in front of her. While Chad ate, she'd talked non-stop, regaling him with every detail of her trip. She'd already told him the highlights of each day when they spoke in the evenings before Lydia got tucked in. Tonight, though, she recounted not only what had happened but also how it had affected her.

She hadn't realized how transformative the journey had been until she synthesized it into words for Chad.

"I'm telling you, Chad, when J.T. came out of that water, he was a different man."

"Well, sure," Chad agreed around a bite of green beans. "That's what the Bible says, right?"

"Yeah. But, I mean, it was so moving to watch the change in him." Alex looked at her plate and realized how ravenous she was. She shoveled a forkful of chicken into her mouth before continuing, covering her mouth with her hand as she spoke. "I thought I was going up there for me… for us. You know, to help me heal from everything I've been through." She paused to swallow, leaving an opening for Chad.

"So, did you? Did you find what you were looking for? Like offering forgiveness? And did it give you the closure you needed?" Chad put his fork down, awaiting her answers and focusing his whole attention on her.

"Yes. And no. With Zeke's help, Terry and I both made our peace with J.T. And it just boggles my mind to think J.T. has also carried this burden. Isn't it amazing how God used our presence to finally open J.T.'s eyes, after all those years Zeke prayed? But, still, there's Mother."

Her eyes lost the sparkle they'd held only a moment before as she recalled how dreadful her mother had looked on the two brief occasions she'd encountered her.

"Y'all didn't get to talk much?" Chad asked, placing his napkin on the empty plate in front of him. Alex shook her head.

"Not at all. She was so combative. She smokes now. She looks awful. She used to be the most fashionable, put-together woman I knew. Even with all her other faults."

Alex remembered her mother's enormous walk-in closet, packed with the latest designer suits, blouses, and shoes. Now, however, she looked sloppy, her hair unkempt and her clothes wrinkled. Alex wondered what had driven her mother to such a drastic change of demeanor.

"You know, babe, you took that trip to forgive people. Maybe forgiving isn't about liking who that person is. I think it's more about liking who we are, despite who or what the other person is."

Alex nodded, considering what Chad said. She'd have to examine her feelings for her mom some other time. Right now, she didn't have time to dwell on the unpleasant aspects of her trip. Based on her discussion with Zeke, she had an idea she wanted to run past Chad, and she wasn't sure how it would be received.

"So, I've been thinking," she began, her gaze focused on the food she pushed around her plate.

"Uh oh. I've learned to be scared when a conversation starts like that," he said, chuckling as he began clearing the table. "You stay there, I'll put these in the dishwasher."

"Thank you, sweetie. Let's not wait for Thanksgiving." Alex spit the words out before she lost her nerve.

"OK," Chad said, looking a little confused. "I'm thankful for you all the time." He rinsed the dishes as he spoke, oblivious to the intended meaning of her statement. "I don't need a day on the calendar to tell me that."

Alex smiled, but her eyes narrowed. She was about to drop a bombshell on him, and she wasn't entirely sure how it'd be received.

"That's not what I'm talking about, dear."

Alex got up and closed the short distance between them. He turned off the water and faced her, questions evident in his eyes.

"How would you feel about not waiting until Thanksgiving to get married? Let's do it sooner." She chewed her lip as she waited for his reply.

"When did you have in mind?" Chad's stone-faced expression gave nothing away regarding how he felt about her suggestion.

"Well," she said, stalling for time while she searched her cavernous purse for the gifts she'd brought back. She kept her tone light when she said, "I was thinking, maybe Labor Day."

Alex glanced up, hoping to see some positive reaction from Chad.

Her heart soared at Chad's huge grin. Within seconds, he swooped her into his arms and spun around several times. She teetered a bit when he put her back down, but Chad paid no attention.

"I can't believe it. Honey, are you sure about this? It's already the second week in June. We'd have to have some kind of miracle to be able to get everything together by then."

"Wait a minute. How do you know what's involved with getting ready for a wedding?" Alex couldn't hide her amusement at her fiancé's sudden knowledge of the intricacies of nuptial planning.

"Char's been telling me all about it. I know we gotta find a venue, pick a caterer, send invitations, taste cakes. That girl has worn me out with wedding-planning advice."

He plopped onto the sofa, obviously exhausted from the mere thought of all that had to get done in a mere ten weeks.

"Maybe we could just do something small. You know. A few friends. Family. A small reception." Alex knew Chad was aware of her distaste for attention, so she didn't think her suggestion would come as a surprise.

"Really? I thought girls thought about their weddings from the time they were little." When Alex shot him a look, he quickly added, "At least, that's what Char says."

"Well, we can iron out the details in the next few days. But, for now, is it decided? Do you think we can shoot for a Labor Day weekend wedding?" Alex joined him on the couch and took his hands in hers.

"I do," Chad said, leaning over to kiss the woman who would be his forever. Very soon.

16
God Provides

Alex punched the screen on her phone to end the call. Heaving a deep breath, she threw the device into her bottomless purse, which served not only as a handbag, but also a briefcase, diaper bag, and filing cabinet. She reached for the coffee pot, only to discover it was empty.

Again.

How many cups have I had this morning?

Her efforts to plan a wedding in ten weeks hadn't gone as smoothly as she'd imagined they would. She'd known it would be tough, finding available and affordable service providers in every wedding-related field. She'd completely struck out with a venue, and her search for a cake baker was looking grim. She'd not even started thinking about flowers.

Or, music.

Grabbing her keys off the hook by the door, she slung the giant purse over her shoulder and locked the door behind her. Maybe talking to Miss Matilda would help calm her mounting nerves.

What was I thinking? Who plans a wedding in ten weeks? And one of those weeks has already slipped away!

Pulling into the long driveway at Together for Good, Alex looked around wondering how she'd gotten there. She'd been so distracted she'd driven on autopilot.

Wow. Better snap out of this fog.

She had things to do. Not only was the wedding date looming closer every day, but she'd received a large order from Brittany, who now worked as a buyer in Charlotte at Penny Wyse Interiors.

Gathering her bag and the wedding planning notebook that was her now-constant companion, Alex smiled as she remembered Brittany's call a few days ago. "Over the moon" didn't begin to describe her excitement at receiving an invitation to interview with Penny. She'd gone to the dean of her school and explained the situation with her internship, leaving out Talia's violent outburst. Apparently, it wasn't the first time the school had had trouble with Talia as a mentor, but they'd never had any proof to support other students' claims of her impropriety. One quick phone call to Penny Wyse verified Alex's pieces had indeed been sent by the sneaky business owner, enough evidence to have Talia's firm removed from the internship list.

"What about graduating?" Alex had asked after hearing all the details of Brittany's dismissal from her job, audience with the dean, and upcoming interview in Charlotte.

"I can submit my last assignment online. Isn't that awesome?" Britt had bubbled with glee. "And forget some ridiculous graduation ceremony! I'm not sitting there for three hours to walk across the stage for ten seconds."

That was last week, the day after Alex and Terry returned to Burton. Not only did Britt get the job. She hit the ground running at Penny's place, contacting Alex immediately about supplying new pieces for the showroom. When Alex mentioned the new wedding date, she'd had to hold the phone away from her ear. Brittany's shriek of joy threatened to burst Alex's eardrum.

A week later, here Alex sat in Miss Matilda's driveway, trying to remind herself why she and Chad didn't simply walk into the courthouse, say their "I do's," and be done with all this craziness. She'd probably regret that plan later, but right now it seemed like sound logic.

As she slammed her car door, Alex caught a glimpse of Miss Matilda in the garden with a few of the current residents. Putting her fingers to her mouth, Alex emitted a loud whistle, sending the chickens into a fit of squawks.

Matilda turned, waving to Alex as she approached. As she often did when she saw the older lady, Alex thanked God for putting this strong woman in her life. Alex cringed to think where she'd be right now had she been left to follow through with the decisions she'd almost made as a scared teenager on the run. She hurried to join the others, early morning dew dampening her sandals.

"Hey, Miss Matilda. Good morning, ladies," Alex said to the women gathering eggs and picking vegetables.

"Hi, sweetie," Matilda said, a smile lighting up her face. "What brings you here this morning?"

"Lydia had pre-school at the church, so I was trying to do some wedding planning."

Alex huffed another long breath, her exasperation with the process getting the best of her. She hoped her wise mentor would be able to give her some perspective. Or, even better, some advice. Alex turned pleading eyes to Miss Matilda, who wiped her hands on her apron before speaking.

"What seems to be the problem, dear?"

"Huh! A better question would be, 'What's not a problem?' I spoke to Reverend Drummond this morning when I took Lydia to pre-school. The church is hosting a missionary conference Labor Day weekend, so we can't have the wedding there.. There's not a single bakery or caterer in town who can fit us into their schedule that weekend. And I haven't even started calling florists." Alex counted the issues off on her fingers.

"So, why not delay the wedding a couple of weeks?" Miss Matilda asked.

"That would be a great idea. Except, we've already sent cards out to the guests asking them to save that date. Rooms have been reserved for out-of-town guests, which I didn't think we'd be able to pull off with it being a holiday weekend."

Alex dragged her fingers through her hair, her agitation apparent. Miss Matilda reached over and patted her shoulder, clicking her tongue against her teeth in a sympathetic sound.

"Riker, dear," Matilda called over her shoulder. Alex's hackles went up at the apparent dismissal of her problems.

"Yes, ma'am. Can I get you something?" Riker was younger than Alex, a small baby bump barely evident.

"You've met Alex, right? Good. I wanted you to tell her about your classes at the technical college."

Matilda looked at the young mother-to-be with encouragement. Alex crossed her arms, still insulted. Miss Matilda always provided the voice of reason for Alex, so her quick change of subject stung.

"Well, I'm almost finished with my classes, but we're having a hard time finding a job. Every place we go says we gotta have experience, but how can we get experience without having a job. I've seen the way they look at my tummy. They know I'll be out soon with the baby. I've been praying a lot lately that we'd find something."

"But, dear," Miss Matilda said, "what exactly is it that you're going to school for?"

"Oh! Duh, I totally forgot to tell you that part, Alex." Riker smacked her head. "I'm getting a certificate in culinary hospitality. Once the baby's born, I'd like to go back and learn some more."

Alex saw Matilda's lips twitch trying to suppress a grin before she spoke again.

"You mentioned someone else was having difficulty finding a position. Who is that?"

"Yeah. Blakely's got the same problem. Isn't that right, B?" Riker called over her shoulder to a girl tucking an egg into her apron.

Blakely joined their group, and Riker restated their problem about securing employment. Blakely nodded, a worried expression crossing her face.

"If I don't find a job, I'm afraid I may have to go back to my parents' house after the baby comes. That terrifies me," the girl said with a shudder.

Alex knew some of the girls in Miss Matilda's care came from backgrounds of hardship and abuse. Her heart broke for these young women, some of them barely more than girls. But she failed to see how their plight had any relevance to her wedding plans. Miss Matilda interrupted Alex's thoughts.

"Blakely, what are you studying?" Matilda kept her gaze intent on the residents, not making eye contact with Alex.

"I'm in culinary hospitality. Just like Riker. Only difference is that I'm concentrating in pastries and baking. Ri's more into the event scene. You know, like buffets and hors d'oeuvres."

With this final piece of information revealed, Miss Matilda at last turned a triumphant gaze to Alex. The obvious question burned in her eyes.

Will you help them the way someone helped you?

Alex fidgeted, uncomfortable at having been put on the spot. Her chirping phone showed an incoming call from Chad, providing Alex the perfect opportunity to excuse herself and process what she'd learned.

"Hey, babe. How's the wedding planning going?"

"About that," Alex said. She heard Chad groan on the other end.

She knew he wasn't too interested in the details. He wanted to help pick the cake and the other food. However, he had no opinion on the décor, flowers, music, or location. While he'd tried to be helpful, making calls when asked, his reluctance to make a decision without Alex's input had at times made him more of a hurdle than a help.

"Alex, you know I want whatever's gonna make you happy." He'd used this cop-out on more than one occasion.

"I know, Chad. But it's been a really hard morning. I couldn't find a caterer or a baker. But...," she let her voice trail off, still trying to decide if it was worth considering.

"But what?"

She explained Riker and Blakely's situation, making a point of mentioning their culinary specialties.

"So, what's the problem?" Chad asked. The tone of his voice indicated the decision had been made.

"Do you think it's wise? I mean, it's our wedding. They have no experience."

Emotions pulled in different directions within Alex. On one hand, she wanted to give these ladies a chance, as Terry had done for her. On the other, what if everything fell apart?

"Babe," Chad's voice turned tender and soothing, the way he talked to her when he wanted to reassure or encourage her. "I think God has again provided. For us. For the girls. Do you want to try to work against that?"

When he put it that way, it became clear what she should do. If Terry hadn't taken a big chance on her, she wouldn't be where she was. Maybe she could be the one to give a big break to other girls.

"You're absolutely right, Chad. I'm going to talk to them right now."

"That's my girl. And, one more thing."

"What?" she asked. What else could he ask her to do under the circumstances?

"Make sure you schedule the food tasting when I'm not working. I'm here to help make the important decisions."

Alex laughed. Maybe they would have a beautiful wedding in a few weeks.

Alex sat in the sunny kitchen of Miss Matilda's little cottage behind the main house sipping tea. Matilda remembered the day four years ago when this beautiful girl had arrived in town, broken and running. The older lady stirred the spoon around her cup, lost in the memory.

"Miss Matilda," Alex waved her hand in front of Matilda's face, causing her to snap back to the present. "Are you feeling well?"

"Oh, sure." She waved Alex's concern off. "I was just thinking about how we had tea at this same table when we first met. Do you remember?" She took a small sip of the strong, sweet brew.

"I remember. That was the day I first saw Lydia." The memory of her first look at her baby's heartbeat never ceased to bring a smile to Alex's face.

Matilda nodded, tipping the cup up for another long sip.

Alex had arranged with Riker and Blakely to do a tasting this Saturday. The bride-to-be had told the girls the number of guests, her and Chad's cake preferences, and Lydia's love of every kind of chicken nugget imaginable.

"Well, it seems some of your worries can be put to rest," Matilda said. She couldn't be happier about how things had worked out for the girls she loved.

"Yes, ma'am," Alex said, nodding. "At least we've got the food taken care of. But, I'm far from finished."

Matilda watched the girl's brow knit together.

"What's left to do?"

She'd thought once the business with food was settled, Alex could coast the rest of the way and enjoy being a bride. She smiled as Alex reached in the suitcase she called a purse and pulled out a notebook. When Alex opened it to a color-coded spreadsheet, Matilda noticed several empty spaces, including one circled in red ink.

"What's that?" she asked, pointing to the red circle.

"Ugh! That's where I'll put the location of the wedding. Minor detail, right?" Alex let her head fall backward and took a deep breath. "Miss Matilda, how am I going to hire those girls to cook if I don't even know where we'll be?"

Matilda recognized panic when she saw it. And Alex was on the edge of falling into despair. She reached out her stiff, gnarled hand and patted Alex's.

"I'd think the location is obvious, dear."

Alex's head snapped to face Matilda. At Alex's perplexed expression, Matilda shook her head and clucked, as if addressing a young child.

"I understand the church would be your first choice. But, what other place holds memories for you and Chad? Where are the girls comfortable cooking? Where would they not have to transport the food any more than a few yards?"

As she spoke, she saw understanding dawn in Alex's eyes. It was quickly replaced with a look of defeat. Alex shook her head.

"Miss Matilda, while I appreciate the offer to have it here more than you can imagine, we can't begin to impose on you like that. You've already done so much for both of us. Really. Thank you, but I'll keep looking."

Matilda knew Alex was simply trying to be polite. What Matilda knew that Alex didn't, however, was how to emerge victorious in a battle of wills with another woman. She had, after all, grown up with a sister and mentored countless young, expectant mothers. Matilda set her face in the sternest expression she could muster.

"Alex Powell, you listen to me, young lady. Would you deny an old lady the joy of watching two of the people she loves most start their lives together in her home? I mean, honestly, the front porch is large enough to accommodate a buffet line, and the back porch would be a perfect dance floor. We could put chairs under the big oak tree for the ceremony." Matilda finished her pitch, her gaze boring into the girl.

Did it work? Did I push too hard?

"Well, Miss Matilda, if you put it that way…"

"Is that a yes?"

Alex nodded, a grin spreading across her face and her shoulders relaxing from releasing the stress of one more decision.

"Good. So, what's that empty square for?" she asked, referring to Alex's elaborate spreadsheet.

"Oh. That's flowers. Miss Matilda, you've been too generous already. I can figure this out. I know you've got a million things to do."

Alex closed the notebook and chugged the last of her now-tepid tea. She stuffed the notebook in her bag, placed the cup in the sink, and reached over to hug her friend.

"I'll walk you out," Matilda said, reaching for the back door. She saw the confusion on Alex's face, knowing her car was parked in front of the main house. "This'll just take a few minutes."

"Where are we going, Miss Matilda?"

"I wanted to show you how beautiful my hydrangeas, snapdragons, and lavender are this year."

The twinkle in her eye elicited a burst of laughter from Alex. This lady knew how to get what she wanted.

17
Who's That Girl?

Chad had found an open table at the downtown café to sip his black coffee. When he'd dropped Alex and Lydia at the dress shop, he'd been told he couldn't accompany them.

"I thought it was just the bride's dress I wasn't supposed to see."

He'd heard all about the superstition surrounding the groom seeing the bride's dress, but he thought he could at least see what Lydia chose.

"Chaddie," Lydia said, rolling her eyes. "I want you to be surprised when you see me, too."

Though still a little girl, Lydia had embraced her role as daughter of the bride with gusto. She had definite ideas on the color of dress she wanted, the type of footwear that would go with said dress, and her favorite food for the buffet.

He grinned as he blew on his piping hot coffee, remembering the little girl's excitement. A hand waving in his face interrupted his thoughts.

"Earth to Chad."

Terry stood on the little patio beside Chad's table. He'd been so deep in thought he hadn't even heard Terry walk up. Chad stood and shook his friend's hand.

"Hey, Terry. Sorry about that. I was thinking about Lydia."

At the sound of his sister's name, Terry's eyes lit up. Chad motioned for Terry to join him, and both men tried to get comfortable in the tiny bistro chairs.

"What brings you downtown?" Terry asked.

He emptied a packet of sugar into the cup he'd brought out of the café and stirred while waiting on Chad's response. Chad noticed he looked more relaxed than before he and Alex had made their trip to North Carolina. Gone were the tense posture and drawn, tight look his face had taken on since the divorce.

"I'm waiting on the girls. They're at the dress shop for Alex's final fitting. They're hoping to find a dress for Lydia while they're at it."

Chad depleted his knowledge of the girls' venture before taking a long gulp from his cup.

"Um, Chad. There's something I've wanted to discuss with you."

Terry looked serious. Chad's stomach knotted.

Good news rarely starts like that.

"OK. Shoot."

Chad watched as Terry set his cup down and rubbed his hands together. He noticed the little white line where his wedding ring used to reside had disappeared. Chad's heart hurt for Terry, but he needed to concentrate on what Terry had to tell him.

"I never got a chance to thank you properly for being so gracious about Alex going to Woodvale with me. I know it couldn't have been easy to watch your fiancée drive away with another man."

You have no idea. Chad wrestled with the decision to play it cool or admit his misgivings. Honesty won.

"Wow, Terry. I gotta tell you, man, it was hard. I didn't understand at all. I kept wondering, 'why him and not me?'" He scrubbed at his neck while Terry acknowledged his admission with a nod.

"I understand. I know you've heard all the details of the trip, but I'm willing to bet Alex didn't tell you what a rock star she was."

Both men knew of Alex's aversion to being singled out. Though she'd told Chad all about J.T.'s salvation experience, she'd never shared details of her personal interaction with her step-father.

Chad shook his head and raised a single eyebrow.

"That's what I thought. Let's just say she started out timid and tentative. Honestly, I wasn't sure she'd be able to go through with it. By the time we left her parents' house, I think she'd finally made peace with not only her past, but also her present and future."

Chad chugged the last of his coffee and let Terry's words sink in. Could making peace with her past allow her to feel more comfortable about their future together? Thinking back to the conversations they'd had on the subject, pieces to a puzzle he hadn't been able to solve began to click into place.

"Man! What an idiot I've been." Chad smacked his forehead.

"I doubt it," Terry said, a grin tugging at the corners of his mouth. "What's the matter?"

"She tried to tell me exactly what you're saying when she was explaining why she had to go. But, when she'd talk, all I saw was a scared girl chasing some crazy dream of restored relationships."

Chad thought he knew everything there was to know about trying to fix broken family ties. He'd tried for years with his dad. He felt certain, however, cancer had motivated the man more than his son's pleas ever did. They'd ended up with a fragile truce, coupled with a budding mutual respect.

Then, he was gone.

Chad remembered Alex pleading with him to understand why she needed to go to Woodvale. He hadn't believed real change could happen in a few short days.

"She's not a scared girl, though," Chad said. "She's a strong, capable woman. She knew what she needed to do. I'm afraid I could've been more supportive."

Guilt gnawed at Chad's insides, but Terry reassured him.

"Listen, Chad. I get it. I feel protective of her, too. But, you'd have been so proud of the way she faced her fears. And the way she put the hurt aside so she could celebrate J.T.'s salvation."

What a scary step she'd taken. Like stepping off a cliff in the darkness. Once again, Chad sat back in his chair, amazed at the woman who would soon be his wife.

Without warning, Chad felt hands reach around him from behind, covering his eyes. The scent that wafted to his nostrils was familiar, but not Alex's.

"Guess who," a throaty female voice whispered in his ear.

Alex laughed at Lydia's childish knock-knock jokes, swinging their intertwined hands as they walked to meet Chad at the café. The fitting had gone well. Only a few alterations were needed, which allowed her plenty of time to concentrate on Lydia's dress. Both mother and daughter had given the thumbs up to the third dress the girl tried.

Pleased with the ease of the appointment and the extra time it afforded her to spend with Chad, joy shone in Alex's face as she turned the corner. Within seconds, the joy turned to confusion, then to anger.

No, wait. Make that jealousy.

Chad stood clasping hands with a woman Alex had never seen. Her high-pitched laughter floated down the street toward the spot where Alex and Lydia stood, now motionless. The woman reached up and placed a hand on Chad's face.

That's it!

Alex tightened her grip on her daughter's hand and stomped the last few yards to the patio. As she neared the object of her pursuit, she noticed Terry sat at the table watching the scene unfold. She'd have to deal with him later.

Had he been complicit in the scenario he sat watching or was he simply an innocent by-stander?

Alex drew in a deep breath, preparing to unleash the full force of her hurt when Lydia piped up, taking the wind out of her mother's sails.

"Hey, Chaddie! Who's that lady you're holding hands with? Mommy won't let me wear a skirt that short. Did her Mommy say it was OK?"

When Alex thought she couldn't feel any worse, Lydia managed to heap a pile of embarrassment on top of the hurt and jealousy. She did, however, provide Chad a convenient exit from the woman's grasp. Alex watched him peel the woman's hands off him before he knelt to address Lydia.

"Hi, sweetie. This is an old friend," a title which made the woman cringe. "She's in town for a reunion."

Alex noticed he didn't address the clothing selection comment. Her ire began to subside a bit as Chad stood and kissed her on the cheek. Wrapping a protective arm around Alex, he made the introductions.

"Yvonne, this is my fiancée, Alex. Alex, Yvonne."

No mention of who Yvonne was in Chad's past. Terry cleared his throat.

"Oh, yeah," Chad rushed on. "This is our friend Terry." Chad clapped a hand on Terry's shoulder.

"He's my Bubba," Lydia declared, pride oozing from her voice as she climbed into Terry's lap.

"I see." Yvonne, obviously confused and miffed at the intrusion, turned her gaze on Chad once more. "Will you be at the reunion?" Her voice sounded more like a purr than a question to Alex.

"Nah. That's not my thing. Besides, we've got a lot of work to do on our wedding planning." Chad pulled Alex a bit closer when he mentioned the wedding.

"Oh, well. That's too bad," Yvonne said.

She slung her purse over her shoulder, turned on her stiletto heel, and swayed her ample hips in time with each step as she retreated up the street.

Alex heard the breath escape Chad like a leaky balloon and felt him relax beside her. Crossing her arms in front of her, Alex turned to face him, one eyebrow raised in question. She saw Terry's amused smirk out the corner of her eye.

He's enjoying this way too much.

"Baby, listen. It's not what it looked like."

"Really? Why don't we start by talking about what it did look like?"

Chad shot a pained glance at Terry, hoping the man would come to his defense. Terry said nothing, though. Instead, he sat listening intently to Lydia's chatter.

"Yvonne was a friend from high school," Chad said, fidgeting and rubbing his neck.

Chad's admission might be the truth, but Alex recognized the signs of evading the whole truth. A friendship wouldn't cause a man to squirm ten years later.

"What kind of friend, exactly?"

Although she had no reason to distrust him, something didn't feel quite right.

"Well, so… Here's the thing… I mean, the truth is…"

Alex watched as Chad fought with himself over how to best begin his explanation. A gnawing feeling developed in her stomach as his discomfort grew.

What could be so bad he'd hidden it from me? Continues to try to hide it from me?

Terry rose from his chair, Lydia clapping with excitement as she settled into the crook of his arm.

"If you'll excuse us, we're going to pop into the pet store down the street and look at the puppies." Terry's amusement had vanished, and he looked at the couple with concern etched on his face. "Take a piece of advice from a guy who's made plenty of mistakes. Get this hammered out. Now. Don't expect it to go away."

Terry turned and strolled away, Lydia's non-stop monologue growing fainter with every step. Alex's shoulders slumped as she dropped into the chair Terry left empty. The initial angry adrenaline rush had passed, replaced by a dull ache. She'd thought she and Chad told each other everything. Now, she wasn't so sure it was a two-way street.

Feeling like a by-stander on the street, Alex watched Chad sit down facing her and reach for her hand. She pulled back, wanting anything but to be close to him right now. She saw the hurt in his eyes, which tugged at her heart.

Alex knew, though, she couldn't let some strange woman waltz down the street and cause her to doubt what she believed to be true about the man she'd marry in a few weeks.

"Are you ready to be honest with me?"

Chad knew from the second Yvonne had whispered in his ear trouble was just around the corner. It had always been that way with Yvonne. He also knew he should've told Alex about her a long time ago. Chad considered how to best recount the story of him and Yvonne. Although he'd not thought of her in years, memories flooded back now, crashing down the walls time had so mercifully constructed. He shuffled through the thoughts running through his mind as he sought the words to explain the relationship and apologize to the woman he loved.

He'd been in the eleventh grade. Yvonne moved to Burton from somewhere out West. Montana, or something like that. With the luxury of a decade of perspective at his disposal, Chad now understood how Yvonne had sniffed him out like a bloodhound. She'd been in search of the most emotionally vulnerable guy in class, determined to make him her project.

Determined to make him love her.

It had worked.

Chad fell for Yvonne's sweet words, lavish attention, and promises for a future together. He'd had nothing to look forward to at home. By the time he'd reached his awkward and formative teen years, his mom had been long gone and his dad was no more than a living, breathing shell of the man he'd once been. His mom's death had sucked the life out of her husband and left her children practically orphaned.

Charmain had adjusted better than the guys had. She'd clung to Miss Matilda's steadying Godly influence. They had regular get-togethers for tea and girl talk. Dad never cared that she spent so much time at a pregnancy care home. He quickly quit caring about anything but getting through each day and hardening his heart against additional agony.

Shaking his head against the memories, Chad blinked as he pulled himself back to the present and looked at the beauty across from him on the café patio. Alex deserved to know everything about Yvonne. Drawing a shaky breath, he steeled himself for the humiliating truth he hadn't relived in years.

"Yvonne and I dated."

It was a start, but even this admission brought with it a flood of pain. Chad looked at his hands fidgeting with the empty sugar packet. He dragged his gaze to meet Alex's.

"Go on." Her voice held no trace of either condemnation or encouragement.

Chad launched into his story. How Yvonne had started flirting with him not long after moving to Burton. How he'd asked her on a date the summer after their junior year. Before he knew it, the summer was over, they were dating each other exclusively, and he was thinking about their future together.

"I was eighteen. I thought I loved her. The kicker was, I thought she loved me." He could hear the pain in his own voice.

"Did she dump you?" Alex leaned forward, obviously captivated by his story.

Chad shook his head.

Oh, if it had only been that easy.

"No. We'd been dating for about six months, and I was saving my money from working at the garage." This next part was what he'd dreaded. How could he tell Alex the truth? How could he not? "I'd saved enough money to buy her a ring." He lowered his eyes before raising them to look at her without flinching. "An engagement ring."

Alex winced at the words. Chad let his head fall backward, praying for the strength to finish the tale.

"The Christmas of our senior year, I asked her to marry me."

Chad had to stop. He wasn't sure he could finish.

"What did she say?" Alex took the sugar packet out of his hands, holding them tightly in her own. Her gesture fortified his resolve. Somewhat.

One more deep breath, then just say it. Get it over with.

"She said she'd answer me after... Well, you know. After we'd been together. Like, you know..."

He couldn't say the words, sitting in the summer breeze on a café patio. He wasn't even sure he could say them if they'd been sitting alone together at home. He felt so foolish. So used.

"Hold on. Let me make sure I understand." Alex slipped one hand free and swiped it through her hair. She lowered her voice to a whisper. "She wouldn't say 'yes' until you slept with her?"

Chad nodded, miserable and spent.

"So, did you tell her to pound sand?" It sounded so simple when Alex said it.

"No. Not at first," Chad shook his head. "I told her that wasn't how I was raised. You know, I spent a lot of time with Miss Matilda, too. I'd seen lives altered forever by an unplanned pregnancy." Alex's expression remained stoic. "I'd also learned about God's design for the marriage relationship. So, she put the ring on and told me she had to go."

"Where did she go?"

"To call all of her friends and tell them we were engaged." The next words stabbed Chad's heart. "And to tell them we'd had sex."

Alex gasped. Chad couldn't look her in the eye.

"I eventually found out about the rumor she'd started, and I ended things between us. She moved back out West not long after that." He pulled his gaze back up, daring to meet her eyes. "Do you hate me?"

"Chad," she reached out and stroked his stubbly cheek. "How could I hate you because some back-stabbing teenage girl took advantage of your morals and emotional vulnerability? I'd really like to run down this street and see if I could find her. You better believe, I'd

151

give her a piece of my mind." Righteous indignation blazed from her eyes.

Chad chuckled, but deep down his heart rejoiced. This part of his past had weighed on his conscience since the day he'd proposed. Many times he'd wanted to tell her. Somehow, though, the topic never presented itself. And he never made a serious effort to broach the subject.

He looked at the woman across from him, and the love he felt for her almost knocked him off his chair. Scooting closer to her, he took her face in his hands and planted a soft kiss on her forehead, then on her nose, then on her lips, lingering for a brief moment.

18
Dredging Up the Past

Alex guided her car down the long, winding driveway leading to Together for Good. Behind her, Lydia bounced and clapped her hands from her car seat. Her injury from a few weeks ago had long since healed, and the little girl had regained her confidence around the chicken coop.

"Yay, Mommy. We're at Miss 'Tilda's."

"We are, sweetie. We won't be staying long. Mommy just needs to go over a few things with Riker and Blakely. We'll find your crayons and coloring book."

Lately, Lydia wanted to color a picture for Miss Matilda every time they visited. The brief distraction gave Alex and her dear friend a few minutes to catch up. Today, though, Alex needed the time to finalize details regarding the menu, table placement, and what seemed like a million other particulars.

Parking in front of the house, Alex caught a glimpse Charmain's car in front of the guest house out back.

"I think Aunt Charmain might be here," she told her daughter, eliciting another round of excited squeals from the child.

Alex freed Lydia from the car seat and shoved everything she'd need to conduct her business into her giant bag. Heaving it over her shoulder, she took her daughter's hand and went up the porch steps and in the front door. Familiar voices and a heavenly aroma greeted the two visitors.

"Yoohoo! What's cooking?" Alex called out, letting Lydia run ahead of her to the kitchen.

"Well, talk about perfect timing," Miss Matilda said, greeting the girls as she moved cookies from a pan to a cooling rack. "I'm just finishing up a double batch of chocolate chip cookies. Lydia, your Bubba usually helps me take care of the duds. Do you think you can take over for him today?"

Lydia looked up at her mom, begging with her eyes for permission to have one of Miss Matilda's cookies. Alex checked her watch and nodded.

"OK. But dinner's only a few hours away, so just one. Riker and Blakely should be here in about fifteen minutes."

She plopped her load on the massive kitchen table before hugging her two friends. Charmain poured Alex a cup of coffee, and all four girls sat around the table reveling in the joy of warm cookies. Alex closed her eyes and groaned.

"Oh, my. I can't have any more of these. I'll never fit into that wedding dress."

"How did the fitting go?" Charmain asked.

Alex hesitated before answering.

"The fitting was fine. It was what happened afterward that wasn't so great."

Charmain and Matilda both raised their eyebrows. Alex didn't want to discuss it with Lydia present, though.

"Sweetie," she said to her daughter, "since you're finished with your cookie, why don't you go color Miss Matilda a picture in the front room?"

Alex helped her little girl out of the booster seat.

"Mommy, don't forget to tell Miss 'Tilda and Aunt Charmain about that lady with the short skirt holding hands with Chaddie."

Alex thought she'd choke. She hadn't intended to go into so much detail, but the cat was out of the bag now. She saw out of the corner of her eye the pair across the table each hold a hand to their mouths to cover their amusement.

"Yes, honey. But, let's not tell people about her short skirt, OK?"

"OK, Mommy."

Lydia's footsteps could be heard running down the hall to the front room. Alex sighed before turning her attention to the two ladies waiting patiently for an explanation.

"Short skirt?" Charmain asked.

"Holding hands?" Miss Matilda followed.

"Yeah. So, I met Yvonne today."

Alex watched the faces of both ladies change from amused and interested to cold and closed. She'd guessed they both knew the whole story about Chad's high school relationship, but their expressions spoke volumes about their feelings for Yvonne.

"Did my brother tell you about her?"

Alex nodded. Still not sure how much they knew, she offered as little information as possible.

"Yeah. He told me about the engagement. And about the horrible rumor she started."

Alex noticed a look pass between Matilda and Charmain.

"What was that? What do y'all know that I don't?"

They both avoided her laser-focused stare. They were keeping something from her, though. She felt it. Why all the secrecy? She needed to get to the bottom of this.

"Someone spill. I want to know what y'all aren't telling me."

Miss Matilda reached over and patted her hand, still unwilling to meet Alex's gaze. The older lady glanced at Charmain, who nodded ever so slightly.

A cold finger of dread snaked its way up Alex's spine. How many more revelations could she endure today? She gave Miss Matilda what she hoped was an expectant look, hoping it didn't come across as a scowl.

"Yvonne was here," Miss Matilda said. No elaboration. No details. Just a single statement.

"What? When? Did she come by today? She's in town for a reunion."

Alex looked at first one lady then the other, trying to gauge their reaction to her questions. Again, the tiny glance they shared. What was she missing? Charmain's shoulders rose and lowered as she took a deep breath.

"Alex, she lived here. After Chad broke up with her."

"What? That doesn't make any sense. This is a crisis pregnancy home. The only reason she'd live here would be…"

The reality of what they told her knocked the wind out of Alex, eliminating her ability to finish her sentence.

"Chad didn't tell me."

"Because he doesn't know." Charmain fairly choked the words out.

How could this be true? He'd told her nothing ever happened between them. Sadness, frustration, humiliation, and a few feelings she couldn't identify welled up within her, causing the kitchen to swim in her vision.

Charmain handed Alex a tissue while Matilda recounted what she knew of the story.

"Yvonne showed up here the February of their senior year. Her family had moved back to Idaho, but she'd stayed. Of course, I'd met her when Chad had brought her out while they were dating. So, when she knocked on my door, I thought she was looking for him."

Miss Matilda rose slowly, moved stiffly to the coffee pot, topped off each cup, and returned the carafe to its place. Looking older than she had when Alex arrived today, Matilda lowered herself back into her seat. Charmain patted her hand reassuringly, nodding for her to continue.

"Her son was born in early August."

Alex did the math in her head. The boy had been conceived around November, a month before Chad asked Yvonne to marry him.

How could the two stories be so different? Had Chad lied to her?

Her breath came in short gasps as she struggled to understand all the information thrust on her today.

"Where is her son now?" Alex hadn't seen a child with Yvonne downtown.

"With his adoptive family. Last I heard, they live about an hour away from here." Miss Matilda finally locked eyes with Alex.

Alex needed to ask one final question, although she dreaded the answer with everything she had. She barely had the strength to give voice to her inquiry, her voice a mere whisper.

"Is Chad the boy's father?"

Both women shook their heads. She wanted to believe them. She wanted to believe Chad. But how could Miss Matilda and Charmain be so sure? There was still something they weren't telling her. Again, looking from one face to the other, she saw the sideways glance.

"How can you be sure? Please, tell me." Alex didn't think she had the strength to beg. But, this thing needed to be in the open. She needed to know.

Charmain watched Miss Matilda's head sag against her chest. Remembering was so painful for her sometimes. But, Alex had known indescribable pain in her life, too. She deserved to know what Yvonne had done to Chad.

"Alex, Yvonne's baby was born here. At the home. Miss Matilda and I delivered him."

Charmain had tried with all her might to forget that day, and had done a pretty good job of it. Until today.

"OK. I still don't understand. Why didn't y'all take her to the hospital? And, how do you know for certain Chad isn't the boy's father?"

Charmain watched the frustration play across Alex's face and heard the desperation in her voice. She knew she needed to get to the point. They'd withheld the truth for too long, thinking they were protecting Chad's feelings. But now that Yvonne had come back and contacted Chad, things had changed. They had other people to consider.

"I was here having tea and doing my Bible study in the cottage with Miss M." Charmain watched her fingers pick at a spot on the table as she spoke. "Yvonne found us there. She was doubled over in pain, trying to catch her breath. It scared the daylights out of me!"

Her body trembled at the memory, and she knew Alex saw it. She continued, drawing strength from Miss Matilda's presence.

"Miss M. asked her a whole bunch of questions. You know, 'When did the contractions start?' 'How far apart were they?' Now, you gotta remember, neither one of us had a very high opinion of her. Miss M. was much more mature than I was. Honestly, I wanted to call an ambulance and send her on her way."

"We couldn't do that, though," Miss Matilda interrupted. "Her contractions were coming too hard and too fast. When she told me the pain had started the day before, I knew we'd be delivering a baby."

Alex sat in stunned silence as each lady contributed a new detail to the account.

Charmain explained how they had drawn a warm bath, eased the girl into the water between contractions, and watched the baby boy make his arrival within minutes. Only then did they have time to call for an ambulance to take both mother and baby to the hospital. They'd never seen her again.

She'd left everything she had behind.

Spent and silent, Charmain sank back in her chair. She wrapped her hands around her coffee cup and stared into it as if searching for the next words to say. Alex beat her to it.

"I don't understand. So, you delivered her baby. What makes you so sure he's not Chad's son?"

"Because," Charmain said, unburdening herself at last of the secret she'd kept for a decade. "The baby we delivered was mixed race. His daddy was a black man. It may not be that unusual now, but ten years ago Yvonne's parents didn't understand. Yvonne cried when she saw him, saying nobody would believe he was Chad's. She admitted to having another boyfriend. She also admitted to knowing she was pregnant when Chad proposed. She'd tried to lure him into a physical relationship so she could make him believe she carried his child. She hadn't counted on Chad refusing to sleep with her."

Charmain had never had the heart to tell her brother. She wondered if he needed to know even now.

"Chad doesn't know about any of this?" Alex asked.

"No." Matilda shook her head, her shoulders slumped. "I'd told him when he and Yvonne first started dating to be careful. I just had a feeling about her. Anyway, when Yvonne broke his heart, he quit coming to see me. I guess after things went wrong, Chad didn't want to hear me say, 'I told you so.' He quit visiting for almost a year. By the time he came back at Thanksgiving, Yvonne and her baby were long gone."

Charmain watched Alex try to process the information she'd been given. She knew it was hard to hear. What she didn't know was what Alex would choose to do with it.

This can't be happening.

The stress of wedding planning coupled with the strain of secrets from her fiancé's past weighed on Alex until she thought she'd snap. Chad had believed Yvonne was giving him an ultimatum. One he'd refused to accept. She had forced him to make a choice, but her goal had been to manipulate him into believing he'd gotten her pregnant. And, by his own admission, Chad had thought he loved her.

Alex understood why Charmain had spared her brother the pain of knowing the truth. She wasn't sure if she agreed with it, but her own judgments would have to wait.

The kitchen door leading to the back porch flew open, and a chattering Riker and Blakely barreled in. They each held notebooks and phones, obviously prepared for their meeting with the bride. Alex swallowed hard, trying to dissolve the lump in her throat. She watched Miss Matilda rise from her chair and motion for Charmain to do the same.

"Well, we'll get out of your way and let y'all have your meeting. We'll be in the front room with Lydia if you need us."

Alex plastered on a smile, but what she intended as a warm welcome sounded stilted and harsh to her own ears, causing the girls to sneak a questioning glance at each other. She drew in a deep breath and tried to release with it all of the questions raging within her.

"I'm sorry, ladies. It's been a really stressful couple of days. How are the food preparations going?"

The tension caused by Alex's terse initial greeting dissipated. The girls relaxed, smiling and talking at once as they opened their notebooks. Alex allowed herself the luxury of letting go of the information she'd been given, tucking it away in her brain to deal with later.

"We've got the menu finalized for your approval," Riker said. "And Blakely has a draft of the cake design for you to look at."

The three ladies went line-by-line through the menu, with Alex agreeing to most of the delicious selections Riker had specified.

"I'm not sure if Chad likes barbecue meatballs," she said, trying to recall if he'd ever expressed an opinion one way or the other.

"I could make a batch this weekend for y'all to taste," Riker suggested.

"Perfect!"

"And when y'all come for that, I'll have a couple of different cake flavors for you to try." Blakely said.

Alex wanted to cry with relief. She didn't know what she'd do without these two talented, industrious girls taking the reins.

"You two are a blessing from the Lord. If I were trying to do this by myself, I'm afraid our guests would end up with sub sandwiches and doughnuts. Not a very elegant way to treat those you want to share the most special day of your life with, huh?"

The girls were laughing at Alex's absurd suggestion of wedding fare when Lydia ran in. Stopping in her tracks at the sight of the three of them doubled over, she approached her mommy and tapped her on the arm.

"Mommy, what's so funny?"

Alex scooped the little girl into her lap.

"Nothing, sweetie. Mommy's just really happy that Riker and Blakely are helping with the wedding."

"Me, too. When do we get to eat cake?"

Lydia's innocent but sincere question started another fit of giggles, which is how Miss Matilda and Charmain found the whole crew when they peeked their heads around the corner.

19
A Ten-Year-Old Secret

Chad had arranged to meet Alex at Together for Good after he left the garage on Saturday. He grinned as he stomped the accelerator, hurrying to make sure he beat her there. Four weeks from today, Miss Matilda's home would be abuzz with the activity and excitement of the wedding. Today, though, Chad was on a mission.

Not just a mission to eat cake.

He parked in the gravel area out front and tucked his phone in his back pocket. Although Miss M. insisted he didn't need to knock, he still felt it important to respect the privacy of the residents. He delivered three quick taps. A voice from within beckoned him to come in.

Knowing the layout of the house almost as well as his own, he strode toward the kitchen. When he heard women's voices, he thought Alex might have beaten him there. The smile he couldn't suppress every time he thought of her stretched across his face. However, the sight that greeted him wiped away his grin and brought him to a dead stop in the kitchen doorway. Panic crept into his gut, causing his stomach to rebel against his lunchtime tacos.

Yvonne sat hunched over, silent sobs shaking her body. Miss M. sat beside her, patting her back and whispering vague reassurances. Charmain stood across the kitchen against the cabinets, back stiff, arms crossed, eyes narrowed. Alex and the catering girls were nowhere to be found.

What in the world is going on here?

"Miss M.?" Chad addressed his longtime friend and protector.

"You can't say you're surprised, can you?" Charmain spit the words out, confusing Chad with the bitterness in her tone.

"Surprised that *she's* here? Yeah, Char. I actually am."

Miss M. had tried to warn him about her before the disastrous end to their relationship. He'd quit coming to visit the home for many months afterwards, too humiliated to face the sweet lady who always had his best interest at heart. But, nobody ever mentioned Yvonne's name to him after he returned. It had almost been as if she'd never existed.

That had suited him fine.

"Even after Alex told you about the baby?" Charmain's question snapped Chad back to the present, and his head jerked in the direction of his sister.

His sister had come unhinged, screaming and punctuating each word with flailing arms. Chad caught the warning look Miss M. shot her. As soon as the words escaped her lips, Charmain clapped her hands over her mouth, her eyes wide in horror.

Alex? What did she have to do with this?

Chad's cell phone vibrated in his pocket. Yanking it out, he read Alex's text saying she'd be here in five minutes.

Good. Maybe she can help me get to the bottom of this.

"Is somebody going to tell me what's going on?"

Chad didn't know how much more he could take of these games. Yvonne raised her tear-streaked face, looking old and defeated. She swiped at her eyes and blew her nose before speaking.

"I'm here to try to find my son."

Chad's knees threatened to buckle. He scraped a chair out and fell into it. Everything around him seemed to be happening in slow motion. He looked to first one woman, then another, and then another. Nobody offered any clarification.

Finally, Yvonne spoke.

"You never told him?"

Miss M. shook her head, her eyes avoiding Yvonne's. Charmain busied herself at the sink, preparing a fresh pot of coffee. Chad's patience, stretched to its limit, threatened to snap.

"Never told me what? What do y'all know that I don't? And why is Yvonne here?"

He'd thought he'd rid himself of her forever. When she showed up out of the blue downtown, he should have known it'd be nothing but trouble. He'd come clean with Alex, though, and believed everything to be settled. The slate wiped clean. Obviously, he'd been mistaken.

The kitchen door flew open, and the music of Lydia's giggle made its way into the room several seconds before she did. Alex followed close behind the toddler, attempting to corral the child before she wreaked destruction on Miss Matilda's kitchen. All her efforts were in vain when Lydia spotted Chad.

"Chaddie!" Her voice reached a pitch reserved for dog whistles. "We're eating cake today! Do you 'member? Today's cake day!"

She ran in circles around Chad's legs. Normally, he'd scoop her up and join in her joy, but his own joy had seeped from him like air out of a punctured tire. He looked at Alex, knowing his gaze held hurt and accusation. He couldn't hide it, no matter how much he wanted to.

Charmain had said Alex knew something about Yvonne and her son. She'd acted so.... What? Had she been covering up her knowledge of Yvonne for his benefit? Or maybe it had been a test to see if he'd tell her about their relationship. He hated airing their problems in front of all these people, but he needed to get to the bottom of this.

"Chad, maybe I should..." Charmain tried to jump in, but Chad didn't want to hear what she had to say. His gaze never left Alex.

"Not now, Charmain." He said, cutting off his sister's attempt to speak. "I want to hear what Alex knows about this situation."

Alex looked around the room, not sure how much information had been revealed to Chad. She knew with certainty that she didn't want Lydia to hear the conversation that was about to transpire. She whispered in her daughter's ear and handed her the little backpack she took to pre-school, then Lydia skipped off to color in the other room.

When Alex turned and met Chad's gaze, the steely glint in his green eyes caught her off guard.

Did he blame her for Yvonne's hurtful ultimatum?

She'd done nothing wrong, yet everything about the way Chad stood – arms crossed, brows knitted, back stiff – indicated he was angry.

At her!

"Are you serious right now, Chad?"

"This looks pretty serious to me, Alex. What about you? What if I lied to you about knowing something deeply personal from your past? How would that make you feel?"

"What are you talking about? I didn't lie to you. You told me about your past when you couldn't hide it any longer."

Alex not only seethed with righteous indignation, but she also had no clue what Chad meant.

"Just answer this one question: Did you know Yvonne had a baby?"

Alex's heart raced. The back of her mind barely registered the other ladies watching the exchange while seeming to hold their collective breath. This information, this dark and painful secret, wasn't hers to share. She dropped her gaze, unable to answer Chad's question.

"That's what I was afraid of." Chad turned on his heel to leave. Before he could, Miss Matilda held up her hand.

"Chad White! You get back here this instant, young man." Alex guessed it was the same stern voice she'd used on him when he'd played pranks as a child, because it worked on the grown man, too.

"Miss Matilda, I appreciate you trying to help. But, you don't understand…" Miss Matilda interrupted him before he could finish his sentence.

166

"No, Chad. You, sir, are the one who doesn't understand. Charmain and I have been very careful to make sure of that for many years now."

Alex watched the emotions play across Chad's face. Confusion. Anger. Hurt. They were the same strong feelings that had tugged at Terry the day Miss Matilda told him he'd been adopted. So many secrets. So much pain.

Chad sank into the nearest chair, and Alex wanted to go to him. She wasn't sure how he'd react, especially after having accused her of lying to him. Tossing her pride and hurt feelings aside, she moved to stand behind Chad and placed her hands on his shoulders. He raised one shoulder and placed his cheek against her hand, his gesture seeming to calm him somewhat. He dipped his head for a moment, then leveled his gaze at the women assembled in front of him.

"Would somebody please tell me what's going on?"

Although Alex couldn't see his eyes, she heard the unmistakable tone of hurt in his voice. She looked at the other three ladies in the kitchen. She knew each one had played a crucial role in shaping Chad into the man he was today, but she also knew she would be the one to walk beside him from now on. Alex begged with her eyes for them to give the man she loved the information, and hopefully the closure, he needed.

Yvonne nodded before she spoke. She kept her story brief and to-the-point, keeping her gaze fixed on the tile floor. Her hollow, emotionless voice droned out the details, seemingly detached from the events she recounted.

"I'd been sleeping with Marquis since the week after I moved to town. We had to sneak around because my parents would have killed me." She paused to grunt a mirthless chuckle.

"The funny thing is, they used to go to football games every Friday night and cheer him on from the stands. They had no idea.

"Honestly, Chad, I started seeing you because you were the perfect smoke screen. While you were busy working at the garage, I could sneak off with Marquis. Then, about a week before you asked me to marry you, I found out I was pregnant."

Yvonne dragged her gaze from the floor and stared at Chad. Unshed tears shone in her eyes.

"I loved him, but he told me there was no way he was getting saddled with a baby. Football was his way out of Burton, and he'd already had several offers from good colleges. So, when you proposed, I saw my chance. And I took it. I had no idea it would backfire so badly."

Yvonne barely got the last words out before she broke down. Alex rubbed Chad's arm, trying to reassure him with her touch they'd get through this.

"She came to me in February," Miss Matilda said.

Knowing the situation as she did, Alex knew it must have been a hard and painful thing to take her in. Miss Matilda's one driving force, however, had always been the lives of innocent babies. She'd do whatever it took to protect them. Even welcome the girl who had used and wounded a boy she'd loved like a son. Alex's heart ached for the lady who must have seen her share of tragedies, scandals, and grief.

"My son was born in August. I didn't even hold him. I knew I wouldn't be able to let him go if I did." Yvonne managed to get her words out around the hiccups brought on by crying.

Alex felt Chad's shoulders rise and fall as he took a steadying breath.

20
Let Them Eat Cake

Seeing her defeated posture and tear-streaked face, Chad almost pitied Yvonne. Her poor decisions had cost her dearly. Now, all she had to show for the last ten years were regrets. And an unquenchable desire to see her son.

Feeling sorry for an ex-girlfriend didn't overcome the growing irritation he felt toward the three women he loved most, though. *Why hadn't someone told him before now?* He wanted nothing more than for Yvonne to leave so he could ask the questions that burned inside him.

"Miss M., have you told Yvonne where her son is?" Chad hoped to steer the conversation to its conclusion, wrapping up this unpleasant encounter.

Miss Matilda shook her head. Everyone present, except Yvonne, was aware the sweet care-giver didn't divulge information. Even if she did know it.

"I was explaining the situation to Yvonne when you came in. Her son was placed in a closed adoption. Normally, that would have been to protect Yvonne's identity. But, according to the attorneys, her son's adoptive parents requested no contact from the boy's birth mother."

"I knew all the details of the arrangement when I signed the papers," Yvonne said, ripping the tear-soaked tissue into tiny pieces. "I guess I was hoping Miss Matilda could give me some clue about the parents. Are they nice? Do they have any other children? Do they live close by?"

"Even if I knew the answers to those questions, Yvonne, I couldn't tell you. Privacy is crucial to this job. Believe me, it's not an easy load to carry sometimes."

Chad recalled the day Matilda had relieved herself of the decades-long secret about Terry's parentage. It had almost shattered her. He wondered about the other secrets she must carry, sworn to protect both the mothers who birthed babies and the loving parents who adopted them.

"Will y'all excuse me, please?" Yvonne rose and walked in the direction of the powder room down the hall.

The group in the kitchen relaxed a bit as they looked at each other without speaking. Alex sank into the chair next to Chad, folded her arms on the table and dropped her head on them.

Chad took the opportunity to pour himself a cup of coffee, not turning from his position at the counter to face the women before he spoke.

"When were y'all going to tell me about this?"

He took a huge gulp of hot coffee, burning his tongue. The pain made him even angrier, as if these women had physically wounded him in addition to wounding his pride and emotions.

"Honestly, Chad," Charmain said. "What difference would it have made? Today was the first time Miss Matilda and I even heard the name of the boy's father."

"That's right," Miss Matilda rose from where she'd sat since he entered and shuffled to stand in front of him. "When she arrived here, you were still so bitter about what she'd put you through. I made the decision not to tell you until you got your head on straight. But, once Yvonne was gone, there didn't seem to be any reason to put you through more pain. Her baby was safe. That was my goal."

Chad set the steaming mug on the counter and stared out the window at the chickens, the picture of contentment as they pecked the ground. Why did life have to get complicated and messy? As he contemplated the benefits of a simpler life, he felt Alex's gentle touch on his back.

"You knew?" he asked, turning to face her.

She nodded.

"It wasn't my information to share, Chad."

"Is this how it's going to be, Alex? Are we going to keep things from each other? I don't think I can go into a marriage like that."

He turned his gaze away, once again envying the chickens and their simple existence.

His words stung.

Alex understood Chad felt humiliated, maybe even betrayed. And by those he loved the most. But Alex stood by her decision. Telling Chad what she'd learned a few days ago would have accomplished little. All her information came from Charmain and Miss Matilda, and Alex still believed they were the ones who should fill him in on the details.

The group heard the door to the powder room click open and Yvonne's shoes tap down the hall. She poked her head in the kitchen, looking better than when she'd left.

"If it's cool with y'all, I'm gonna hit the road. Miss Matilda, here's my contact information if you remember anything you can tell me, or if, you know, someday he wants to…" She trailed off without finishing, shrugging at the possibility that her son may seek her out one day.

Matilda crossed the room, took the slip of paper Yvonne extended toward her, then pulled the woman into a huge hug.

"You take care of yourself, you hear?"

Yvonne nodded. She turned and was gone.

No goodbye. No apology for Chad.

No thanks to Miss Matilda for all she'd done during the pregnancy.

Alex tried to imagine the hurt Yvonne felt. First to be dismissed by the child's father. Then, abandoned by her own parents. And now, after a decade, she longed to see the child she'd carried. Alex didn't know what she'd do without Lydia. Every hectic day, sleepless night, and countless raisin pulled from between her sofa cushions were blessings from above.

Even as Alex pondered the joy her daughter brought to her life, she couldn't shake the niggling sensation that something wasn't quite right.

"I'm going to check on Lydia."

Heading out of the kitchen, Alex realized what seemed off. She'd never heard the massive front door open and shut with Yvonne's exit. She quickened her pace to the front room where Lydia's crayons, coloring books, and nap mat stayed stashed in the giant built-ins.

When Alex reached the doorway, she had to restrain herself. Lydia had taken her mat out and lay asleep in the middle of the floor. Yvonne knelt beside her, stroking her cheek. The urge to scoop her daughter up in her arms overwhelmed Alex, but she watched the scene before her unfold, trying mightily to remain calm.

"I never got to do this to my baby." Yvonne's words were muffled by the sob in her voice.

Shaking off her initial sense of dread, Alex tried to see this woman before her not as the person who had cruelly and shamelessly devastated her husband-to-be. Instead, she saw her as a woman who'd felt trapped, backed into a corner, and forced to make decisions she'd later regret.

Alex understood. She, too, had felt trapped and afraid. She, too, had almost made a decision she would have regretted forever.

God had led both girls to Together for Good. Their stories, however, couldn't have ended more differently. Alex considered the best way to pose her next question.

"What gave you the courage to place your son up for adoption, Yvonne?"

Yvonne grunted out a laugh devoid of humor. When she turned to look up at Alex, the freshness of the pain in her eyes shocked Alex.

"I wasn't courageous. I was young and scared. And angry. All I wanted to do was get back to Marquis. I loved him, and I thought if I didn't have a baby weighing me down, he'd come back to me."

"What happened?" Alex felt she'd been plopped into some bizarre nightmare.

"After my son was born, I went to the college where Marquis was playing football. He took one look at me and told me he couldn't deal with me or my problems. He didn't ask about the baby. He didn't want any reminders of his 'past mistakes.'" Yvonne made quotes in the air. "Those were his words."

"Did you go back to Idaho?"

Yvonne shook her head. "No. My parents didn't want anything to do with me either. I've got two perfect siblings. A lawyer and a teacher. I was just the black sheep."

Alex heard the hurt of her family's abandonment in Yvonne's voice, though she tried to hide it.

"I settled in that little college town, got a job as a waitress, and worked my way through school. I never saw Marquis again. He was injured his sophomore year and lost his football scholarship. I think he moved back here. Even though he rejected me, though, I never stopped loving him.

"Anyway, I'm a CPA in north Georgia. I do OK most days, but sometimes I think about him." She stroked Lydia's soft curls, longing glowing in her eyes.

They really weren't that different. Choices made at crucial junctures determined how their stories played out. The pivotal distinction, Alex believed, was her own trust in God's provision and sovereignty. It carried her through the tough days.

"Yvonne, did Miss Matilda talk to you about God when you lived here?"

Yvonne nodded, but wouldn't look Alex in the eye. "I was awful to that sweet lady when I was here at Together for Good. I told her to take her religious bull… Well, you can imagine what I said. Anyway, I told her I didn't need someone else lecturing me and telling me what a horrible person I was." At the memory of her behavior, Yvonne put her face in her hands, too ashamed to say anymore.

Alex knelt beside the hurting woman and rested her hand on Yvonne's back. "Would you please sit here with Lydia for just a second. If she wakes up, tell her I'll be right back"

Alex hoped she was right about her next move. If not, it could back-fire, causing more pain to Miss Matilda than this particular resident had already caused.

"Miss Matilda," Alex said, peeking around the kitchen doorway.

"Yes, dear." The light had gone out of the old lady's countenance. The emotional weight, constant stress, and heavy burden of this job had begun to take its toll on the lady.

"I have a feeling Yvonne may finally be ready to hear what you tried to tell her ten years ago."

As the meaning of what Alex was saying dawned on their older friend, Alex, Chad, and Charmain watched her face break into a radiant smile. She had her arms raised in the air as she scooted down the hallway to tell Yvonne the best news she'd ever heard.

Not long after Miss Matilda disappeared to the front room, Blakely came running in the kitchen door, apologizing repeatedly for running late. The bride- and groom-to-be watched in fascination as she unpacked sample after sample of beautifully-decorated miniature cakes.

"Where do we begin?" Charmain asked, lightening the mood and snapping the couple back to reality.

Blakely handed Chad and Alex a list. As they read, they saw it contained a description of each creation: the flavor of the cake, the type of filling between layers, the kind of icing, and the types of flowers and details intricately piped on the tiny pieces of perfection before them.

Chad and Alex looked at each other. Within seconds, they were doubled over in laughter. Charmain rolled her eyes; Blakely looked as if she'd cry. Alex reined in her giggles, trying to regain her composure before they could hurt the talented young baker's feelings.

"Oh, Blakely," Alex said. "These are stunning! Chad and I thought we were just going to get a few slices of cake, pick which one we liked, and be done with it."

"Yeah," Chad agreed. "I had no idea we'd be eating works of art."

At their words, Blakely released a huge sigh and smiled.

"I'm so glad you like the way they look. I wasn't sure how much detail you were looking for, so I went all out."

"You certainly did," Alex said, watching the artist wield her knife to begin portioning out the cake.

The sound of little feet racing down the hall announced Lydia's entrance to the kitchen and cut short Alex's affirmations. The child came to a screeching halt the second she saw the array of breath-taking confections.

"Oh, my," she breathed, putting both hands to her mouth. "Mommy, you didn't tell me we were having lots of cakes. Can you and Chaddie get married again soon so we can do this again?"

The grown-ups laughed at her childish logic, but Alex lifted a quick prayer of thanks. This afternoon had tested their relationship, with Chad even questioning the wisdom of going through with the wedding. The one thing Alex knew for sure was she didn't want to go through life without Chad.

They had some issues to work out. Like communication. That much was clear after the spats they'd had over the last few weeks. Reverend Drummond was addressing this and other potential relationship pitfalls during their pre-marital counseling. Alex prayed that once the stress of finishing school, travelling to North Carolina, and planning the wedding was behind them, things would get smoother.

She took Chad's hand, squeezed it, and gave him a quick kiss on the cheek. He looked surprised, but he returned the squeeze. Then he mouthed the words, "I love you." The whole sweet encounter may as well have happened on the moon. The others were so engrossed in cutting, serving, and tasting cake they paid no attention to the couple.

The group sat savoring each delectable bite, vowing each time that the one they were tasting was definitely their favorite. Soon Miss Matilda and Yvonne slipped in and took a place at the table.

"Would you ladies like to try some cake?" Blakely asked, serving up two plates.

"That would be lovely, Blakely. Thank you." Miss Matilda passed a plate to Yvonne. "I know we're here to figure out what cake to have at the wedding, but I think another bit of celebrating is in order today." She popped a bite into her mouth and raised her fork high, as if in victory.

It took a couple of seconds for the cake eaters to process the meaning of her statement, but when they did, everybody erupted in shouts of joy, fits of clapping, and cries of congratulations for Yvonne's salvation. This day had started full of tension, accusations, and heart break. Although the kitchen in Together for Good looked as if a cake factory had exploded, and the couple couldn't agree on what cake to serve, everyone knew it had indeed been a day worth celebrating.

21
Flowers and Surprises

The next few weeks seemed to evaporate.

"It's like, one minute we're tasting cake, the next minute our wedding is six days away." Walking hand-in-hand with Chad to the church nursery after the service, Alex marveled at how the time had sped by.

"I know what you mean. We've been so busy getting ready for the wedding, I'm ready to be married so we can see each other again."

Alex laughed, but an unease gripped her. She thought Chad meant his comment as a joke. In truth, though, they'd seen little of one another lately. She'd been working day and night to get everything ready for the wedding, including her special surprise. She'd even told her retail customers she wouldn't have any new pieces ready until early Fall.

"Chad," Alex stopped and looked at him. "Do you regret our decision to move the wedding up?" She needed to know this was what he wanted, too.

"Are you kidding? It's one of the best decisions we've ever made. Well, except for deciding to get married in the first place, that is."

Reassured, she squeezed his hand and told him she and Lydia would meet him in the parking lot. He promised to have the air conditioner cranked up by the time they got there.

Alex signed in on the computer screen outside the children's Sunday school area, following the church's safety protocols for checking in and releasing the children. No sooner had she finished tapping in her info than Mrs. Drummond materialized at the door, beaming at Alex.

"Good morning, our lovely bride!" A warm hug accompanied her sweet greeting. "Alex, tell the girls at Together for Good what a lovely job they did on your shower. Everything was so beautiful, and you received some wonderful gifts. People love you and Chad very much, you know."

"Thanks, Mrs. Drummond. I'll be sure to pass along your kind words."

Miss Matilda and the girls had thrown a lovely party for her and Lydia yesterday, complete with tons of finger sandwiches, cheese straws, and lime sherbet punch. The quintessential Southern affair. Although Alex normally shunned the spotlight, she'd enjoyed being honored as the bride.

Lydia burst from the classroom area, waving the craft she'd made in Sunday school above her head and snapping Alex back to the present.

"Mommy, look what I made today. It's a bride. Mrs. Drummond says I'm a bride, too!"

"We learned today that the Church is the bride of Christ. It may be a little confusing for her, considering the current circumstances." Mrs. Drummond and Alex shared a chuckle.

"That's beautiful, sweetie. Can you tell Mrs. Drummond goodbye and you'll see her at the wedding?"

"'Bye, Mrs. Drummond. See you at the wedding." Lydia ran over to her beloved Sunday school teacher and whispered conspiratorially to her, "Mommy will be dressed like a bride, but my dress is just as pretty."

Mrs. Drummond's mouth twitched with barely-contained amusement. "I'm sure it is, dear. I can't wait to see how beautiful you both are."

Alex mouthed a thank you to the pastor's wife and took Lydia's hand. There was so much to do between now and next Saturday. First, though, Sunday dinner at Miss Matilda's.

Walking across the scorching parking lot to where Chad had the air conditioner blasting, Alex smiled thinking about the next time they would spend Sunday afternoon at Together for Good. They would officially be a family.

While the residents cleaned up, Chad and Lydia wandered through the vegetable garden, giving Miss Matilda and Alex a chance to check out the selection of blooms available for next weekend.

"We'll need enough for your bouquet," Miss Matilda counted off the required arrangements with gnarled fingers. "Charmain and Brittany's bouquets, and a single flower for Chad's lapel. What about centerpieces? Have you talked to Riker about them? How many tables is she having set up? We'll need something for each one. Oh, and the buffet table. Another arrangement for that."

Miss Matilda spoke as fast as Lydia as she went through the list. Alex's head spun with the number of details still left to complete. It must have shown on her face because Miss Matilda stopped her barrage of questions long enough to pat her young friend's arm.

"It's going to be fine, dear. It'll all get done. It always does."

Alex nodded, feeling no more reassured now than when she and Chad had decided to move the wedding up.

"Miss Matilda, I have no idea what I'm doing. I kind of feel like I'm drowning here. And it sounds like so much work. Are you sure you're up for it?" Alex had no qualms baring her true feelings to her trusted friend. Miss Matilda nodded and smiled.

"Of course, I'm up for it. I can't remember when I've had this much fun." Then she turned and resumed her flower inspection. "So, I think we'll use these beautiful hydrangeas. The white ones for your bouquet and pink for the others. Maybe we can add some lavender sprigs to them. Oooh, these gladiolas will be stunning on the tables."

She babbled on, Alex's head still swimming with the information overload. She was thankful someone else was running this show.

If Chad and Alex thought the month before the wedding had sped by, then the week before went at light speed.

Brittany arrived on Wednesday to lend her assistance with the final preparations. Her design flair calmed the bride somewhat. Alex knew when her friend joined forces with Riker and Blakely, she'd have the elegant yet welcoming day she wanted. Miss Matilda welcomed Brittany with open arms, allowing her to use one of the vacant rooms at the home while she was in town.

Preparations kicked into full gear on Thursday. The tables for the reception, borrowed from the church, arrived in a fleet of pick-up trucks. When several of the guys from Chad's men's group had volunteered to bring them to Miss Matilda's place and set them up, Alex gladly accepted.

Meanwhile, in the kitchen at Together for Good, Riker and Blakely called all the shots. They'd created a spreadsheet itemizing a schedule for every task to be accomplished, and everyone had their marching orders. Things moved like a well-oiled machine, with Riker checking off one detail after another as they were completed.

Miss Matilda walked in the kitchen door carrying a basket heavy with freshly cut flowers, their aroma filling the room. She placed the basket in the huge farm sink with a sigh, her brow knitted together in worry.

"What's wrong, Miss Matilda?" Alex asked, fresh panic gripping her.

The constant up-beat attitude the older lady had provided over the past weeks had been Alex's lifeline. If something was amiss, she wasn't sure she'd be able to cope.

"Oh, nothing, dear. We really need to get all of the flowers cut soon. The sky's beginning to look very dark."

"Won't they be fine if it rains?" Riker asked, not even looking up from her job of piping filling into mushroom caps at a breakneck pace. Miss Matilda shook her head.

"I'm worried that with the predicted winds, they may get damaged." She continued to rinse each bloom, trim the stems, and place them in large buckets of water. "I don't think I can get the rest of them before the storm hits."

Riker abandoned her piping bag and wiped her hands on her apron before emitting an ear-splitting whistle.

"Everybody to the kitchen." She yelled, going into drill sergeant mode. It scared Alex a little.

The three girls who'd been ironing tablecloths came scurrying in from the front room. Brittany, Blakely, and Miss Matilda froze, their work forgotten. Alex abandoned her job tying up little tulle circles with birdseed for the moment. Everyone looked at one another as Riker paced, her hands resting on her growing bump.

"Ladies, here's the situation. The flowers all need to be gathered. Now."

Riker barked orders in fast succession, her voice and her body language making it clear there was no time to waste. She gave Brittany and Alex the job of clipping the blooms. Each of them had a couple of girls assigned to assist by holding a basket and transporting the precious cargo inside, where Miss Matilda and Blakely would prepare the flowers and put them into water-filled buckets.

"What will we do with all of the buckets," Blakely asked. "I barely have the space for my cooling racks. And the cake layers should be done in about twenty minutes."

Even with the kitchen's enormous dimensions, large enough to prepare meals for an army of expectant ladies, the space was beginning to shrink as more and more wedding-related items piled up.

"There's the shelf Alex built out on the screen porch," Miss Matilda reminded them. "We could put them out there."

"Perfect." Riker grabbed a basket and headed out the door. "What are y'all waiting for? Let's go, ladies. That storm's not gonna wait on us!"

Within seconds, each woman armed herself with a basket, clippers, or bucket, prepared to work together to accomplish the task at hand.

Or, risk facing Riker's wrath.

The angry pelting of fat raindrops on the screen porch roof confirmed they'd made the right decision to drop everything and harvest the flowers. The blooms now sat, secure and beautiful, in a dozen buckets on the back porch, awaiting the next step in the process – arranging into bouquets, corsages, boutonnieres, and centerpieces. Brittany would spend all day Friday working her design and floral magic.

"I'm exhausted," Alex's best friend said, blowing on her coffee to cool it before taking an experimental taste.

"Me, too," Alex agreed. "I don't know how Riker and Blakely are doing it. They're both late in their second trimester. They'll probably want to sleep for a week once this short-fuse wedding is over."

"Alex," Brittany set her cup on the table and took her friend's hands in her own. "I can't thank you enough for everything you've done for me. I'm so happy for you and so glad to be sharing in this craziness with you."

Britt's eyes sparkled, and Alex swallowed hard, trying not to cry.

"Britt, I literally couldn't get through all this wedding prep without you. Besides, I wouldn't want to. You've been there for me through it all. I can't imagine true sisters being any closer than we are."

Alex squeezed Brittany's hands, thanking God again for this special lady in her life.

A booming clap of thunder interrupted Alex and Lydia's breakfast Friday morning. Alex peeked out the window, a frown pinching her face. She'd tried not to watch any weather forecasts all week for precisely this reason. She couldn't handle the stress of worrying about what they'd do if tomorrow brought with it a deluge.

"Mommy, I hope it doesn't rain tomorrow. I don't want our pretty dresses to get wet. It's OK, though. Chaddie likes the rain."

Lydia's matter-of-fact pronouncement reminded Alex of the true purpose for tomorrow. Rain or shine, she and Chad would be married. It didn't matter if it happened outside under the huge oak tree or on Miss Matilda's spacious porch. Tomorrow, she would marry the man she loved more than anything.

"Our dresses will be fine, honey. But, let's hurry up so we can get the surprise loaded and over to Miss Matilda's, OK?"

At the mention of the surprise, Lydia shoved the last bite of yogurt in her mouth, squirming in her booster seat with excitement. Alex released her daughter from the confines of the seat and watched her run to her room for her backpack. Looking around the place that had been her home for almost four years, she heaved a deep sigh.

She'd taken this little cottage from a dated, unused structure to the cozy place she and Lydia had called home. Now, surrounded by stacks of boxes containing most of her possessions, a melancholy assailed her heart knowing she'd live here only a short time more.

Fear quickly replaced the sadness. Despite months in counseling with Reverend Drummond, the reality of all that being married entailed still scared Alex. Could she let her guard down after what had happened to her and be the wife Chad deserved?

"Ready, Mommy!"

Alex hadn't even heard Lydia's quick little footsteps returning, but she stood before her mom, backpack in place and a huge grin on her face. Alex pushed her troubling thoughts to the back of her mind and smiled at the adorable little curly-haired girl before her.

"Well, let's go, then. We need to get the surprise from the workshop and load it into my car."

Alex had been careful not to let Lydia into her garage-turned-workshop while working on the large piece she'd made especially for the wedding. She smiled as Lydia rushed to the door, jumping up and down in anticipation of finally being allowed to see the secret her mother had kept.

Pushing the button to raise the garage door, Alex instructed Lydia to get in her car seat. She picked up a few tools she'd need then turned to begin loading her car, colliding with Chad.

"We've got to stop running into each other like this," Chad said, his dad-joke game already strong. Alex grinned at his silly sense of humor.

"Hey, you. What are you doing here?"

She'd not told him what she was up to, but here he was. No time like the present to let him in on her surprise build. Besides, she could use his help assembling it at Miss Matilda's.

"I was in the neighborhood. You know? Like, I live twenty feet away. I thought I'd check in and see if you needed any help with things today."

"Well, that's a silly question. But now that you asked, you can help me load this into my car."

As she spoke, she pulled a huge tarp off a pile of boards. They were tapered on the ends and had been whitewashed.

"What is it?" The look of uncertainty on Chad's face made Alex laugh out loud.

"It's our wedding arch. I made it out of an old pergola someone was throwing out. I'm going to set it up under the oak tree at Miss Matilda's and leave it there for her."

As she spoke, she scrolled through the pictures on her phone and showed him the finished product. She'd disassembled it for easy transport.

"Babe, that's beautiful." She heard the awe in Chad's voice. He took her face in his hands and kissed her gently. "I have no idea why God blessed me with you, but I'm so glad He did."

"Back at ya, my love. Now, can we get going? The day's wasting away." She lingered a second longer in his embrace before pulling away.

"Um, sweetie. Where do you think all of this wood is going?" Chad asked.

"In my car."

She'd used her dependable SUV to transport all of her projects for four years now. However, looking at first the pile and then at her vehicle, Alex saw she'd need to make two or three trips to get everything over to Together for Good.

"Hm, I guess I didn't think about how much there was to take."

"Lucky for you I've got a huge pick-up," Chad said, rolling the tarp into a ball and taking it to his truck. He smoothed it across the bed before returning to start the loading process, dropping a quick kiss on Lydia's head as he walked by the open car door, where she sat waiting to be buckled in.

"Hey, Chaddie. The wedding is tomorrow!"

"I know," he said, pulling her from her seat and twirling her around in his arms. Her giggles brought a smile to Alex's face. "Are you ready for the wedding?" he asked the little girl, returning her to the car seat. Her face was solemn as she nodded.

"I'm helping Mommy with the surprise and it's OK if our dresses get wet."

Alex laughed again at the perplexed look on Chad's face as he attempted to follow toddler logic.

"Enough goofing off, you two," she teased. "Let's get this loaded and over to Miss Matilda's."

"Yes, ma'am," Chad and Lydia said in unison.

Securing the final bolt, Alex wondered how she'd thought she would get this huge structure in place by herself. It had been so much easier in her workshop, where she had a solid floor and equipment around to assist her.

"It's amazing, Alex. Let's go get Miss M. now and show it to her." Chad's excitement rivaled Alex's. She'd waited and worked a long time to have the structure in place under the oak tree. She couldn't wait to see the look on Miss Matilda's face when she saw it.

She and Chad walked hand-in-hand through the front door, calling out to find out where everyone was. They followed the voices to the kitchen. They recognized Miss Matilda's and Brittany's, but they couldn't identify the soft-spoken man's voice.

When Alex stepped into the kitchen, her knees almost buckled. She tightened her grip on Chad's hand, using it to steady her faltering balance. There sat Zeke at the huge table, sipping coffee amidst the flowers, cake, birdseed bags, and empty platters. Lydia sat in his lap. Miss Matilda and Brittany seemed to be deep in conversation with him.

"Zeke," she said. "What are you doing here? Is everything OK at home?"

Alex's mind immediately latched onto all kinds of possibilities. *Was J.T.'s health deteriorating? Was Mother sick?* She couldn't reconcile his presence in this setting.

"Hey, there, Lexie Bug," Zeke said, rising from his seat to greet Alex. He held Lydia in his arms as he hugged Alex. "Everything's fine back at home."

Alex saw him falter a beat. She thought he was trying to hide something from her, but she didn't press him on it. Instead, she remembered the manners drilled into her by Karen and introduced her fiancé to the kind man she'd known most of her life.

"Terry called me after y'all left Woodvale. Told me you're getting married and asked if I could come down and help your pastor at the ceremony." He looked a bit uncertain as he realized they'd cooked up the plot without the bride's knowledge. "I hope you're good with that."

Unable to speak with the lump in her throat, Alex nodded, her eyes shining.

"Mommy, Zeke says if you're Lexie Bug, I must be Lyddie Bug. Chaddie, you can be Chaddie Bug, if you want." Lydia's proposed nickname for Chad made the ladies laugh and Chad blush.

When they could breathe again, Miss Matilda offered everyone cookies, with coffee for the adults and milk for Lydia. As everyone dug in, Alex pulled Zeke aside.

"When did you get here? I didn't see your car out front."

"I left Woodvale on Tuesday. The drive down took me right by two of my daughter's homes, so I stopped in and visited with each of them for a bit. I got to Burton this morning. My car's at Terry's house. He brought me over and introduced me."

Alex shook her head, not able to believe Terry had pulled off a surprise like this. At the thought of a surprise, Alex gasped.

"Oh, my goodness! I completely forgot. Miss Matilda, I've got a surprise for you."

"Land sakes, child. How many surprises do you think an old lady can handle in one day?" Her smile belied her protest. Alex helped her up from the hard wooden chair.

"It's outside, but you can't peek."

Alex and Chad flanked the older lady as they walked out on the wide wrap-around porch. Miss Matilda covered her eyes, protesting at having to do so but grinning the entire time.

They positioned her at the back corner of the porch, the perfect vantage point for seeing the newly constructed pergola where this time tomorrow a wedding would take place.

"Open your eyes," Alex said. "I hope you like it."

Miss Matilda sucked in a breath and covered her mouth with both hands.

"It's beautiful."

"We'll get married underneath it. But, it stays after that. I wanted to give you something to remember these last few crazy months. And to thank you for all you've done for me."

Alex hugged the kind lady who'd rescued her following her run-in with a deer, who'd saved her child from a decision driven by fear, and who had loved her beyond anything she'd ever known. Miss Matilda returned the embrace, continuing to surprise Alex with the strength remaining in her frail-looking frame.

"It's one of the nicest surprises anyone's ever given me."

Looking around her at the surprise she gave and the one she received today, Alex thought maybe she could learn to enjoy surprises instead of being annoyed by them.

She'd soon change her mind.

22
Unexpected and Uninvited

Alex couldn't believe their wedding day had arrived! She'd finally broken down and checked the weather forecast for today, raising her hands in praise at the promise of a sunny day ahead of them.

Four years ago, she'd jump-started Chad's business out of sheer desperation. She smiled at her own car-themed pun. Today, they'd become husband and wife. Before rising to start the day she'd remember for the rest of her life, she closed her eyes in prayer and thanksgiving.

Insistent rapping on her front door interrupted her prayer, making Alex bolt from her bed, throw on her ratty robe, and race to the door before the noise woke Lydia. Charmain stood on her doorstep, beaming and holding two huge cups of coffee from Alex's favorite downtown café.

"Good morning, you beautiful bride!" Charmain greeted Alex, breezing into the tiny kitchen and handing one of the cups to her friend. "Are you ready to go?"

Alex looked down at her bathrobe then back at Charmain, accepting the cup and taking a long gulp.

"Do I look ready, Charmain?"

"No," she said, drawing the syllable out. "I thought I was supposed to pick up you and Lydia at nine o'clock and take you out to Miss Matilda's." She looked at her watch, immediately realizing her mistake. "Oops. I'm an hour early, huh?"

Alex nodded, but she couldn't be mad at Charmain's willingness to help her. Besides, she _had_ brought delicious coffee.

"Since you're here, you might as well make yourself useful," Alex said, hearing Lydia's bare feet pad down the short hallway. "If you could get a yogurt and a sippy cup of juice for Lydia, I can get a quick shower."

Charmain agreed.

After she'd dropped a good morning kiss on her baby's head, Alex hurried down the hall to shower and pack everything she and Lydia would need for the wedding. Tossing her tattered robe into her bag, she heard Chad's ringtone on her phone. She grabbed it off the dresser and tapped the screen with a smile on her face.

"Good morning, handsome. Got any plans for the day?" she teased.

"Nope. Maybe go fishing or take a nap. Hey, wait a minute. I think I'll get married today."

This was one of the many things she loved about him. He rolled with the punches, taking on life with his sense of humor and calm demeanor.

"That's a great idea," she played along. "Mind if I join you?"

"I'd be honored." Alex heard the husky tone his voice got when his emotions bubbled to the surface. She couldn't start crying this early in the day. She knew she needed to keep the tears at bay, at least for a little while longer.

"Hey, I'll see you under the arch in a few hours. Have a great day. I love you."

He promised to be there, and she tapped the screen to end the call. Time to get this day underway. She chugged the last of her coffee before turning on the shower.

An hour later, she stood in the room at the top of the stairs of Together for Good, getting dressed for her wedding surrounded by her two closest friends, her daughter, and Miss Matilda.

"Where are y'all going on your honeymoon?" Brittany asked, helping Alex slip into her wedding gown.

"I don't know. Chad says it's a surprise." Alex bit her lip, nervous about the expectations and responsibilities ahead of her. "What if I can't go through with it, Britt?"

Her fear had plagued her since the night of the attack, but she'd been able to either squelch it or ignore it. Now, neither tactic would work much longer. From now on, she had to cope and move forward. She owed that to Chad. She owed it to herself.

"Alex, you'll be fine. Chad loves you. I've seen how patient he is with you and Lydia. Everything will work out and you'll wonder why you ever worried about it at all."

Alex heard the words Brittany said. She wanted to believe them. Still, the thought made her stomach turn somersaults.

Would everything really work out?

She trusted Chad completely. They'd worked through so many issues. Like establishing open communication, something they both agreed needed work after the missteps they'd had in recent weeks.

The time for them to be united as husband and wife–in every way–was almost here, and Alex wasn't sure she'd be able to go through with it. She was too ashamed, though, to say anything to Chad about her fears.

I guess I've still got a ways to go on the whole communication thing.

Chad hung his suit on the hook in Miss Matilda's cottage and slipped the plastic bag off, inspecting it one more time. He wanted this day to be perfect, and even though all eyes would be on his gorgeous bride, he thought Alex might appreciate seeing him looking nice, wearing something other than the jeans and greasy T-shirt he normally wore.

"It looks fine," Terry said, relaxing in the chair across the room where he sipped coffee and munched on one of the delicious muffins Riker had brought them. "Just like it did the last three times you checked it. If I didn't know better, I'd say you're a little nervous."

Chad grinned at the older man while Zeke reached for another muffin from the loveseat.

"That's OK," Zeke said, closing his eyes and let the taste of lemon blueberry bliss burst in his mouth. "You should be nervous. This is a huge step. But I'm guessing once you see that pretty Lexie Bug walking down the aisle, your nerves will vanish," he snapped his fingers, "like that!"

"I hope you're right, Zeke."

Since Zeke's arrival yesterday, Chad had come to admire the man who'd dropped everything and driven eight hours to be here for Alex.

Walking across the room to grab one of the mouth-watering muffins and ease the grumbling of his stomach, Chad's eye caught a glint of sunlight bounce off the windshield of a car driving up to the cottage. He pulled back the curtain to get a better look.

"Were we expecting any more deliveries? I thought everything was here." He couldn't understand why some stranger was here.

Today, of all days…

Terry joined Chad at the window. "Uh oh."

He dropped the curtain and turned to Zeke, but not before Chad caught the look of concern on his face.

"What? Don't say 'uh oh' today, Terry. Who is that?" Chad tried to keep his emotions reined in, but he utterly failed.

"Who is it?" Zeke repeated, still concentrating on his muffin more than the situation at the window.

"It's Karen," Terry said.

Zeke dropped his muffin and started choking.

"What? Why in the name of all things holy would that woman be here today?" Zeke bolted from the loveseat and started pacing. By this time, Karen's shoes tapped across the front porch, followed by an insistent knock at the door.

The men looked at one another, eyes wide, mouths hanging open, and unsure what to do next.

"Karen? Who's Karen?" Chad had no idea what was going on, but, taking his cue from the others, dread gripped his heart.

"Alex's mom." Terry offered no other explanation. None was needed.

"What?!" Chad's raised voice alerted their visitor that someone was indeed inside. She rapped again, this time longer and harder.

"I know someone's in there." The closed door muffled her voice, but did nothing to disguise her demanding tone. "I need to speak to Alex Powell right this minute."

Chad blanched at her words.

No. Not today. Her mother will not ruin this perfect day.

Terry motioned for Chad to go into the kitchen, putting his finger to his lips to indicate he should remain quiet. Chad complied, more than willing to let someone else take the lead.

He sat at the kitchen table, bowed his head, and prayed God would somehow take the woman away from this place.

Before she did any damage.

"Good morning, Mrs. Wickham. What a surprise to see you here." Terry greeted Karen as if she were a wedding guest they hadn't expected. She was neither invited nor expected.

Karen swore at Terry as she pushed past him into the cottage's small living room.

"Cut the crap, you sick man. I know you and my daughter have some kind of thing going on." She was gaining steam, spewing her self-concocted, hate-filled lies, when she saw Zeke. "You!" she shrieked. "I should have known you had something to do with this. Ever since Alex and this cradle-robber came to the house, things haven't been the same."

She advanced on Zeke, fury in her eyes, but Terry extended his arm and halted her progress. Karen glared at Terry and hurled more profanity at him.

"That's quite enough, Mrs. Wickham. If you'd like to have a conversation, I'll be happy to do so. I will not tolerate such language in this house, though."

Terry thought the woman would blow a gasket. Her eyes blazed, and he smelled her stale, cigarette-tainted breath as she huffed like an angry bull, her nostrils flaring. He stood his ground without flinching. Years of dealing with his ex-wife Gail had taught him one thing: never show weakness to a bully.

"Where is my daughter. I demand to see her right now." She'd lowered her voice to a whisper, never taking her eyes off Terry.

"Actually, she's getting ready for her wedding."

Terry's announcement sent Karen into another fit of cursing. Raising one eyebrow, Terry reminded her she was wearing out her welcome. Or rather, she would be wearing out her welcome _if_ she'd ever been welcome in the first place.

"I knew it," she said, her anger simmering for a moment. She still pointed an accusatory finger at Terry. "You two came to Woodvale to flaunt what you've been doing since she ran away. Well, you may have fooled J.T., but you don't fool me. I'll fight this. You'll be sorry you messed with me, mister."

She'd gotten spun up again, and the more she yelled, the louder and more agitated she became. Terry looked at Zeke to see if he had any idea what she was ranting about. Zeke shrugged and raised his brows, content to stay on the fringe of this encounter.

Terry turned when he heard heavy footsteps behind him. Closing his eyes, he braced himself for the battle that would surely ensue when Chad defended his fiancée's honor.

"Who's this kid?" Karen asked, gesturing toward Chad.

Terry looked at his friend, seriously concerned Chad may punch Karen. It was no longer any secret how she'd repeatedly hurt Alex. And now she had the audacity to come here and hurl unfounded accusations about the woman Chad loved. Terry placed a steadying hand on Chad's shoulder, hoping to remind him of his manners and the life that awaited him. He felt Chad relax under his touch and heard him swallow hard.

"Mrs. Wickham," Chad said, his voice eerily calm, "we've never met, but I'm the man your daughter is marrying today. If you have a problem with that, well, I'm sorry. Nothing is stopping this wedding. We've waited too long."

An evil, sickening grin spread across Karen's face. She raked her gaze deliberately from Chad's head to his feet and back again.

"Huh." She grunted her dismissive response to Chad's declaration and crossed her arms. "I don't believe you. Why would he," she jabbed her thumb in at Terry's direction, "come up to Woodvale with her? And why would J.T. change his will?"

Her second question hit the men like a bombshell, rendering them speechless as they stared at Karen. Terry watched Zeke sink back onto the loveseat he'd abandoned, while Chad shook his head, his eyes narrowed in confusion.

"What are you talking about, Mrs. Wickham?" Terry's social aplomb kicked into high gear, enabling him to remain cool despite the questions jumbling his head. Even he, however, flinched in disbelief at what Karen announced next.

"J.T. died yesterday."

Zeke took two long strides to stand in front of Karen before grabbing her by the shoulders.

"What did you say?" He hoped he'd heard her wrong. J.T. had been weak but stable when Zeke had left Woodvale on Tuesday morning.

Could his health have really deteriorated that quickly?

"That's right, Zeke. He's gone. And so is your cushy job. I'd appreciate you removing your hands from me." Karen wiggled her shoulders in an attempt to loosen his grip.

Grief-stricken, he dropped his hands from the loathsome woman. J.T. had been his boss and his friend.

At least someone will grieve him.

Zeke looked at Karen's cold, calculating expression, unable to fathom what J.T. had ever seen in her.

"Excuse me for asking," Terry spoke up. "What happened? More importantly, why are you here? Don't you have more pressing matters to attend to? Like planning his funeral? Or settling his estate?"

Zeke's stomach lurched. He knew the reason for Karen's fury. *I never thought she'd find out so soon.*

"I'm here because I spoke to J.T.'s attorney last night. It seems he changed his will a few weeks ago." She fixed Zeke's hazel-green eyes with her accusing stare, deftly side-stepping the question about how J.T. had died. "You knew about this, didn't you?" Her icy voice targeted J.T.'s trusted employee and confidant. Zeke nodded.

"Yes, ma'am. I did. He asked me to witness it when he made the change a few weeks ago."

"How dare you…" she started, but a soft knock on the door interrupted her fury.

"Chaddie. Bubba. Can I come in?" Lydia's little voice called out.

Zeke winced to think Karen would lay eyes on the child, after Alex had been so careful to prevent it. He watched in numb silence as Chad hurried to the door before Karen could reach it.

"Hey, princess," he said, scooping her into his arms.

"Hey, Chaddie. Mommy said to tell you she's almost ready for her pictures, so don't peek at her pretty dress."

Zeke saw Karen's face light up with wicked delight as she took in the scene before her. He prayed Alex's daughter didn't say anything in her childish enthusiasm that would provide too much information to this vile woman.

"Thanks, sweetie," he kissed her cheek and put her down. "You tell her I'll behave and not peek even once." His strained smile was convincing enough for Lydia, who bolted out the door laughing.

"Who was that?" Karen's glare shot daggers at each man, demanding an answer.

Overcome with the news Karen had brought, Zeke hung his head and gripped the door frame, sobs racking his body and rendering him unable to provide any information. Chad clenched and unclenched his fists, his jaw set in a firm line.

Terry spoke up, his answer clipped. Terse.

"That's my sister."

"You expect me to believe you? You're almost old enough to be her grand-father. I know that's your child. She looks just like you." Karen attempted to make sense of Terry's statement, her wild-eyed stare searching for some clue from the others.

"She looks like me because we have the same father." When Terry spoke the words, Zeke whipped his head up, terrified of what was to come.

"Yeah, right. And who would that be?"

Zeke knew Alex had guarded the truth about both her painful past and her daughter like a mama bear. He believed Karen would be more likely to leave when she finally heard the truth. Besides, she needed to know the facts to make sense of J.T.'s final decisions, even if knowing did nothing to help her accept his choices.

"James Terrence Wickham."

It was Zeke who spoke, and his words hung in the air. Alex could be angry with him. He could accept and handle her ire. But she needed to know these two men who meant the world to her hadn't betrayed her closely-guarded secret.

Karen staggered backward as if punched, struggling to catch her breath. Understanding slowly dawned on her face as her mind processed Zeke's statement. She shook her head, denying what she'd heard.

"No," she said, the rage that had earlier fueled her screams giving way to a deep, quiet disbelief. "You're lying. This is some kind of sick joke."

"Trust me, Mrs. Wickham, raping a minor is no joke. It's a crime."

Karen's eyes darted around the room, seeming to search for some other way to explain Alex's sudden departure four years ago.

"He knew all along." Her statement caused her shoulders to sag under the weight of the truth she struggled to acknowledge. She looked old and defeated.

For a moment, Zeke almost felt sorry for her. She'd endured a lot in the past twenty-four hours. Becoming a widow. Finding out her daughter was getting married. Discovering she had a grand-daughter. Learning her late husband had assaulted her daughter.

Zeke confirmed J.T. had been told of both Alex's child and Terry on their recent visit to Woodvale. Karen stared past him, her head shaking in denial.

"Is that the reason you came to Woodvale?" Her eyes bore into Terry.

"Yes. Alex needed to forgive both of you before moving on with her life. I wanted to meet the man who fathered me."

Karen pondered Terry's response before pulling her shoulders back and staring at the men in defiance.

"I don't believe you. Any of you," she said, her voice more subdued than when she'd arrived. Denial rang in every word. "I'll contest the revision of his final wishes every step of the way."

"It won't do you any good," Zeke said. "It was all legal. The lawyer was there when I witnessed him sign it."

"Wait. I don't understand. What is there to contest?" Chad held his hands out before him palms up, almost as if surrendering to his confusion. Zeke needed to let the guys in on what Karen had discovered, which would affect them both beyond their wildest imagination, before she hurled any more accusations at them.

"J.T.'s revised will, which left almost everything to Alex and Terry."

"Chaddie promised to behave," Lydia called out, climbing the steep stairs to the room where her mom and the other ladies were dressing.

"Thanks, sweetie," Alex said, hugging her daughter gently to avoid wrinkling her luminous satin gown.

"Mommy, you look beautiful." The little girl breathed her praise, her eyes affixed to Alex.

The ladies laughed at the girl's rapt expression before agreeing how lovely the bride was.

"Well, you look very pretty, too," Alex complimented her daughter. "Is Chad ready?"

"No, Mommy. They're talking to some lady who smells funny."

"Who?" Alex tried to imagine who would have shown up today, of all days. The image of a woman flashed in her mind. "Lydia, was it the same woman we saw hugging Chad downtown?"

Yvonne had been wearing too much cheap perfume the day they'd met her. But Lydia confirmed it wasn't Yvonne. She'd never seen this lady.

Alex snatched her phone out of her bag and speed-dialed Chad. It went straight to voice mail. She slipped on her beaded sandals and stomped toward the door.

"Alex, what are you doing? You're about to get your pictures taken." Charmain snagged Alex's hand and squeezed, trying to reason with her. "Don't go getting upset and ruin all Brittany's hard work. Your hair and makeup look perfect."

There was no reasoning with the jittery bride, though.

"Dear, I'm sure there's a perfectly good explanation," Miss Matilda placed her hand on Alex's arm and used her most soothing voice to try to dissuade her. "Besides, you don't want Chad to see you, do you?"

Her final argument almost worked. Almost. Alex shook Miss Matilda's hand off and hurried down the stairs.

"I'll be right back," she called over her shoulder.

Was there another girl in Chad's past he'd forgotten to tell her about? Could it be Yvonne, and Lydia hadn't recognized her? Why would a woman come here to see Chad? Today?

Sandals pounding across the kitchen to the back door, Alex decided: they would settle this before any wedding took place here today.

Outside the cottage door, Chad saw his hand tremble as he pulled it shut, the click sounding like a death knell. He drew a shaky breath. In. Out. He needed to calm his nerves before searching for his bride. This was not how he'd imagined today's events unfolding.

He turned and put a foot on the top porch step, but he halted before making any progress. Blinking, he willed his brain to confirm the sight that met his eyes. A vision, beautiful and ethereal. And she stalked off the main home's back porch.

He saw her lips set in a grim line and her eyes blazing. Her arms as straight and stiff as boards by her side, she clenched and unclenched her fists.

"Alex," he said, his voice squeaking out an octave higher than normal. He gulped. "What are you doing? I thought you were getting pictures taken."

He wanted to hold her, to remind her of his love. To do whatever he could to soften the blow of the news he was sure would shake her. He didn't dare, though. He'd seen that look before, and he hoped he wasn't on the receiving end of the chewing out that would soon take place.

"Who is she, Chad? I know there's a woman in there," she pointed at the cottage, her other hand firmly planted on her hip.

Chad felt like a rug had been yanked out from under him. He stalled, stammered, shifted his weight. Anything to avoid answering her question. He'd volunteered to find Alex and tell her about her mother's visit. He was almost her husband, and she should hear this kind of news from him. But he'd planned on devising the best strategy for breaking the news on his brief walk over to the main house.

Now, he had to sink or swim, following his instincts as he spoke.

"Alex, why would you think there's someone here?" He winced as he said it, aware his deflection made him sound as if he were hiding something.

She planted her feet and shoved both hands on her hips, sunlight shimmering off the satin.

"Look, Alex," he moved toward her, reaching for her with both arms as he prepared to deliver the news of J.T.'s death.

"Don't touch me, Chad. Who is in the cottage? And why is it such a big secret?"

The last question died on her lips, and Chad looked in the direction of her gaping stare at the open cottage door. When Karen appeared in the doorway, Alex swayed as if her knees might buckle. Despite her recent rebuff, Chad stepped to her side, looping a steadying arm around her waist.

"Mother." Alex's voice, flat and quiet, held no emotion. No hurt. No accusation. No surprise. No love. "What are you doing here?"

"I assumed your young man would have told you by now."

Chad saw the hurt and confusion in her Alex's brown eyes when she looked to him, questions swimming in the tears threatening to slip down her face.

"She showed up out of the blue, honey." He pulled a tissue from his pocket. He'd stashed it there in case he lost control of his emotions at the wedding. Now, though, he handed it to her, certain she'd need it before he did. "I didn't even know who she was."

"We did, though," Terry spoke up, squeezing past Karen to stand on the porch. Zeke followed closely behind, dabbing his eyes with a handkerchief.

"He went to be with Jesus, Lexie Bug." Zeke hardly got the words out before another wave of sobs overtook him.

Pulling her close to him, Chad felt Alex's body stiffen at Zeke's words. He knew she'd understand what Zeke meant. What he didn't know was how she'd react to it.

Alex expected a roller coaster of emotions on her wedding day. The ones she'd prepared for, though – happiness, nervousness, excitement – gave way in an instant to others.

Sadness. Pain. Confusion.

201

Information swirled in her mind like a feather caught in a tornado. No matter how hard she tried, though, Alex couldn't force the pieces to fit together in her brain.

Somebody — maybe Terry or Zeke, she couldn't be sure, the ringing in her ears was so loud — announced J.T. died yesterday.

Why is Mother here?

It didn't make any sense. Shaking her head, Alex tried to concentrate. To get a grasp on the situation.

"How did it happen?" Alex directed her question to no one in particular.

When no one spoke up, Karen heaved a sigh and crossed her arms before responding.

"Well, the nurse said he'd been fine the night before. But when she checked on him when she got back the next morning, he was gone. The doctor thinks he had a heart attack in his sleep."

Karen displayed no hint of the grief typically associated with the loss of a spouse. The makeup on her lined face wasn't streaked. Her eyes, though bloodshot, weren't puffy from crying or ringed with runny mascara.

"The nurse? Didn't you normally look in on him at night or in the morning?"

Even as Alex asked her mother the question, she saw Zeke shaking his head. He would know Karen's routine of caring for, or <u>not</u> caring for, her husband.

"Do I look like I have Florence Nightingale tattooed on my forehead, Alex?"

Sarcasm, Alex knew from experience, was one of Karen's most powerful and often used tools to deflect, belittle, and demean. The fact that she chose to wield it now told Alex everything she needed to know.

"So, that would be a 'no,' Mother."

If Alex had to guess, Karen wasn't even sad he was gone. She might even be glad. Glad to be rid of the burden he'd become. Glad to be free to live as she wished without having Zeke or a nurse constantly attending to her husband's failing health. But her mother's face didn't read as "glad." No.

She's livid.

What could make her angry enough to drive for hours the day after her husband died?

"What do you want from me, Mother? And how did you find me?"

Karen stomped down the porch steps. Chad stepped protectively in front of Alex, but she touched his arm to stop him. Looking up at him with a grateful smile and a brief shake of her head, she stepped around him, ready to battle if necessary. Karen reached into her coat pocket and extracted one of the old, tattered envelopes from Carol Ann. Alex shook her head, confused how it had lead Karen here or why she even had it.

"I found a stack of these on the bed next to J.T. I figured I could use the return address to get to the bottom of his recent behavior. And, I see I was correct."

As she had when they'd arrived in Woodvale and been greeted by a bitter and rude Karen, Alex again felt an unbidden urge to slap her mother.

"How dare you come here." The words hissed through Alex's pursed lips halted Karen's progress. "I think you need to leave now, Mother. You're not welcome here."

The very same words Miss Matilda had spoken to Gail a few years ago hung in the air. Karen blinked, obviously confused by a harshness she'd never heard before in Alex's voice.

"Believe me, I'm leaving. But you haven't heard the last of this." Karen's nostrils flared as her shrieked threat echoed off the houses.

The people putting a few final touches on the wedding preparations under the oak tree heard the outburst and looked to see what was going on. Alex cringed.

"Please, keep your voice down. What else could you possibly have to say? He's gone, Mother. Go home and give him a proper burial." Drained and exhausted from the confrontation, Alex's shoulders slumped as she exhaled.

Why doesn't she just leave me alone?

She watched Terry bound down the porch steps two at a time, by her side in a second. A premonition of doom squeezed her heart.

Now what? Could it get any worse?

"Oh, I forgot," Karen said, her sugar-coated voice in stark contrast to her rage-contorted face. "You haven't heard the really big news, have you?" She crossed her arms, assuming a defiant, aggressive stance.

As baffling as her mother's presence was, her question made even less sense. Alex's head whipped from side to side, looking at first Chad then Terry. Twice.

What do they know that I don't?

Terry cleared his throat.

"J.T. changed his will, Alex," Terry said, barely loud enough for her to hear. "Zeke witnessed it."

Zeke still stood on the porch, his shoulders shaking. Alex saw him nod his head behind the handkerchief.

Terry and Zeke quickly pieced together the details of J.T. revising his will, while Alex listened, stunned and barely able to process their words. Terry would receive the construction business, which made Alex smile. It had been her childhood dream to take over J.T.'s business. But plans changed. Dreams changed. She had new dreams now.

The revised will explained the true reason for her mother's fury. Whether out of guilt, gratitude, or a combination of the two, J.T. had willed the bulk of his fortune to Alex. Her knees felt like soup. She was to receive most of his money, several land holdings, a cabin in the mountains, and his truck.

During Alex and Terry's trip to Woodvale, Zeke had told her of Karen's eagerness to liquidate the company's assets. She wanted the cash to buy a house on the coast, take extravagant trips, update her wardrobe. Things she felt she'd missed out on during J.T.'s extended illness.

J.T. hadn't planned to begin liquidating his assets until next year. Despite his ever-deteriorating condition, he didn't allow his business to be sold. Instead, he'd put Zeke in charge of the company.

It was now up to Terry to decide what would happen to Wickham Land Holdings.

"Karen received the house and a generous annual allowance," Zeke said, seeming to regain control of his emotions.

"I had no idea." Alex stared into space and spoke to no one in particular, her voice small.

"Right! You really expect me to believe that?" Karen hurled the venomous accusation at her daughter. "For all I know, you've been in contact with him the whole time you've been gone."

Does she truly not know what he did?

Alex grasped the truth of her mother's self-deception, at once loathing and pitying the woman before her. Closing her eyes, she prayed for the strength to finally extend grace and forgiveness, regardless of the hurt her mother had inflicted.

Before she whispered her "Amen," quick little footsteps crunched in the gravel driveway.

"Mommy, Miss 'Tilda told me to find you. She says you shouldn't see Chaddie yet because..." Lydia's mouth snapped shut and she skidded to a halt when she saw the grownups in the yard between the main house and Miss Matilda's cottage. "Mommy," she whispered. "That's the lady I told you about."

"I know, sweetie. It's fine." Alex held her hand out, and Lydia grabbed it with both of her own chubby hands, squeezing with all her might. "Why don't you let Bubba hold you?"

Terry reached down in invitation to the little girl, and she flung herself into her brother's safe, strong arms. She laid her head on his shoulder, facing away from Karen.

"Well, what a happy little family." Sarcasm dripped from Karen's words. "Your sugar daddy here tried to convince me that little girl isn't his. Do y'all think I'm stupid?" Still seething, she dragged her angry scrutiny across the people in front of her.

Karen's accusation told Alex Terry had already denied being Lydia's father.

How much more did he tell her?

"My daughter," Alex began, careful to avoid saying Lydia's name, "is Terry's half-sister, Mother. Terry's mother used to live in Woodvale and was sent here, to the pregnancy care home, by her family."

She saw her mother start to speak before her mouth clamped shut. Although she continued to look from one member of the group to another, each time she'd try to form a question, all she could manage was ineffective sputtering. Finally, after several failed attempts, she found her voice.

"Why didn't you tell me?" Her question implied Alex was to blame. For J.T.'s criminal behavior. For his illegitimate child.

"Would you have believed me? I doubt it. I did what I had to do, Mother. And I'm glad I did."

"But... when? How? I don't understand." Karen continued to wrestle with the revelation, placing one hand on her head as if it would help her think.

"Mother, just go. None of the details matter now. You weren't there. You rarely were." Alex saw Karen flinch. "But that's the past. I've got a beautiful daughter. I'm marrying the man I love." She reached out and took Chad's hand. "I'm very happy. And very blessed."

"You haven't heard the last from me." Despite knowing what her late husband had done to her daughter, Karen still intended to follow through on her threat of legal action. Alex shrugged.

"Do what you need to do, Mother. Just know, I forgive you for all you did and didn't do throughout my childhood. And for all you will do in the future. I've learned some powerful lessons from you."

Alex turned and stepped gingerly over the rocky surface and up the back steps, allowing the screen door to slam behind her. Noticing that Zeke had already slipped back into the cottage, Chad and Terry looked at each other, shrugged and followed in Alex's wake, leaving Karen standing alone in the sunshine.

23
Soft-Hearted Guys

Matilda stood in the upstairs hall wringing her hands. From the window in the bedroom where the ladies in the bridal party were getting ready, they'd watched the whole scene in the yard between the main house and her cottage unfold. According to Brittany, the mystery woman was Alex's mother. Although they couldn't hear what was being said through the double-paned glass, the body language left no doubt a tense situation existed below.

Hearing the slam of the screen door, Matilda inched closer to the stairs, prepared to offer the bride encouragement, advice, or a shoulder to cry on. Based on the waving arms and tense expressions she'd just witnessed, Matilda guessed one or more calming tactics may be needed. She watched Alex grip the banister, place her foot on the first step, and hang her head.

"Alex, sweetie. Is everything OK?" Matilda knew better, but she wasn't sure how to voice her concerns. Alex shook her head before looking up, a forlorn expression clouding her features.

Not the expression a bride should be wearing on her wedding day.

"J.T. died yesterday, Miss Matilda."

Matilda heard the girl's voice crack, and her heart broke for this young woman who'd been forced to deal with so much. While Matilda considered what to say to offer her condolences, Chad slipped into the hallway at Alex's side, pulling her into his arms and whispering softly in her ear.

Not wishing to intrude on the young couple, Matilda tiptoed backward in hopes of making a quiet escape. Before she'd made it back to the dressing room, however, an insistent knock on the front door was quickly followed by the click of it opening.

"Um, Miss Powell. I'm really sorry to interrupt, but I'm ready to shoot your photos under the oak tree. If we don't get going, I'm gonna lose my lighting and the guests may start to arrive before we're done."

Alex glanced at her watch and sucked in a breath. Raj, the young photographer from Riker and Blakely's school, stood in the doorway fidgeting. He'd been fantastic all morning, capturing excellent candid shots of the pre-wedding action. Now they had only a few hours before the ceremony. Charmain's early arrival this morning seemed a million years ago.

Alex made a difficult decision. She'd have time to grieve J.T.'s loss, deal with her mother's threats, and figure out her next move… tomorrow. Or maybe next week. Today, though, she was getting married. She resolved to put the sadness and uncertainty out of her mind for today. The only thing that mattered today was marrying Chad. She prayed Zeke and Terry would be able to do the same. They'd be hurting, too.

"Wait a minute," Brittany yelled from the room upstairs. "Alex Powell, don't you go out there until I've had a chance to touch up your hair and makeup. I'll be there in just a sec."

Her friend's obsession with perfection made Alex chuckle. Brittany, barely able to keep her balance under the weight of her makeup bag and various other tools, ran down the wooden steps, Charmain trailing close behind. The quick clicks of their shoes hitting each stair tread announced their descent.

"Hey, I've got a great idea," Charmain said. "I know y'all didn't plan to do a 'first look' shoot before the wedding, but that plan's obviously fallen apart. Why don't you let Raj get some shots of the two of you together? Lydia too."

"Actually, Charmain," Alex said, her lips barely moving as Brittany attempted to reapply lipstick, "that is a great idea."

She looked at Chad, who stood watching the whole exchange with a looked of stunned terror.

"You go put your suit on, honey. Comb your hair. Do whatever it is you need to do to get ready," she said. "I'll meet you under the oak tree in ten minutes." He nodded and bolted for the back door. "Oh, wait! Where's Lydia?" He froze mid-stride at Alex's question.

Alex didn't know how they could take photos of her if she didn't know where she was. And, what kind of mom was she, anyway? Not even knowing where her child was?

"She's asleep," he said. "Terry's walking her around in the shade while she takes a nap."

Chad had twisted his upper body toward Alex to answer her, but his feet still faced the back door, poised for a quick exit. Alex nodded, which was all the encouragement he needed to beat a hasty retreat. The screen door slammed, announcing his departure just seconds later.

"Turn around and bend down a little bit. I'm going to put your veil on." Brittany ordered, taking her role of stylist very seriously. As she always had.

She'd embellished the beautiful antique comb Alex had purchased by adding a small gathering of tulle that barely brushed Alex's shoulders. After tucking the comb into the bride's curled, teased, and sprayed hair, she scooted Alex to stand in front of the hall tree mirror. Charmain had slipped out to the porch to retrieve Alex's bouquet and now handed it to her soon-to-be sister-in-law.

"Wow," Alex breathed, taking in the full effect. "I'm really a bride. I'm getting married."

It was the break from the tension they needed, and the ladies dissolved into giggles. Alex marveled at how liberating it felt to laugh. The hard times made the good times sweeter, without a doubt. She wondered, though, why they so often seemed to occur on the heels of one another, taking her on a roller coaster of joy and sorrow.

"Well, ladies," she said, beaming. "Let's not keep Raj waiting any longer. We don't want him to lose the light."

Raj ran ahead of the group of ladies. Walking backwards, he shifted the camera to best capture the sun shining over their shoulders as they walked, laughing as they approached the ceremony site.

Miss Matilda and the bridesmaids settled themselves in guests' chairs while Raj directed Alex through a series of natural-looking poses under the arch. Hearing the cottage's screen door bang shut and the porch steps creak, Alex turned her head to find the source of the noise. Raj snapped a close-up of her face the moment she saw Chad, now immaculate in his freshly pressed suit.

The sun shone bright in Chad's eyes, and Alex noticed he squinted to find her in the shade of the huge tree. Raj moved into position to capture him stepping into the canopy of the branches. The second he did, Raj snapped away feverishly.

A shy smile curved Alex's lips as she watched Chad's jaw drop before he clapped his hand to his mouth.

He'd already seen her dress, and it was stunning. He'd known it would be. But with the veil and the flowers, Alex had transformed from beautiful to breathtaking. Chad was positive there'd never been a more beautiful bride. Overcome with his love for her and gratitude to God, tears stung his eyes. He swiped at his face, remembering he'd given Alex his tissue.

Alex seemed to float toward him, unwrapping a fine lace handkerchief from around her bouquet and extending it to him. He laughed through his tears.

"You sure you want to let me use this delicate thing?" He couldn't believe he'd started blubbering before the ceremony even began.

"Chad White, we're going to share a whole lot of tears. Some happy ones and some sad ones. And, yes, I'll always share my hanky with you."

That did it. Her words obliterated the final shred of self-control he'd managed to cling to. He put his head in his hands, his whole body trembling with the force of his sobs.

"Honey," Alex said, worry tingeing her voice. "Are you OK?"

Chad sniffed hard and took a deep breath. Nodding, he grunted a little self-conscious laugh.

"Wow, what a big baby I am."

"No," Alex shook her head, her own eyes glimmering with moisture. "You're a sweet, sensitive, loving man. And I get to spend the rest of my life with you."

Chad took Alex's face in his hands, but was halted by shrieks coming from the back row.

"Chad, what do you think you're doing?" Charmain swooped in and pulled him away. "You can't kiss her until the wedding!"

"Besides," Brittany chimed in, "you'll ruin her lipstick."

With a shrug, Raj directed the couple to the arch, where they were soon joined by a sleepy-eyed Lydia. Plied with the assurance of Riker's cookies awaiting her after she had lunch, Lydia did exactly as Raj instructed, smiling and hamming it up for the camera.

Finally, Raj released his camera and let it hang from the strap around his neck.

"OK, Miss Powell, I think that'll do it for now."

While Miss Matilda and the bridesmaids took Lydia back to the house for a light lunch and the promised goodies, Chad pulled Alex close, intoxicated. By her perfume. By her beauty. By her strength. He placed a light kiss on her forehead.

"Meet me back here?" he asked, his voice still husky with emotion.

Smiling as she looked up at him, her long lashes almost touching her eyebrows, she nodded, kissed his cheek, and followed the others, her wispy veil fluttering in the wind.

Terry, who'd also been waiting in a back row chair, sidled up beside Chad and clapped him on the back.

"So, whaddya want to do for the next couple of hours?" Terry asked.

"I'm starving!"

Laughing, they wandered back to the cottage, where they devoured the sandwiches and lemonade Riker had brought over for them.

"Where's Zeke?" Chad asked around a huge bite.

"He went back to the guest room to lie down."

"Will he be able to make it through the ceremony?"

Chad knew Zeke had received a huge shock today. He understood the pain in losing people you cared about, and he wouldn't blame the man if he wanted to bow out. Terry nodded.

"I was worried about that, too. But he said he'll be fine."

The two sat in silence, each lost in his own thoughts, when they heard stirring from the back part of the cottage. They glanced at each other before they saw Zeke standing in the doorway. His eyes were still swollen, but he was no longer crying.

"Zeke," Chad began, "listen, man, if you can't…"

Zeke interrupted him before Chad could excuse him from the privilege of performing the service.

"I came here to get you and Lexie Bug married. I intend to do just that." Zeke drew a ragged breath before continuing. "Ever since J.T. was saved, I've been at peace about where he'll spend eternity. I just can't believe I wasn't there with him when he passed."

"Zeke, Karen didn't say when he died. He could've gone in his sleep." Terry tried to console him with logic. Zeke nodded.

"I know. Still, I'm pretty sure she wasn't holding his hand, or whispering assurances of her love for him."

Chad and Terry both shook their heads. Without warning, Zeke's face split into a huge grin, the first they'd seen on his normally-smiling face in hours.

"At least we know he's out of pain. And, he's back with your mama," he said, looking at Terry.

"Everything's happened so fast today, I hadn't even thought about that. You're right, Zeke."

"And, don't y'all worry about Karen. J.T.'s directions concerning his estate are air-tight. There's not one thing she can do about the fact she's not inheriting everything."

Chad didn't have the mental faculties today to consider what Alex's inheritance would mean for her. Or him. He simply knew he didn't want her to have to deal with a long, drawn-out legal battle.

He appreciated Zeke's reassurance.

He glanced at his watch and saw it was ticking closer and closer to ceremony time. With a flutter in his stomach, he felt the grin that had been on his face since Alex came home from North Carolina slip back onto his face. Looking at Zeke and Terry, he asked if they could have a quick prayer before the ceremony.

"I'd like nothing more," Zeke said, bowing his head and resting his hands on Chad and Terry's shoulders.

24
I Do, I Do, and I Do

An hour later, the time to start taking their places had arrived. Terry, who'd been tasked with alerting the ladies, rapped at the bedroom door. Aunt Tilley flung it open, beaming.

"It's time?"

"Yes, ma'am. You ladies ready?"

His aunt, nodding her answer and gathering her things, looked almost as radiant as the bride. Terry noticed a color to her cheeks he hadn't seen in a long time. She'd bought a lovely plum-colored dress for the occasion. It played up her silvery hair, which Brittany had coaxed into a sophisticated updo.

Terry, feeling a bit playful after the tension of the morning, decided to tease her a little bit.

"I'm sorry, ma'am. I'm not here for the bride yet. Are you, perhaps, a bridesmaid?"

Aunt Tilley waved him off, giggling like a teenager. He loved seeing her this happy. A pang of guilt stabbed his heart, knowing he'd been a major source of her recent sorrow. Overcome with his love for this lady who'd given him all she had, he scooped her up and twirled her around. She kicked her feet like a puppy learning to swim, her whoops a mixture of joy and consternation.

"Put me down this instant, you naughty boy!"

He set her gently on her feet, holding her by the elbows until she stopped swaying. She waved her hand in front of her, fanning to ward off the flush creeping into her cheeks and laughing as she gave him a sideways glance.

"What has come over you, Terry Lovell? Do you want me to break a hip? All that twirling foolishness." She almost pulled off her stern reproof before the laughter bubbled up. "That was, as my girls would say, awesome."

He bent down and kissed her cheek.

"I'm glad, Aunt Tilley. Have I told you lately how thankful I am for you? Can you forgive me for being such a pig-headed idiot?"

"Sweetie," she placed a cool, wrinkled hand on his cheek. "You weren't a pig-headed idiot. You had so much to work through. And, of course, I forgive you. I only hope you can find it in that big heart of yours to do the same for me."

"Already done."

He offered his arm and she tucked her hand in the crook of his elbow.

Terry smiled, feeling as if his life was back on track at last.

Matilda felt like a young girl again. All dressed up, made up, and coifed. And on the arm of a very handsome man. Her only concern today was that her heart may explode with happiness. That would be fine with her, but she begged the Lord to let her see the wedding from this side of heaven.

Floating down the aisle between the white folding chairs, Matilda clung to Terry as she surveyed the guests. Sunlight filtered through the enormous branches overhead, dappling the guests' heads with puddles of gently swaying radiance. These people meant so much to the beautiful couple pledging their love to one another. Her mind drifted back to another wedding where she'd occupied the seat of honor in the front row.

Terry and Gail's wedding had been more of a gala event than a celebration of love. Gail's elaborate gown - encrusted with seed pearls, sequins, and crystals – rivaled any royal gown Matilda had ever seen. The fifteen bridesmaids wore voluminous black taffeta dresses and carried bouquets as enormous as a casket spray. Terry's baseball teammates stood with him, many looking either hung-over or bored, in elegant black tails.

The day had foreshadowed Terry's married life. Matilda sat by in mute silence as Gail played both bride and wedding director, so great her need for complete control. She'd already informed Terry they'd take a two-week honeymoon in Hawaii, a gift from her parents, despite his protests of not having the time off from work. Through it all, Terry smiled, handsome and unruffled, and followed Gail's every decree.

Looking up at the nephew she loved as a son, her heart ached for the years he'd lost. She knew how he'd longed for children, just as she herself had. But God had different plans for both of them.

Matilda trusted those plans.

And today, she received a reward for her obedience. She had the privilege of a front row seat at the union of these precious young people she'd loved with all her might.

God is so good!

Chad stood behind the big oak tree, inhaling and exhaling. Bobbing his head from one side to the other. Shaking his hands as if trying to get something off of them. Doing whatever it took to calm his nerves. Reverend Drummond and Zeke stood off to his left, chatting in quiet voices, chuckling occasionally.

How can they laugh? I'm about to make the biggest commitment of my life! Am I ready to take on the responsibility of a wife? And a child?

The more he thought of it, the faster his heart raced. Terry walked up behind him and tapped him on the back, startling Chad.

"Whoa, bud. Why so jumpy?" Terry's eyes held a mischievous glint.

"Terry, I knew I'd be nervous, but this is ridiculous. What if I'm not what Alex needs? What if we don't agree on how to fold the towels, or fight over the toothpaste cap? I want to be a great husband and dad. How will I know how to do that?" The words tumbled out, barely making any sense even to his own ears.

Trying to verbalize his fears – his perceived inadequacies – seemed futile. He'd watched other guys get married, and they'd always seemed cool and calm. What was wrong with him?

"I just got Aunt Tilley to her seat, so it's almost time for us to head out there. You look a little chalky." Terry reached up and squeezed Chad's shoulder. "Listen, Chad. You and Alex have something special. Your relationship has already been tested. More than once. And look how much you love each other. It's only going to get better."

Chad swallowed hard and nodded.

"You're right. She's the best thing that's ever happened to me. I just have to trust God I'll be the man He wants me to be." He drew one final ragged breath. "Let's do this."

Terry motioned to the ministers, who walked from behind the tree to stand in front of the assembled crowd.

Chad rubbed his sweat-dampened hands on his pants before shaking Terry's hand.

"Thanks, man. Your pep talk must've done the trick. I'm ready to marry that girl!"

"That's more like it. After you," Terry motioned for Chad to lead the way, and the grinning men took their places beside the ministers.

Alex couldn't believe the time had finally come. In a few minutes she'd be Chad's wife.

Who would've guessed?

She remembered the day she'd bargained with Chad for the cost of her car repairs, promising to turn his business around with a waiting room re-model and a schedule overhaul. The folly, the boldness even, of her proposition mortified her now. She hadn't even known him.

God had plans, though. Even then. Before then.

As Alex had learned over the last few years, His plans were always best. Not always the easiest, but always the best.

A brief knock sounded at the door before Riker poked her head in.

"They're ready for y'all," she said. Alex heard her daughter and friends squeal with excitement.

Little ringlets clung to Riker's face. She and Blakely had worked around the clock for days to pull off this wedding, not an easy accomplishment for two young women heading into their third trimester and going to school. Alex made a mental note to do something special for the girls. They were more than earning the price they'd quoted for their services.

"Are you ready to go, sweetie?" Alex clutched her bouquet in one hand and reached out and rubbed Lydia's back with the other. Her daughter nodded.

"You really are the most glowing bride I've ever seen," Charmain said, pausing in front of Alex. "I'm so glad to finally be getting a sister."

Alex wanted to hug this woman who would soon officially be family, but she didn't dare send Brittany into fits with even the thought of messing up a single detail of her look. Instead, she grasped Charmain's hand and squeezed, trying to convey the gratitude she felt.

She remembered the day they'd met. Chad's grand re-opening had been winding down, and Charmain had breezed in. Alex recalled being very pregnant and very jealous of the girl who held Chad's attention. How mortified she was to learn she'd been envious of his sister! Within a few months, they were forever friends. Charmain had even held Alex's hand during labor, helping her welcome her precious baby girl into the world.

"I love you, Char. Thanks for helping me get to today." Alex kissed the air beside both of Charmain's cheeks. The lovely bridesmaid made her exit, ready to take her place under the tree.

"Alex," Brittany began, and Alex could see the puddles forming in her eyes.

"Britt, don't. Not now. You haven't got time to touch up my mascara."

"You're right," Brittany sniffed. "Anyway, I wanted you to know how proud I am to call you my friend. You're a remarkable woman."

"Thanks, Britt. I couldn't have done any of this without you."

It was so true. The day Alex discovered she was pregnant, she and Brittany had pulled an all-nighter planning her escape. Of course, Brittany had been a crucial contributor to the wedding preparations.

Alex air-kissed her best friend, promising to be right behind her, then looked down at her little girl.

"Are you ready, little missy?"

Lydia nodded again, her cheeks flushed and her feet dancing. She held her own tiny nosegay, a miniature version of her mother's bouquet, and looked very ladylike. Chalk up another win for Brittany.

"Me, too," Alex winked. "Let's go, shall we?"

Hand in hand, they walked out of the room as a duo for the last time. In a few moments they'd be a party of three.

A guitarist from church played their favorite hymns and worship songs. Chad shifted his weight from one foot to the other, ready to get this wedding going. Then he saw his sister.

It's happening.

Charmain walked slowly down the aisle to the arch, and Chad raised one eyebrow at her. A slight nod from her told him their plan was a go. Glancing up, he looked at the beautiful arch Alex had built as a surprise for him and Miss M.

She's not the only one with surprises up her sleeve.

He smiled and relaxed a bit, watching Brittany follow in Char's footsteps. Both girls took their places before all eyes turned to watch the bride make her entrance.

Chad thanked God he'd already seen Alex. If he'd been hit with the joy of seeing her for the first time in his current emotional state, he would've dissolved into a puddle in front of all these people. Watching her now, escorted by her sweet little girl, he was a bit more prepared for the onslaught of feelings and quickly dabbed both eyes with a knuckle.

She smiled up at him as they took their places. Then Zeke began to speak.

He opened with a prayer, thanking God for the perfect weather, for the loving guests who'd chosen to share this day with the bride and groom, and, finally, for the happy couple. When he'd finished, he looked at Chad, who nodded at the ministers while carefully avoiding Alex's questioning stare.

"Who gives this woman to be married?" Reverend Drummond asked in his clear, strong preacher voice.

"I do," Lydia pronounced, just as they'd rehearsed last night. Before she could turn to take her seat next to Miss Matilda, Chad knelt down and took her hand.

"Chaddie," she whispered loud enough for the guests to hear her, "this isn't how we practiced it." A ripple of laughter ran through the crowd.

"I know," he said, taking a small velvet box Charmain handed him. He reached down and lifted the little girl in his arms. Standing, he prayed he'd be able to get through this part, which Alex knew nothing about. At the look of confusion on Alex's face, he smiled at her and mouthed the words, "I got this." Lydia waved at her mommy, sending more murmurs of amusement through the crowd.

"Lydia," his voice cracked and he had to swallow hard a couple of times. He almost came undone when she put one tiny hand on his cheek. Huffing a breath, he continued. "On this special day, I'm marrying your mommy. In a few minutes, we'll promise to love each other forever. But I want you to know that today I promise to love you forever, too. I'll be here for you when you're happy, when you're sad, and even when you're angry. Do you understand?"

"I do!"

The crowd couldn't contain their joy. Some laughed, some whooped, some clapped. When the excitement died down, Chad continued, noticing out the corner of his eye Alex smiling at the two of them.

"Sweetie, your mom and I will exchange rings, but I'd like to give you this locket to remind you of the promise I'm making to you today."

He held up the velvet box and she opened it, her mouth forming a tiny circle when she saw the white gold locket on a delicate chain. Alex peeked over to see.

"It has an 'L' on it," she said to her daughter. "That's the letter your name starts with."

"This belonged to my mommy," Chad explained to Lydia. Alex's eyes widened in question. "Her maiden name was Littleton."

Charmain handed her bouquet to Brittany and put the necklace on Lydia.

"I love you, Chaddie." She flung her arms around Chad's neck and squeezed.

"I love you, too, Lyddie." He kissed her cheek and set her down. She skipped to her seat on the front row with Miss M., climbed up, and gently fingered her new jewelry.

Chad turned to Zeke and Reverend Drummond. He nodded, swallowing back his emotions for what seemed like the millionth time today.

How could she have ever doubted this man standing before her. Alex wanted her wedding day to be free from tears, but the joy welling up inside her threatened to spill down her cheeks.

She handed her bouquet to Brittany, who'd returned Charmain's after the necklace surprise. Turning to face Chad, she placed her hands in his own upturned ones. Then she heard Zeke speak the vows she and Chad had written.

"Chad, do you promise to love and cherish Lex...um, I mean, Alex every day for the rest of your life? Do you commit to being the man God intended you to be for her? To be prepared to support her in every way possible? To be ready to forgive and to be forgiven, even when things get tough? To stand beside her in sunshine and in shadows, in hopes fulfilled and dreams shattered. And do you promise to put your commitment to your family second only to your commitment to God?"

"I do." She heard the emotion in his voice, but it still rang clear and loud enough for those on the back row to hear.

"And, Lexie Bug," he grinned before whispering to her, "I had to say it just once." Then he continued in his preacher voice. "Do you promise to love and cherish Chad every day for the rest of your life? Do you commit to being the woman God intended you to be for him? To be prepared to support him in every way possible? To be ready to forgive and to be forgiven, even when things get tough? To stand beside him in sunshine and in shadows, in hopes fulfilled and dreams shattered. And do you promise to put your commitment to your family second only to your commitment to God?"

"I do."

Reverend Drummond took the rings from Terry and Brittany and held them high for the assembly to see.

"The wedding ring is a perfect circle, with no beginning and no end. It symbolizes Jesus' eternal love for his own bride, the Church."

Alex heard Lydia clap from her seat, recognizing her Sunday school lesson. Then, Reverend Drummond addressed the couple in front of him.

"Chad, place this ring on Alex's finger and repeat after me. Alex, I give you this ring as a symbol of my love… and of my devotion and faithfulness to you alone…. Take it today and let it be a reminder …. that you can always count on me to be your husband and your friend…. until the day God calls us home." Chad finished making his vows and slipped the ring on Alex's finger.

Next, it was Alex's turn, and she repeated the sacred words, promising to be loving, devoted, and faithful forever. After she slipped it onto Chad's finger, she looked up into his eyes, knowing she'd didn't deserve the blessing of this man, but elated to finally be married to him.

"And, now," the pastor began, "by the power vested in me by the state of South Carolina, I pronounce you husband and wife. You may…"

He didn't get to finish.

Chad swept Alex into his arms, twirled her a half-turn, and dipped her low before planting a long celebratory kiss on his wife. He swept her, blushing and breathless, back to a standing position to the cheers and applause of the crowd.

Alex felt the flush creep into her cheeks but refrained from fanning herself. She retrieved her bouquet and raised it in the air in a victorious gesture.

"We did it!" she exclaimed, to even more cheering from their closest friends.

Walking out on Chad's arm as the recessional played, she wondered if anyone had ever been this happy.

25
Why Wait?

C had pulled Alex close as they swayed in time to the music of their first dance. They'd stood on this porch many times, together and separately, but tonight was different. Tonight, they celebrated their love, commitment, and – the thought made him smile wider – their marriage. He had no idea what song the DJ played, but he knew this woman in his arms was all he'd ever need.

"What're you thinking?" Alex asked, her face tilted up to watch him as thoughts meandered around his brain.

"I'm thinking that I'm the most blessed man to ever live." He pressed his lips to the top of her head and inhaled the heavenly aroma of her hair.

Somewhere in the distance, he heard the repeated click of Raj snapping pictures of their guests having a good time.

"What about you?" he asked. "Today's been kind of like emotional whiplash."

Alex nodded and rested her cheek against his chest, swaying in time to the music while the guests looked on.

"It has. But I'm at peace with everything. At least for today. We've got some challenges ahead of us, though."

"And we'll face them together," he said.

Releasing his hold on her, he raised her hand in his and spun her around before pulling her back to him. He then dipped her as he had under the arch, his loving kiss interrupting Alex's laughter. This time, when he stood her upright, she did fan herself with her hand, which drew cheers and applause from their onlooking friends.

The DJ shifted gears and played an upbeat tune, encouraging folks to cut loose and have a good time.

"I'm going to get us some punch. I'll meet you on the other side front of the porch where it's quiet," Chad said, kissing her hand before letting her go.

"Perfect."

Alex rested her elbows on the porch rail, gazing out over the field in front of Together for Good. Closing her eyes, she breathed a short prayer of thanks for her husband and the beautiful day. When she opened them, she had to blink a few times to understand what she saw.

A car had pulled into the long, winding driveway and was coming toward the house. Dusk had already started to give way to evening, so the car's headlights obscured Alex's view of the vehicle.

Could that be Mother? Surely not! She's already embarrassed herself enough today. No way she'd come back for more?

Or... would she?

Alex heard Chad's footsteps approach but didn't turn to look at him. Her eyes stayed trained on the approaching car.

"Were you expecting someone?" Chad asked. She shook her head as he handed her the punch cup. She chugged it in one gulp, thankful for the hydration and the sugar.

"Miss Matilda told me the new resident wasn't moving in until Monday," she said.

Alex had felt a twinge of guilt at possibly delaying a scared pregnant girl from settling into her new home, but Miss Matilda had assured her the girl wouldn't be able to come any sooner.

The closer the car got, the more certain Alex was that her mother hadn't turned around and returned to the home. It was an older model car with a few dents and a yellow ribbon tied to the radio antenna, flapping in the breeze. The gravel driveway crunched under the tires; the emergency brake screeched as it engaged.

Alex watched a tall, well-dressed man, probably around Chad's age, exit the driver's side and walk around to the passenger door. In the glow of the lanterns hung around the porch, she saw the deep mocha color of his skin, his high cheekbones, and his closely cropped hair. When he opened the door, a woman in a knee-length white dress and French-braided blond hair took his hand as she emerged.

Alex gasped. Chad choked on his punch.

Yvonne! What was she doing here?

Chad recovered his manners before she did, moving down the steps to greet them. She watched and listened from her perch beside the rail.

"Yvonne. Marquis. What a great surprise." He extended his hand in greeting to the tall black man.

Marquis! Yvonne's high school boyfriend.

"Hey, man," Marquis said, placing his hand on the small of Yvonne's back. "Yvonne just wanted to come out and share some news with Miss Matilda."

Alex glanced at Yvonne, almost unrecognizable from the distressed woman who'd sat in the kitchen a few weeks ago. Tonight, she looked relaxed, radiant, and happy. She wrapped her arm around Marquis and stared up at him, love shining on her face.

She really does still love him.

The thought tugged at Alex's heart, knowing she herself got to spend the rest of her life with the man she loved. She waved and called to the couple.

"Hi, you two. We're glad you could join us." Even as Alex said the words, she realized she truly meant them. "Come and have some cake. It's delicious."

When the pair saw Alex, their faces froze. They looked quickly at each other, then back at Alex.

"Oh, Alex," Yvonne said, covering her mouth with both hands. "I'm so sorry. We had no idea today was your wedding. When we drove in, I thought Miss Matilda was throwing some kind of Labor

Day party. I didn't understand why Chad had dressed up for something like that."

"Don't be silly," Chad swept his arm, palm up, toward the porch, ushering them up the steps. "Come and join us."

Once Chad had introduced Marquis to his new wife, Yvonne shook her head, the need to apologize etched in her features.

"Alex, there's no way I'd intrude on your beautiful wedding day. We just wanted to tell Miss Matilda our news. We're getting married!" She took Marquis' hand as she spoke.

"Yvonne," Alex clapped, sincerely happy for them. "That's wonderful. When?"

"Now! We got our license yesterday. We're headed to a little all-night chapel about half an hour away." The joy on Yvonne's face was undeniable. "We've wasted so many years, we don't want to let another day slip by."

Alex understood about second chances. And the need to follow God's leading. And wanting to be with the one you love for the rest of time. She searched her heart for enmity or animosity toward Yvonne. On this day of celebration, though, all she felt was a sad tug at her heart. It was true this couple had hurt Chad and, by extension, Alex.

Seeing them so obviously in love and excited to start their life together at last, Alex wished for them a joyous beginning to their marriage. Not a somber ceremony in a tiny chapel with no friends to share their happiness.

Alex glanced up at Chad, now standing by her side. She raised an eyebrow in question, and he seemed to understand.

Maybe we're getting better with communication.

He nodded almost imperceptibly, and it was all the encouragement Alex needed. She raised up on her tiptoes to plant a quick kiss on her husband's cheek.

"Why don't y'all get married here?" she suggested, clapping her hands in delight.

Yvonne and Marquis glanced at each other, hesitant.

"I don't know. This is your special day. We'll just get back in the car and tell Miss Matilda tomorrow some time." Marquis looked uncomfortable at having crashed the wedding, but Alex wasn't about to let the couple get married in some seedy chapel with no friends.

"Nonsense. We insist, don't we, honey?"

"Absolutely," Chad chimed in. "The arch is decorated, there's a minister here. Two actually. And, you're already dressed for the occasion."

As he counted off the advantages for changing their wedding plans, Alex reached up and pulled the comb out of her hair. She stepped behind Yvonne and secured it into her French braid, fluffing up the veil.

"Wow," Marquis breathed, looking at his bride. Yvonne beamed, but still looked doubtful.

"Now," Alex said, grabbing her bouquet off the little table beside the rockers, where she'd put it earlier. "All you need are flowers, and you're ready!"

"Alex, no. That's too much. You're supposed to throw that." Yvonne looked uncomfortable at Alex's generosity.

"You're right." Alex nodded before she turned around and walked a few steps away from Yvonne and Marquis. Without warning, she turned back around and shouted, "Catch!" before lobbing the flowers toward Yvonne.

Startled, Yvonne's reflexes took over, and she caught the projectile of blooms. They all laughed at Alex's not-so-subtle ploy.

"I guess that old wives' tale about the bouquet toss was right this time. You <u>are</u> the next one to be married."

Yvonne stepped forward and hugged Alex. "I don't know why you're doing this or how I can ever thank you," she whispered in Alex's ear.

"Enjoy your wedding day as much as I've enjoyed mine," Alex whispered in reply.

231

"Chad. Alex. I don't know where you two have disappeared to, but Raj needs pictures with…" Matilda's lips clamped shut mid-scold when she rounded the corner of the porch.

The look on her face made the young people giggle. Chad stepped to her side and guided her toward the group. She noticed a tall, handsome young man standing with Yvonne. Most of all, though, she noticed how beautiful Yvonne looked. Very bridal, in her white dress and little veil and bouquet. Her face radiated a happiness Matilda had never seen there, even when the girl had lived at the home.

"Miss Matilda," Yvonne said, beaming. "Marquis and I are getting married. We still love each other after all these years apart." As she spoke, Marquis draped an arm around her shoulders and pulled her close to him.

Matilda shook her head, not able to believe what she heard.

"You young folks confuse me sometimes," she admitted. "When are you getting married?"

"Right now!" Four voices rang out in a chorus before they all started laughing again.

"Miss Matilda, would you stand beside me? It would make me so happy for you to be my maid of honor."

Matilda's hand touched her chest, her disbelief evident. "Of course, dear. It would be my pleasure."

"Chad, I know I did you wrong all those years ago, and I'm so sorry," Marquis said. "You don't owe me a thing, but I'd really like to ask your forgiveness. And maybe I could steal you away from your groom responsibilities for a few minutes? I'd love to have you stand with me." Marquis extended his hand, and Chad grasped it, pumping it up and down as he answered.

"Sure, man. I'd be honored. And, of course, I forgive you."

Having seen Chad's complete heartbreak over this woman standing before her, Matilda understood the depths of grace he'd finally achieved. Her heart swelled again with love and admiration for the bride and groom. Both brides and both grooms, in fact.

"Well, this wonderful day just got even better," Matilda said, the lines beside her eyes deepening with her broad smile.

"I'll go talk to Reverend Drummond. Yvonne, you can freshen up in the room at the top of the stairs." Alex went into wedding-planner mode, as she'd watched Brittany do for days. "Miss Matilda, Chad can walk you down to the tree. The chairs are still set up, so you can rest there until they're ready to begin."

Chad placed his hand on Marquis' back. "Well, man, looks like your single days are officially over."

Chad and Marquis both offered an arm to escort Matilda to the wedding arch. She accepted both, beaming as she took the long walk down to the oak tree, this time escorted by two handsome men.

"I can't believe y'all did this."

Alex smiled at Charmain, who seemed incapable of understanding why she and Chad would share their wedding day. And with Yvonne and Marquis, of all people. Alex slipped her sandals off and rubbed her feet, sore from running around making sure everything and everyone were in place for the impromptu wedding.

Alex had seen the couple at church a few times since the day Yvonne had been at Together for Good. Alex, however, had never had the time or, if she were honest with herself, the inclination to greet them after the service. She was always rushing to the nursery to pick up Lydia. But Reverend Drummond had been delighted to perform the ceremony, so Alex guessed he'd been aware of their elopement plans.

Brittany touched up Yvonne's makeup to perfection, and Raj agreed to get some great shots of the nuptials. Terry had the foresight to have a few of the solar-powered outdoor lamps moved to the arch so there would be adequate lighting. Alex's biggest surprise, however, still awaited the happy couple.

She'd found Blakely removing the top layer of their cake to prepare it for freezing. Alex knew tradition dictated she and Chad eat it on their first anniversary.

But Alex had other plans.

"Blakely, is there another serving plate in the kitchen? Something nice. Crystal or silver, maybe."

"There is. Why?" Blakely's hands hovered over the small cake tier.

"Don't freeze the cake, please. Could you put it on the plate for Yvonne and Marquis to cut?"

Blakely, in the hormonal rush of late-term pregnancy, burst into tears. Alarmed, Alex wrapped her arms around the girl and patted her back until the crying passed.

"Alex, that's one of the sweetest things I've ever seen anyone do." The girl swiped at her cheeks with the heel of her hand. "I'll make you another cake for your anniversary. Free of charge."

"That's really not necessary," Alex argued. She understood how tight finances would be during the first year of single motherhood.

Now Alex stood with Charmain at the porch rail overlooking the side yard. Brittany joined them, and together they watched another happy couple get married under the arch by the oak tree.

Although they couldn't hear a word of the ceremony, they saw Yvonne hand the bouquet to Miss Matilda before taking Marquis' hands. They watched Chad pull the ring from his pocket and hand it to the groom, who slipped it on his bride's finger.

They watched the couple begin their marriage with a sweet, tender kiss. Cheers erupted from the guests on the porch, and Alex smiled to know she and her bridesmaids weren't the only ones celebrating the day's second wedding.

Terry, elated for his friends but exhausted from toting his little sister around all day, had placed the sleeping girl on her mat in the front room. Riker's feet were swollen from days of being on them, and she offered to sit with the little girl before clean-up started.

Yvonne's reaction to Alex's wedding cake surprise made Terry smile. First, a look of confusion crossed the woman's face. Then disbelief. And, finally, elation and the tears that overwhelming emotion tended to generate. He knew this day was more than Yvonne and Marquis ever dreamed of.

Terry also knew although Alex had had a glorious wedding day, she still had a lot left to process. He'd put his own emotions on the back burner for the day, but he knew the grief, regret, and 'what ifs' would hit him all too soon. He wondered: if he'd been able to forgive as gracefully as Alex had, would the last few years have turned out any differently? Maybe. Maybe not.

No sense in fretting over such futile questions after the fact.

Regardless, Terry's respect for Alex and Chad, already deep and sincere, grew even more as he watched Chad forgive people who'd wronged him, just as Alex had done with J.T. and Karen. Terry knew he could learn a lot about forgiveness by watching them and following their example.

With that thought in mind, Terry went in search of his Aunt Tilley, intent on taking her for a spin around the dance floor.

26
Departing

"Are you sure there's nothing I can do to help clean up?"

Riker looked at Alex as if she had two heads. "Alex, you're the bride. You don't clean up. Leave that to us."

Alex, now in the lacy white sundress she'd packed for travelling, stalled a minute longer. Riker was right, and Alex knew it. She couldn't admit to Riker the reason for her hesitancy to leave. Leaving meant being alone with Chad for the first time as his wife. Her stomach lurched.

"I guess you're right, Riker."

She wandered into the front room where Chad waited for her. It was time for them to make their exit. She found him on the couch with Lydia on his lap, her head resting on his broad chest as they sang a song together softly.

Alex's heart melted. "What are y'all singing?"

"Hey, Mommy. We're singing *Jesus Loves Me*. Chaddie told me I can sing this while y'all are on the moon and I won't be sad."

Alex almost giggled, but Lydia was so serious, she didn't dare. She'd tried numerous times to explain it was called a honeymoon, but Lydia remained steadfast in her belief they were going to the moon.

Eyes wide, Chad shrugged one shoulder, clearly out of ideas for trying to explain the concept.

"That's a great idea, sweetie." Alex decided Chad had the best idea: give her a coping skill and try to explain it to her some other time.

Although, at this point, mere moments before they made their way through a tunnel of bubbles courtesy of the tiny vials given to each guest, Alex thought they indeed might as well be going to the moon. Chad had kept their destination under wraps, refusing to budge when she asked for even a hint.

He knew she worried about being too far away from Lydia, especially after the chicken wire incident. She knew he was due back at the shop by Wednesday, meaning their honeymoon would be brief. Her secret hope was that he hadn't planned some back-to-nature camping trip.

I need indoor plumbing and air conditioning.

Alex chided herself for acting like the spoiled rich kid she'd been when she arrived in Burton. If a camping trip made Chad happy, she'd figure out a way to deal with it for a few days.

"So, my husband," she wondered if the novelty of saying that would wear off. "Where are you taking me?" She hoped her attempt at sounding casual worked.

"Well, um... About that."

Uh-oh. Again, a sinking feeling punched her in the stomach.

"Exactly what does that mean?" Even to her own ears she sounded guarded. Cautious.

Riker interrupted the tension, apologizing for the intrusion.

"Hey, Lydia. I've got a chicken strip in here, if you're hungry."

Alex looked at the young woman who'd helped save their wedding day with appreciation as Lydia bounded off Chad's lap and made a beeline for the kitchen. Riker gestured toward the little girl's retreating back, indicating she'd follow her before backing out of the room.

"My plans for our trip have changed a little," Chad admitted, rising from the sofa to stand in front of Alex.

"Oh." It was more a statement than a question.

Chad rubbed the back of his neck, a sure tell he was nervous. Alex let him stutter over his explanation for a few seconds before rescuing him.

"Honey, I know wherever you've chosen will be fine."

Reassured by her words, he relaxed. A little bit.

"I'm so glad to hear you say that. Because, to tell you the truth, I've never laid eyes on the place we're going. In fact, I just found out about it today."

"What?" Alex took a step backward, dumb-founded. "You mean, you've been all secretive for weeks, but you didn't even have a placed booked until today?"

She crossed her arms and thrust one hip out, her stance telegraphing her ire. She avoided looking at Chad when he reached out and rubbed her upper arms, obviously attempting to calm her.

"No. It's not like that," he explained. "I've had a place overlooking the beach booked for weeks. Which wasn't easy to get on Labor Day weekend, let me tell you." She glared at him, so he surged ahead in his account. "Gosh, Alex. I really wanted this to be a surprise, but I guess I'd better tell you now.

"Earlier today, after your mom left, Zeke pulled me aside. You remember Zeke telling you about the cabin you've inherited?"

Alex narrowed her eyes and nodded, not sure she was liking this turn of events. When she'd been in Woodvale, Zeke had told her J.T. had bought a hunting cabin many years ago to fix up. Could Chad really have thought a smelly old hunting cabin would be a better place for their honeymoon than a beach front cottage? Trying to reserve judgment until he finished his explanation, she remained statue-like.

"Yeah. Well, funny coincidence. When J.T. found out Zeke was coming down for the wedding, he asked Zeke to call the care-takers and have the place spruced up for us to use this weekend. Zeke brought the key with him." Chad reached in his pocket and pulled out a single key on a rabbit's foot keychain.

So, we are going to a smelly old hunting cabin. Alex swallowed and took a deep breath. Then another. She needed to get her thoughts together and try to be understanding. *But, a hunting cabin?*

"Listen, Chad. I think it's very sweet of Zeke to offer us a hunting cabin for the weekend, but…"

Alex's attempt at being understanding was interrupted by the front door opening. Alex glanced at her watch, remembering the guests were waiting to send them off in style. She looked up and saw Zeke standing in the doorway.

"Hey, there, Lexie Bug. Did Chad tell you the big surprise?" He looked surprisingly happy for a man whose dear friend had recently died. Alex guessed he too would be hit with overwhelming grief at some point soon.

"Um, Zeke. That's really sweet, but Chad already got us a place at the beach for a few days." Alex tried to politely extricate them from the prospect of the next few days spent with an outhouse and cold water.

"Yeah, about that, babe," Chad whispered. "I canceled the beach house reservation."

Alex's head whipped toward Chad to see if this was a joke. He looked so forlorn she felt sorry for him. How could he have known he'd committed them to some dump for their honeymoon?

"In that case, we accept," Alex said, drawing her shoulders back as she resolved to make the best of the situation. If nothing else, they'd have a great story to tell their grandkids.

"Oh, that's wonderful. I know you'll love it."

Zeke seemed truly delighted to hear they'd accepted, and Alex understood how Chad had been convinced into going. Zeke tapped a few times on his phone before saying, "I think I forgot to send the photos of the place to Chad. How do you like it?"

He held his screen toward the newlyweds for them to see. Their mouths dropped as Zeke scrolled through the photos.

"Zeke," Alex said, stunned. "Are you sure this is the right place? This doesn't look like a rickety old hunting cabin."

"Of course, it's not!" Zeke said. "Who told you it was rickety? And who told you it was a hunting cabin? This was a rental property J.T. kept in the mountains. He fixed it up through the years with leftovers from different projects, and now it's pretty nice. What do y'all think?"

Alex and Chad looked at each other, neither able to speak. Every picture of the house looked like it had been staged for a magazine.

From the spacious kitchen to the soaring stone fireplace to the back porch overlooking the Great Smokies, everything about the place screamed cozy elegance. Alex was the first to start giggling. Chad soon joined her. Zeke looked baffled at what was so funny, his gaze shifting from one to the other.

"Are you two feeling OK?"

"I'm sorry, Zeke." Alex tried to catch her breath before continuing. "After everything that's happened today, I thought we were heading off to some gross old cabin in the woods with no running water. Instead, we're going to a mansion." She took Chad's hand and squeezed.

"Actually, Lexie, if you remember, it's your mansion now." Zeke sobered, reminding Alex of the terms of J.T.'s will. "Of course, there will be some legal matters to get it properly transferred to you, but, for all intents and purposes, it's yours."

"Wow." Barely audible, it was the only thought Alex could formulate.

How would it feel to step into the house, knowing it now belonged to her? To them, actually, now that they were married. They'd just have to deal with that matter in a few hours. For now, Chad had his hand on her back guiding her toward the door.

"Oh, one more thing." Zeke snapped his fingers, remembering a final detail to tell the couple. "Don't bother stopping for groceries. I had the property management folks stock the fridge and pantry. You should find everything you need."

"Thank you, Zeke. How can I ever thank you for all you've done for us?" Alex hugged the man who'd been J.T.'s best friend and most loyal employee. He glanced down, shy at the praise being heaped on him.

"Lexie Bug, you don't have to thank me. I should be thanking you for finally opening J.T.'s heart to the truth." His eyes held puddles now. "I'm telling you, if that hadn't happened, I'd be feeling a whole lot sadder now. But I know I'll see him again."

He placed a gentle kiss on her cheek before shaking Chad's hand. Then he opened the door and announced the couple's impending departure to the gathered crowd.

Terry watched Alex and Chad kiss Lydia goodbye. He chuckled to see her fascination in the bubbles far exceeded her interest in saying goodbye. She puffed at the little wand furiously, sending tiny rainbow-glinting orbs dancing on the evening breeze. Charmain stood close behind her with a backup vial, in case she ran out.

"Y'all be careful," he said to Chad, hugging them both.

"We will. And, Terry, thanks for being there for me. Not just today, but ... well, always."

"Glad to do it," Terry said, clapping Chad on the back. "Now, go on. Get outta here."

Chad grinned and grabbed Alex by the hand. They sprinted to her SUV and, before long, their taillights had disappeared in the late summer night. The guests waved and blew bubbles for several seconds after they lost sight of them.

"Wasn't it a beautiful day?" Aunt Tilley asked, stepping up to Terry's side and placing her soft, bent hand on his arm.

"Yes, ma'am. It definitely was a day of surprises."

They'd arrived that morning to prepare for a wedding. Through the day, they'd received heartbreaking news, discovered they were beneficiaries of a huge estate, watched a touching ceremony – two, in fact – and celebrated in style.

"Aunt Tilley, how do you suppose Alex got to be so wise at such a young age?"

"What do you mean, dear?"

"I look back at the last few months and I see how strong she's been. She's the one who encouraged me and accompanied me on my trek to meet J.T. She's the one who helped him see how much he needed Jesus. And she's the one who shared her wedding day with another bride."

Terry shook his head as he stared out over the front field toward the place the headlights had recently disappeared. Aunt Tilley reached up and touched his cheek in a feather-soft caress.

"Sweetie, I think Alex is a fine example of what God can do with our lives when we're ready to forgive." The light in her eyes made Terry grin.

"You're so right, Aunt Tilley. Now, how about another turn on the dance floor?"

He tucked her hand in the crook of his arm, and they laughed all the way back to the porch.

Ready to Forgive

<u>Reader Questions</u>

Thank you for continuing this journey with Alex and her friends. Below you'll find a few questions to help you delve deeper into the main themes of the book and to encourage discussion with others. Each question set is divided into information you gleaned from the book and truths you've experienced in your own life.

I hope you enjoy diving a little deeper.

B = Questions related to the book.
P = Questions related to your personal experience.

1. *Forgiveness is a major theme in <u>Ready to Forgive</u>. Ephesians 4:32 says, "Be kind and compassionate to one another, forgiving each other, just as in Christ God forgave you."*
   B. What are some ways the characters in *Ready to Forgive* were kind and compassionate to each other? What examples of forgiveness did you see?

   P. When were you called to forgive someone as God has forgiven you? Had you held onto unforgiveness for a long time? How easy/difficult was it to forgive?

2. *Alex and Chad had issues with communication, especially when it came to letting one another in on either their past (Yvonne) or their plans (trip to Woodvale).*
   B. How did Alex and Chad's relationship with God enable them to forgive each other and move forward in their relationship with one another?

   P. What situation have you been in that was a result of a breakdown in communication? How did you move past it?

3. *As in <u>All Your Heart</u>, characters in <u>Ready to Forgive</u> reveal the secrets they've kept for a long time.*
   B. What could be some reasons Chad, Charmain, Yvonne, and Matilda kept their secrets for so long?

   P. What are the circumstances, if any, under which it's acceptable to keep information secret from someone?

4. *Zeke had prayed for the Wickham family's salvation for years.*

B. What factors do you believe had the greatest impact in J.T.'s decision to accept Christ? Why might God have allowed J.T. to delay in his decision for so long?

P. For what have you prayed for a long time, only to be told "No" or "Wait"? How did you deal with these answers?

5. *The timing of J.T.'s death had the potential to ruin Alex and Chad's wedding day.*

B. How do you think Alex, Zeke, and the others were able to carry on with the wedding? What previous events had happened that potentially influenced their decision?

P. What life-altering event have you had to deal with on the surface, or postpone dealing with altogether, so you could be present in the moment? How did this change your handling of the situation, if at all?

6. *Alex, Chad, and Terry's lives will change with the inheritance of J.T.'s estate.*

B. Knowing the characters, how do you think it will change their lives? What about their lives will remain the same?

P. What gift have you received or goal have you achieved that allowed you to do something you would have otherwise never considered doing?

LeighAnne Clifton and her husband Bill call South Carolina home. After meeting while both earning their degrees in chemical engineering at the University of South Carolina, the pair married and settled in Aiken. They have two grown children, a son-in-law, and a pair of spoiled cats. Before writing *All Your Heart*, LeighAnne wrote *The Little Vessel*, a modern-day parable for all who need reminding that God has a unique purpose for their lives.

LeighAnne, like Alex Powell, loves to upcycle old junk into beautiful, one-of-a-kind pieces. She shares her thoughts on Christian living, DIY projects, and the latest book news on her blog:

https://alive-leighjourney.com

Made in the USA
Columbia, SC
20 February 2022

56506145R00143